"What do you think of him, Wayne?" she asked him as he loosened the girth to remove the saddle.

"He was one of my top picks," he said simply.

Charlotte took the opportunity to study Wayne. Yes, he had some years on him, but he was still a handsome man with a strong profile and, in her mind, a wealth of experience that she was interested in tapping into.

Wayne felt her studying him and he turned his face to look at her. Their eyes met and Charlotte felt an undeniable spark. She felt an attraction to him; she couldn't remember the last time she had been attracted to anybody. It felt uncomfortable, so she shifted her attention back to her purpose: horses.

"If Cash was on the top of your list," she said, "what other horses made the cut?"

Wayne felt respected by Charlotte and it only confirmed his decision to bring his talent and resources to her ranch for the summer and, perhaps, early fall. She was sharp as a tack, quick-witted and grounded in the homestead lifestyle. And, she was real pretty to look at. She had an infectious smile, ocean-blue eyes that gave him glimpses into the depths of her soul and her character; he was attracted to her beyond the physical even though that was there too.

Dear Reader,

Thank you for choosing *Big Sky Cowboy*, the seventeenth Harlequin Special Edition book featuring the Brand family.

Charlotte "Charlie" Brand is a fearless, capable woman who is trying to save Hideaway Ranch, which has been in her family for five generations. With creditors at the door and time running out, Charlotte must make the most out of a short Montana summer to convert her cattle ranch into a short-term destination rental for companies looking for a winter retreat. Unable to do it alone, Charlotte hires cowboy Wayne Westbrook to help her rebuild the ranch. Although their chemistry is undeniable and their attraction difficult to resist, Charlotte can't be distracted by romance when her family's legacy is on the line.

Wayne Westbrook lives a nomadic life as a cowboy for hire who never stays in one place for long. When Charlotte offers him work, Wayne has to fight a battle within himself. One side wants to help Charlotte rehab her ranch, while the other wants to drive off in the opposite direction, leaving the attraction he feels for this fierce cowgirl behind. Confident he can fight his attraction to Charlotte, Wayne accepts the job, believing that he can rescue this beautiful cowgirl before he rolls on to the next town. But before long, Wayne comes to realize that Charlotte was the one who rescued him...and that this rolling stone cowboy has finally found a home.

You can connect with me at my website: joannasimsromance.com.

Happy reading!

Joanna

Big Sky Cowboy

JOANNA SIMS

Recycling programs
for this product may
not exist in your area.

ISBN-13: 978-1-335-59450-1

Big Sky Cowboy

Copyright © 2024 by Joanna Sims

For questions and comments about the quality of this book, please contact us at CustomerService@Harlequin.com.

Harlequin Enterprises ULC
22 Adelaide St. West, 41st Floor
Toronto, Ontario M5H 4E3, Canada
www.Harlequin.com

Printed in U.S.A.

Joanna Sims is proud to pen contemporary romance for Harlequin Special Edition. Joanna's series, The Brands of Montana, features hardworking characters with hometown values. You are cordially invited to join the Brands of Montana as they wrangle their own happily-ever-afters. And, as always, Joanna welcomes you to visit her at her website, joannasimsromance.com.

Books by Joanna Sims

Harlequin Special Edition

The Brands of Montana

A Match Made in Montana
High Country Christmas
High Country Baby
Meet Me at the Chapel
Thankful for You
A Wedding to Remember
A Bride for Liam Brand
High Country Cowgirl
The Sergeant's Christmas Mission
Her Second Forever
His Christmas Eve Homecoming
She Dreamed of a Cowboy
The Marine's Christmas Wish
Her Outback Rancher
Big Sky Cowboy

Visit the Author Profile page
at Harlequin.com for more titles.

This book is dedicated to:

Yvonne Campbell (aka *Mama*)

Thank you for your love, kindness, generosity and prayers!

You are truly an angel in this world.

We love you so very much.

Prologue

Hideaway Ranch, Big Sky, Montana

"Sounds like we have company," Charlotte Brand said to her mother, Rose. The driveway alarm mounted on the main gate chimed. Bowie, their five-year-old pit bull and rottweiler mix, leaped up out of his bed growling and raced to the door, where he barked and pawed to be let out.

"Were you—" Rose Brand had to pause to catch her breath before she continued in a wheezy voice "—expecting someone?"

"No," Charlotte answered her mother and then said to Bowie calmly, "Quiet."

The dog sat down, continued to growl in a low tone, his concerned eyes watching hers. Charlotte looked out the kitchen window and saw a gentleman pulling up to the house in an early-model faded green Ford truck.

"I don't recognize him." Charlotte pulled a small

handgun out of the kitchen drawer, lifted up the tail of her T-shirt and slipped the gun into a waistband holster.

Their ranch was situated in a valley near the base of Lone Mountain; it was isolated. Folks didn't just pop by unannounced.

"Could be," her mother said teasingly with a weak smile, "Prince Charming."

"Bite your tongue, Mama," Charlotte retorted playfully, then asked, "Are you going to be okay?"

Rose had been battling her third bout of pneumonia since her diagnosis of emphysema, and she had just come through a nasty coughing spell.

"Quit…fussing." Her mother said from her hospital bed that now took up much of the space in the small family room adjacent to the kitchen. "I'm…fine."

Rose had lived her life strong and stoic, so even if she weren't fine, she wouldn't admit to it. Thinking that it would be short work to send this unwanted visitor packing, Charlotte headed toward the front door and gave Bowie a rewarding pat on the head for his patience before she shrugged into her late father's tan and orange canvas Carhartt jacket. She zipped up the jacket and flipped the brown collar up to protect her neck from the cold.

Her hand on the door, Charlotte said, "I'll be right back."

Rose waved her hand and then, seemingly sapped of energy from the short exchange, she closed her eyes.

"Love ya, Mama," she said out of habit.

"Love you."

Charlotte opened the door and stepped outside into the wintery April air with Bowie at her heel. The melting snow on the porch made a crunching sound beneath her feet as she walked the short distance to the rough-hewn railing. Bowie sat down beside her, his hackles standing upright, and a low, consistent growl in his throat. Bowie had always been leery of strangers; between his strong muscular frame and his extensive training, Charlotte always felt protected with her dog by her side.

The man behind the wheel gave her a quick wave in greeting; she judged his age to be in the late forties or early fifties by the salt-and-pepper he had in his bushy goatee. The black Lab in his front-passenger seat, that also had some salt in his coat, was sticking his nose out of the cracked window, catching the scents of the ranch.

The man took a cowboy hat off the dashboard, put it on his head as he opened his door and said to the dog, "You stay put, Mick."

"Howdy," the man said after he shoved his creaky driver's door shut.

"You lost?" she asked in a tone deliberately unfriendly.

The stranger was tall and lean; beneath his sheepskin denim jacket he wore a button-up checkered shirt tucked neatly into his faded jeans. There was a gray bandanna around his neck, and his pointy brown cowboy boots were scuffed from use. The chocolate brown hat was most likely a Stetson, and it looked new.

"Well, I don't believe I'm lost." He cracked a small smile, barely visible behind his unruly facial hair.

"Then, what are you doing here?"

"I'm looking for Charlie Brand." He hooked his right thumb into his front pocket and cocked his hip in a relaxed stance. "Am I in the right spot?"

"Why are you looking for Charlie?"

"The name's Wayne. I'm looking for work." The man fished a piece of paper from the front pocket of his shirt. "I got this from the post office up in Gallatin Gateway."

She *had* left an advertisement for ranch help, but that was quite a while back. For her, it seemed like a lifetime ago.

"We don't have work now." She said in a blunt tone, "A phone call would've saved you the trip."

"I tried the number." Wayne held the small piece of paper up between two fingers.

Charlotte worked to keep her expression neutral; she had changed her number last year in an attempt to slow down the collection calls.

"Well," Wayne said, a ring of disappointment in his voice, "nothing ventured, nothing gained, I suppose."

She gave the slightest of nods.

"Beautiful place you've got here." He looked around, taking in the empty pastures and horse corrals covered in layers of undisturbed snow. "You folks selling?"

Her face and voice devoid of emotion, Charlotte said, "You can find your way out the same way you came in."

"Well," he said and gave her a nod, lifting up his hands a bit in surrender, "I apologize for the imposition."

In her gut, she didn't fear this man, but she still stood her ground at her post. Wayne turned on his heel to head back to his truck, and for the first time in his life, Bowie left her side, barreled down the steps and chased after the man.

"Bowie!" Charlotte shouted his name followed by the do-not-attack command. "Leave!"

Wayne spun around, his eyes trained on Bowie, and quick as a whip, a knife appeared in the man's hand.

Charlotte pulled her gun, pointed it at the man, her hand steady, and yelled, "If you hurt my dog, mister, I'll shoot you where you stand!"

"Then call him off!" Wayne barked back at her.

The air seemed to crackle with tension; her assertive voice mixed with the urgent, piercing sound of Wayne's dog barking and scratching at the truck window made it difficult for her to keep her focus solely on Wayne. She gave the return command to Bowie, but instead of attacking or returning to her, he slid to a stop at Wayne's feet, barked once, and then dropped onto the ground and rolled onto his back in the snow, his big, fat paws curled downward, his white, grayish-blue and light orange belly exposed. Bowie's big tongue slid out of his mouth, and he seemed to smile at Wayne.

"Well, I'll be damned." Wayne seemed as stunned as she felt. The cowboy chuckled, put away his knife and knelt down on one knee to give the dog a scratch on his belly. Then, Bowie rolled up to a sitting position, his back wet with crystalized snow, and licked Wayne's goatee. Wayne petted Bowie's large head and floppy ears. "Bark worse than your bite, big fella?"

Not amused, Charlotte holstered her gun and said, "Bowie. Come."

Bowie looked over at her, gave a small, unhappy whine, but finally did as he was commanded and returned to his post by her side.

Wayne walked back to the driver's side of his truck, but instead of getting behind the wheel, he leaned in, seemed to search for something and then emerged with a pen. Using the hood of his truck as a makeshift desk, he wrote something on the back of the slip of paper he had taken from her advertisement. When he was done, he stuck the pen in the front pocket of his shirt and then walked over to where she was standing. Bowie started wagging his tail again but didn't move.

Wayne handed the piece of paper to Charlotte, and she took it.

"Please pass this on to Charlie for me." He pushed the brim of his hat up and caught her eye. "Winter's gonna break before we know it, and there might be work to be had here. I could surely use it."

She nodded her head wordlessly. The man had the most intense blue deep-set eyes she had ever seen; in fact, for a split second she was actually distracted by them.

Wayne seemed reluctant to leave; he took one more look around, caught her eye again, rapped the knuckles of his right hand on the hood of his truck a couple of times, then climbed behind the wheel. He cranked the engine and revved it several times before backing up. Wayne gave her one last wave before he drove slowly down the long dirt driveway that would lead him back to the highway.

When her unexpected visitor disappeared from view, Charlotte looked down at Bowie and asked, "Seriously? I thought for a minute there you were going to go with him!"

Bowie seemed to smile back at her, his tongue hanging out the side of his mouth, his eyes loving and soft, as if he was convinced that he had done a very good job.

"All right. I love you anyway." She couldn't resist the sweet, eager look in Bowie's oddly colored eyes—one blue and one brown. She petted him on the head affectionately as she balled up the piece of paper and stuffed it into the side pocket of her jacket.

She wiped her boots on the doormat before quickly entering followed by Bowie and then shut the door behind them to keep the warm air in.

"I hate to disappoint you," she said to her mom as she

shrugged out of her coat and hung it up on the horseshoe hook by the door. "Not Prince Charming after all. Just another broken-down cowboy looking for work."

Instead of returning to his own bed, Bowie made a beeline for Rose; he started to whine and nuzzle Rose's hand, which had slipped off the side of the bed.

"Bowie! No!" Charlotte whispered harshly. Her mother's eyes were closed; she was resting peacefully and Charlotte didn't want Bowie to awaken her.

She snapped her fingers and pointed to his bed. Still whining in a way she hadn't heard before, Bowie went over and sat there but didn't lie down, his eyes still trained on Rose. That's when a warning light flashing in her brain and the question mark behind Bowie's odd behavior sent her quickly to her mother's side. She picked up her mother's hand: it felt frail and limp. Rose's rest seemed almost *too* peaceful.

"Mama?" She patted her mother's hand, but Rose didn't rouse. "Mama!"

Charlotte felt for a pulse and couldn't find one. A sense of dread washed over her body, adrenaline pumping through her veins. Her hands were shaky when she dialed 9-1-1. She put the phone on Speaker and then began to perform CPR on her mother.

"Come on, Mama!" Charlotte screamed, tears rolling off her cheeks onto her mother's flowered nightgown. "No, Mama! Please, God! *No!* Wake up, Mama!"

"9-1-1. What is your emergency?"

Chapter One

Three weeks later

"This is as far as we can go." Charlotte parked her rust bucket of a farm truck at the end of an overgrown road that hadn't been used for several years. "We'll have to hoof it to the bluff from here."

"You mean hike?" her younger sister Danica asked, her hands tightly holding their father's wooden urn.

Their father, Butch Brand, had passed away nearly ten years ago; it was his final wish that one day he be reunited with his beloved Rose on the bluff where he had first professed his love for her. Today was the day that their father's request would be carried out.

"The fresh air will do us some good," Rayna, the baby of the family, said, her fingers turning pale pink and white from the grip she had on their mother's urn; Rose's was made from a lighter wood than their father's and was smaller in size.

Danica said, "I really don't think that saying's true. I'm used to a bit of smog in my air. Ever since I arrived in Montana, I feel like I'm getting too much *air* in my air. Do you know what I mean?"

Charlotte and Rayna said in unison, "No."

After Rayna got out, Danica scooted herself over to the passenger seat, carefully balancing in oversize rubber boots she had borrowed from Charlotte while still holding on to their father's urn. She wobbled for a second with a frown on her face.

"These boots are bringing up some trauma for me," Danica said sincerely.

"You'll be fine." Charlotte grabbed a machete from the bed of the truck.

Forty years ago, Rose had brought three girls into the world within thirty minutes of each other. There was one fraternal twin, Charlotte, and identical twins, Danica and Rayna. Their father, Butch, had always proudly said that life had given him a royal flush.

"So says you." Danica hugged the container to her body.

Danica had always been the girliest triplet: she loved fashion and makeup, and she had loathed ranch chores, especially when they involved mud and manure. As soon as Danica could, she escaped to California and rarely ever looked back.

"Do you want to trade?" Charlotte offered the machete to her.

"No." Danica jutted her chin out a bit. "I'll get the hang of it."

It was a somber day, but Charlotte couldn't help but

smile at Danica, who had donned a slim-fit black designer suit for the occasion; but, in her haste to get to Montana, she hadn't considered footwear for hiking. Now, the slacks of her pricey suit were tucked into faded black rubber boots.

"Are we going?" Rayna asked, an anxious quiver in her voice. "I'm afraid I'm going to drop Mom."

"Don't drop her!" Charlotte and Danica said.

"Well, I wouldn't do it on purpose," Rayna said, "now, would I?"

"Do you want to swap?" Danica asked.

"Nobody's swapping," the youngest of them said. "This is the configuration we agreed upon."

Charlotte began the task of clearing the way, whacking the overgrowth with the machete to reveal the path their parents had walked when they had first fallen in love. At one time she glanced back and saw Rayna, bringing up the rear, clutching their mother's urn, with tears streaming down her cleanly scrubbed face. She stopped hacking at the overgrowth.

"Are you okay, Ray?"

Rayna sniffed several times loudly. "No. I need a tissue. Can you get it out of my jacket pocket?"

"Just hold Mom in one arm," Danica suggested.

"No!" Rayna sniffed again.

Charlotte put down the machete so she could fish around in Rayna's pocket. She found the tissue, swapped the urn for the tissue, so their youngest sister could wipe her face and blow her nose.

After she was finished, Rayna put the balled-up tissue into her pocket and then took their mother's urn back into her arms.

"Better?" Danica asked her.

Rayna nodded. "I know that we were raised not to show our feelings when we're sad or upset or hurt. That's just what we do."

"Don't cry," Danica and Charlotte echoed their mother's saying, "do something."

Rayna nodded. "But this is really sad. I mean, *really* sad."

Rayna had always been the sensible, rule-following, sensitive triplet; she had gotten straight A's all the way through school, graduated with her bachelor's degree magna cum laude, married her college sweetheart, moved to Connecticut and worked several minimum-wage jobs so her husband, Ben, could get through medical school, all while raising twin boys. Now that her boys, Ryder and Rowdy, were off to college, Rayna and Ben would have to adjust to their new life as empty nesters.

"It *is* sad, Ray." Charlotte gave her sister a quick hug. "We're all sad."

"I'd hug you too if I could, Rayna," Danica said, her own eyes starting to tear up at the sight of her identical twin crying. "You have a right to show your feelings. Mom and Dad were great parents. But they *were* wrong about that."

Rayna collected herself, rolled her shoulders back and then, nodding, said, "I'm ready."

Charlotte picked up the machete and continued to forge the path upward. The ground was still mushy from the melted snow, and the larger rocks on the path still had spots of glistening, slippery ice.

As they progressed up the hill to the bluff, the path became rockier and steeper, and Charlotte warned her sisters to be cautious of how and where they put their feet. Even though there was still a nip in the air as they climbed higher, her body felt warm and she had developed a film of sweat on her face and under her clothing. As she stopped to wipe her brow, she looked up ahead and then spotted what she had been looking for.

"Look." She pointed to a large, wizened oak tree with a trace of a heart and initials carved into its bark. "Dad carved that the day Mama said *yes* when he asked her to marry him."

"Wow," Danica and Rayna said together.

As if they had just found themselves in church, the three of them went silent as they made their way to the tree that had meant so much to all of their lives. When they reached it, wordlessly they all put their hands on the heart, running their fingers along the grooves of the initials Butch had carved.

After a couple of moments in communion with what Rose had always referred to as their Love Tree, Charlotte cleared the rest of the path until they could see the rocky bluff that looked over the main house, the livestock barns and the pastures.

"This is it." Charlotte stood on the massive granite plateau that gave them a bird's-eye view of their family's homestead. It was Brand land for as far as their eyes could see; it had been in their family for five generations, and the enormity of that thought, the fact that they were standing on the shoulders of their ancestors—brave, adventurous homesteaders—made Charlotte feel inextricably tied to this ranch. It was more than just a ranch: it was their family legacy.

Danica and Rayna joined her on the bluff.

"This is where it really all began for them," Danica said quietly, her eyes drinking in the vastness of the land below.

"And for us, as well," Rayna said softly. "We wouldn't be here now if it weren't for them."

Several quiet moments followed marked by the sorrowful sound of a red-tailed hawk gliding through the expansive blue Montana sky.

Charlotte fought back her own tears as she pulled a folded piece of paper out of the front pocket of her jeans. Slowly, she unfolded it; she cleared her throat several times before she began to read Butch Brand's final love letter to his beloved wife, Rose.

"'My beautiful, lovely, sweet Rose. I knew I loved you the minute I saw you, and I only had eyes for you for all of my days after. If this letter is seeing the light of day, that means you have finally come home to me, my love, and that means our souls have joined and our bodies will now become a part of the land that we cherished. To my incredible girls, my greatest gifts, I know that you will now lean on each other and gain strength from one another, knowing that our love for you is never-ending. You will see each of us in your sisters: hold on tight to each other. Never let go. And always remember that we love you as we loved each other. Deeply and completely.'"

Charlotte's voice wavered with emotion as she read their father's final written words aloud. When she was done, she folded the letter and put it back in her pocket.

"It's time," Danica said.

"It is time," Rayna agreed.

Quietly, reverently, Charlotte untwisted the lids from the urns and put them at the base of the tree. Inside of each urn was a thick plastic bag that held the ashes of their parents. Charlotte took a recently sharpened pocketknife out of her coat and sliced open each bag.

"Goodbye, Mom. Goodbye, Dad," Danica and Rayna

said, their voices blending together in a way that made it sound like one melodic voice.

"Goodbye," Charlotte whispered.

"We love you," they each said.

Then, Danica and Rayna tipped over the urns and released their parents' remains onto the rocks and shrubbery below the bluff. Some of their ashes were caught on a gust of wind, mingling together in a beautiful dance before they floated away. The empty urns at their feet, the three of them stood together on the bluff holding hands; Charlotte could feel her sisters' broken hearts beat as if they were in her own body.

It was difficult for her to gauge how much time had passed, but after a while Charlotte gave Danica's hand a quick squeeze. Danica and Rayna held the urns while she screwed the lids back into place. One by one, and with Charlotte in the lead, they carefully made their way down to the truck. Charlotte took the empty urns and put them in the small space behind the truck bench. Danica and Rayna, each looking uncharacteristically dazed and fragile, were hugging each other; when Charlotte came over to join them, her sisters opened their arms to make room for her. They had a special hug. Based on Rose's report, they had given each other a triplet hug as soon as they could stand: they stood in a circle, their arms around each other's shoulders, the crowns of their heads touching. Butch said that they looked like they were in their own little football huddle.

"It's just us now," Rayna said mournfully.

"We need to do better," Danica said. "Touch base more often. Take vacations together."

"I've always *wanted* to take vacations together," Rayna said. "We've always been so busy."

"We didn't even spend our fortieth birthday together," Charlotte said.

At the same time, they broke their triplet huddle and then reached forward with their hands and made a tower out of them.

"We will do better," Charlotte said.

"Yes, we will," the two younger sisters responded.

As she drove them back to their childhood home, a log cabin that their great-grandfather had built, Charlotte feared that as their grief faded, so too would their renewed pledge to make space in their busy, disparate lives for each other. After high school, they had purposely chosen paths that had stretched their triplet bond to the point of breaking. Now having lost both of their parents, if this didn't compel them to strengthen their bond as sisters and multiples, Charlotte feared that nothing ever would.

Bowie greeted them at the door, ready for pets and licks. Rayna left her winter boots outside of the front door, lay back on the hospital bed and hugged one of their mother's pillows to her body.

"When are they coming for the bed?" Rayna asked.

Charlotte, putting on a pot of coffee, said, "Sometime next week."

For quite a while, she had found the whirring sound of Rose's oxygen machine to be a bit irritating; now, the house seemed eerily quiet without it.

"I can still smell her shampoo." Rayna smelled the pillowcase.

Danica returned from the room she had shared with Rayna wearing a pair of black Chanel pumps that matched the black suit perfectly; she had also fixed the eyeliner distorted by her tears. Danica put her nose into the pillow and breathed in.

"I always love that scent. Lilacs," Danica said, taking three mugs out of the kitchen cabinet and setting them by the coffeepot.

Once the coffee was brewed, Charlotte poured black coffee for Danica and herself, and added a tablespoon of sugar and cream for Rayna. Each with a piping hot mug of coffee to warm their bodies, they sat down at the round table that their father had made from wood harvested from the ranch.

"Why does everything look so small now?" Rayna asked between cooling blows on her coffee. "I don't remember our room being so tiny."

"I know," Danica agreed. "I remember everything so much bigger than it actually is."

Charlotte wrapped her hands around her mug; she hadn't slept much the night before. Today wasn't pivotal just because of their trip to the bluff to carry out their father's final wish; they would also discuss Rose's last will and testament. Charlotte believed that none of them wanted to wade through that document, but unlike her sisters, this ranch had been her whole life. She didn't have a life to return to at the end of the week; Hideaway Ranch *was* her life. It was the only life she had ever known— or wanted to know.

"Well," Danica said with a sigh, her perfectly polished, glossy crimson nails tapping on the clay of the mug, "I suppose we should just get to it."

Rayna nodded; her blue eyes looked worried behind the John Lennon frames of her glasses. Rayna played distractedly with her mahogany ponytail before she got up to get a refill.

"Do me a favor," Danica said. "Grab the stack of papers that are in Mom's junk drawer."

Rayna did as requested; she handed the pile to Danica and then brought her mug full of steaming coffee back to her seat at the table.

"I hate this," she said, her eyes welling up again.

"I do too." Danica stacked her hands on top of the papers. "But you and I are leaving at the end of the week. We shouldn't put this off. We have some pretty big decisions to make."

Charlotte took a deep breath in, her hands gripping the mug as if it were an anchor that tethered her to the table instead of letting her float away on a cloud of despair. Danica pulled a document from a large manila envelope, looked it over and then looked at the both of them.

"Are we ready?" she asked.

Rayna chewed on a cuticle; her nails were short, clean and unpolished. She nodded. "Let's just get it over with."

"Agreed," Charlotte said, noticing that her own nails were chipped, with traces of dirt under the nails.

"Okay." Danica tucked her straight blunt-cut wheat-blond hair behind one ear, which was adorned with a large sparkly diamond stud. "Here we go."

Because they were all estate executors, all decisions had to be made together, no split decisions, no majority rules. That also included the fate of Hideaway Ranch. Ownership of the ranch was now split in three equal parts.

"I've taken a look at the financials," Danica said, catching her eye. "It's pretty bleak."

Charlotte did her best to keep her expression calm and her tone civil; it was hard to discuss the last few years at the ranch with anyone, even her sisters, who hadn't been fighting tooth and nail not to be dragged under and drowned by the monthly nut of the ranch. She had been fighting the good fight alone, taking on more debt every year until her credit ran out.

"I think," Danica said gingerly but firmly, "we need to consider selling."

"No." Charlotte crossed her arms in front of her body.

"You've taken on an enormous amount of debt, Charlie," Danica said, using their father's nickname for her. Butch had given them all boyish nicknames: she had been Charlie, Danica had been Danny, and Rayna had been Ray.

"I know that," Charlotte snapped defensively. "Don't you think that I know that? I've been doing this all on my own. Taking care of the ranch, taking care of our parents—"

"Here we go," Danica interrupted, her jaw setting in preparation for a fight.

"I've done the best I could with what I had. I sold the cattle, I sold the horses, I've let everything go that I could, just to make sure that Mama and Dad were able to live out their lives here. I did what Dad and Mama wanted; I kept this ranch intact. I haven't sold *one acre*—" she held up her finger "—not a one!"

"Maybe you should have," Danica said, her tone more controlled after Rayna had reached over to put her hand on her arm.

"Don't say that." Charlotte's brow wrinkled in anger. "Don't ever say that. This land has been in our family for generations. This land is sacred. It must remain in the family. Every last acre of it."

"Things change," Danica said. "Times change."

"I'm not selling." Charlotte shrugged and gave a shake of her head.

"Then, what do you intend to do?" her sister asked. "Get back into cattle?"

"No," she said. "I want to turn this into an Airbnb, tap into some of that corporate money that comes to Big Sky every winter."

Danica's periwinkle eyes widened in surprise. "Do you have any idea how much it would take to convert this place into a corporate destination? You have not one but two mortgages on the property, and if something doesn't change like right now, the bank will foreclose, and then we're all screwed. The thing that makes me absolutely nuts is that you let it get this bad. Why didn't you reach out to me before things got this serious?"

"That's the way Mama wanted it. Bottom line." She could hear the defensiveness in her own voice. All of them knew that, in the past, Danica was the triplet with a head for business and numbers, while she was *not*.

Danica looked out the window, seeming to make mental calculations. After a minute or two of thought, she said, "You'll need a revenue stream."

Charlotte abruptly pushed back from the table, walked the short distance to the kitchen sink and put her empty mug into it. Her back turned to her sisters, she admitted, "I've already been to the bank. Several of them, actually."

She turned around, arms crossed in front of her body, and said, "You've been awfully quiet, Ray. This involves you too."

Rayna had been nervously playing with the ring finger of her left hand, and when Charlotte took a closer look, she was temporarily distracted.

"Where is your ring, Ray?" she asked. "Why aren't you wearing your ring?"

She returned to the table; now all of Danica's attention and hers was trained on their little sister.

"It's back in Connecticut," Rayna said, still fiddling with her unadorned ring finger.

Charlotte and Danica both looked at their younger sister, waiting for her to continue.

"Ben and I are getting a divorce," she finally said. There was a slight waver in her voice, but there was also determination.

"Why didn't you tell us before?" Danica asked, reaching for Rayna's hand.

"Yes, why?" Charlotte reached for her other one.

"Because Mom died." Rayna had tears in her eyes again. "What else really mattered?"

"I'm so sorry, Ray," Charlotte said.

"So sorry," Danica echoed and nodded her agreement. "What's your plan? Do you have one?"

"We took out a second mortgage on the house to pay for Ben's medical-school debt, so when we sell it, I think we'll just break even. *Stay-at-home mom* doesn't exactly wow employers. I think when all is said and done, I'll have the clothes on my back and my car and no income or career prospects." Rayna looked over at Charlotte. "I was hoping to sell the ranch so I could just be okay. I'm sorry for even thinking that. Now I think that we should keep the ranch. Of course we should keep it. Dad and Mom would want us to keep it in the family. Maybe if we do make this a business, I would be able to build a little nest egg for myself while I figure out the rest of my life."

"You don't have anything to be sorry about," Charlotte said. "We're going to figure this out, Ray. I promise you we will."

The three sisters went silent and Charlotte had a horrible feeling in her gut about selling the ranch, paying off the debt and then splitting whatever funds were leftover into three equal parts. Because of her mother's wishes and, perhaps, her own pride, she hadn't reached out to Danica, the most financially successful sister. But, now, with the threat of losing the ranch she loved so dearly, Charlotte pushed through her pride and asked Danica for help.

"Would you consider funding the business?" she asked with a slight waver in her voice. "Just until I can get it up and running."

Danica looked down at her hands holding the coffee mug, all the while giving a slight shake of her head. Time dragged by while Charlotte waited for her sister's response; she had hated the asking and she hated the waiting.

Danica raised her gaze. "And you wouldn't reconsider selling some land off?"

Charlotte's arms were crossed tightly in front of her body while she did her best to keep her frustration from bubbling over.

"It's not a bad solution," Rayna chimed in. "It's not best-case scenario, but isn't selling a part better than losing the whole?"

Charlotte knew it was unreasonable to hold the line as she was, but every fiber in her body rebelled against the thought of selling one acre of Hideaway Ranch.

There was another lull in the conversation before Danica said, matter-of-fact, "But you won't sell."

"No." Charlotte said easily, firmly. "I've held the line. While the two of you were building your lives elsewhere, I've been right here. I've literally shed blood, sweat and tears for this land and I'm not going to walk away while I still have some fight left in me."

Danica's lips thinned while she absorbed what she had said. In the vacuum left by her two older sisters, Rayna said, "We rise together, we fall together. I don't know how I can help, Charlie, I've got so many of my own problems. But, I can't—no, I won't—pad my nest by chipping away at this ranch that has meant so much to you."

When Rayna spoke, Danica and Charlotte tended to listen. She had always been the calm voice of reason, the mature triplet, and she typically broke the vote.

Rayna continued, her voice soft and reflective, "Danny, you don't have to help Charlotte, but I think you should. We've never asked you for anything before."

Danica frowned. "So you saved them all up for one giant ask."

"I suppose that's true," Rayna said. "But, I know you, Danny. If you don't help Charlotte now, you will always regret it."

Their mother's cuckoo clock struck the hour and the little bird, one of their mother's favorite possessions, came out of its cave and seemed to chime in. This broke the tension and made them all laugh.

"I'm clearly outnumbered," Danica said. "And I think this idea may be just as 'cuckoo' as mom's clock, but… okay."

"Okay?" Charlotte asked.

Danica nodded slightly as she picked up her cell phone, scrolled through her contacts and pushed the green phone to call. "Hi, Lenwood…Yes, thank you very much for the flowers. They were lovely. Listen, my sisters and I are going into business together. So I'll need some funds." There was a pause, and then Danica said, "I'll be setting up a business account, and then I think I'll need you to free up five hundred thousand to start."

When Danica hung up, Charlotte asked her, "Danny— are you sure?"

"Of course I am," she said. "My business is booming. I'm completely comfortable. What good is my success if I can't use it to help family?

"So?" Danica leaned forward and stretched out her arms to them. "Are we going to do this thing?"

"Yes," Charlotte and Rayna said after they took Danica's hands. "We are!"

"I have one stipulation as the financial backer of this business," Danica said in a serious tone. "If we don't turn a profit in two years, and after we've paid down some debt, we reconvene and put selling the ranch up to a vote."

After they had all agreed to the plan, Danica said to Rayna, "If you want to come to LA and be a Realtor to the stars with me, nepotism is a very Hollywood thing to do."

"Or," Charlotte said with a smile, "you could come back to Montana and get knee-deep in manure again. Breathe in all of that fresh air."

"Thank you." Rayna smiled at both of them, holding on tightly to their hands. "It feels amazing to be connected with you like this. It really does. I've missed you. I've missed *us*. I love you guys so much."

In unison, Charlotte and Danica said, "And we love you."

Chapter Two

"What can we do to help, Charlie?" Aspen asked via video chat.

Aspen Hernandez and her twin sister, Aurora, were two of Charlotte's closest friends. Aspen was a skiing instructor who had a side hustle as a food blogger and influencer. Aurora was a fashion-and-decor blogger, which had allowed her to stay at home with her two-year-old fraternal twins, her daughter, Arabella, and her son, Axel. And even though Aspen and Aurora were thirty and she had just crossed her own personal Rubicon when she reached forty, their age difference didn't impact their friendship.

"I was hoping that you could develop a menu for me—maybe two weeks of meals, easy for a disaster in the kitchen like me to learn."

"I would love to do that for you," Aspen said. "I really would. And I'll give you the family discount."

Charlotte smiled. "Thank you. I'll take any break I can get."

"So what do you have in mind?"

She leaned her hip on the kitchen counter. "The meals I really loved that Mom used to make were all stick-to-the-ribs, down-home, backcountry food."

"Gotcha," Aspen said. "Old Montana prairie food."

"Exactly."

"Do you happen to have any of your mom's recipes?"

"I think so." Charlotte walked over to the cabinet where Rose had kept her cookbooks. "I don't see it right off the bat. Can I get back to you on that?"

"Absolutely," her friend said. "I think I have plenty to go on for now. I'll also give you some vegetarian and vegan options for the meals."

"All easy to make," Charlotte reiterated.

Aspen laughed. "So easy a toddler could make them, yes."

After she hung up with her friend, she sat down at the kitchen table, crossed off a couple of items on her yellow legal pad from her to-do list and then added a couple other points. She sat back in her chair with a sigh and smiled when Bowie came over to check on her.

"Hi, my good boy." She petted his wide, grayish-blue head. "It's pretty quiet here now, isn't it?"

She was used to living a life that was filled with more land and space than people. That was the life she had signed up for; she was carrying on her ancestors' ranching lifestyle. But this was the first time she had actually begun to feel isolated and lonely. Her sisters had returned to their own lives in California and Connecticut while she tied up the final threads of her mother's life, and that included making arrangements for all of Rose's medical equipment to be picked up. As strange as it was to have her mother sleep in the living room, Charlotte found it more unsettling to see the empty space left behind when the medical equipment company had arrived the preceding week to remove it.

Charlotte stood up and walked the short distance into the snug living room; even though the bed was no longer taking up the lion's share of the space, Charlotte hadn't moved the furniture back into place. In a way, it felt almost disrespectful, as if she were callously moving on without a sincere mourning period. She sat down on the couch that had been one of the first furniture items Rose had purchased as a newlywed; she had refused to replace it even when it was stained and threadbare and had springs poking through the flattened cushions. Bowie jumped up to sit next to her, and she hugged him, grateful for the companionship.

"I miss her," she told her canine friend. "I know you do too."

Charlotte wrapped her arms around Bowie and held on tightly to him. The pain of losing her mother was nearly unbearable. Fixing up the ranch to be a short-term rental was the distraction she needed to help her adjust to life without Rose. And yet, with so many quiet moments alone, Charlotte had a daily fight not to let her sorrow drag her down into a deep well of depression.

"Okay. Enough of this," she said to Bowie as she wiped the tears from her face.

Then her phone rang, and she received a text at the same time.

"Hey, sis," Danica said brightly. "You were on my mind. How's it going?"

"It's going," she said, reading the text that had just come in. It was from Rayna, checking in as well.

"You're sad," Danica said. "Let's do a three-way call with Rayna. I have some news that might just cheer you up a bit."

By the time she got off the phone with her sisters, Charlotte did feel better. Danica had been working with an attorney in Bozeman to set up the business and file all of the necessary paperwork with the county and the state. That news cheered her up, and the call had given her impetus to sit back down and cold-call the ranch hands that had moved on once she'd sold the cattle and horses. But an hour later, she had exhausted those contacts without any luck. Many of the phone numbers had changed; the men she did reach had moved on, many finding work out of state.

"Who are we going to get to help us fix this place up?" She ruffled Bowie's ears, which made him look up at her with his sweet, odd eyes and smile with his tongue hanging out.

In that moment, Wayne flashed through her mind. Was it possible that the cowboy was still in the area? Had he found work nearby? Or had he, like most of the cowboys she had called, moved on like tumbleweeds on a windy day?

"Do you know what?" she said to Bowie. "Maybe, just maybe, you were actually onto something, handsome boy."

Charlotte went to retrieve her jacket that was now stored in the closet because it had finally started to warm up. She fished around in the pocket, a nervous anticipation in her gut, silently praying that she hadn't tossed away the piece of paper with Wayne's number scrawled on it. After a moment or two of frantic searching, Charlotte pulled out the tiny balled-up note triumphantly.

"You see there, Bowie?" She held up her trophy for her dog to see. "Mama would say this is a sign! Divine intervention."

She had never really believed in divine intervention or destiny, but Rose had. Her mother had believed so strongly that, now that she was gone, it made Charlotte want to at least *try* to believe. And if she couldn't go as far as believing, at least she could willingly follow any breadcrumbs the universe appeared to be putting in her path.

Charlotte sat down at the table with her phone and the crumpled scrap of paper. "I'm actually nervous. Why am I nervous?"

Bowie titled his head and lifted up his floppy ears curiously as she listened to the phone ringing on the other end of the line.

"Wayne here."

Charlotte was so caught off guard by how quickly he had answered the phone she had the odd experience of her words getting jammed up in her throat.

"Hello?" Wayne asked.

She cleared her throat and swallowed several times and then finally managed to squeak out, "Hello."

There was an awkward pause while Wayne waited for her to say something, and then she did.

"This is Charlotte Brand."

He waited for her to continue.

"Hideaway Ranch," she said. "You were here looking for work about a month ago."

"Big Sky," he said.

"Yes."

"The woman with a quick draw and steady hand."

She smiled sheepishly. "Yes. That's me. I'm sorry about that."

"Don't be. I would've done the same," he said with an honest, almost appreciative timbre to his voice. "What can I do for you?"

"I was actually wondering…"

"If I found work?"

"Yes."

"I did."

"Oh," she said, deflated. "Well, thank you for your time. I wish you the best of luck."

Charlotte ended the call, dropped her head into her hands and began to rub her temples to stop the stress headache that was lurking in the background. She could not fix the infrastructure by herself; she needed a jack-of-all-trades like Butch.

"Okay," she said aloud, "so, *not* divine intervention."

Her phone rang and when she checked the number, she was genuinely shocked.

"Hello?"

"Is this Charlotte?"

"Yes, it is." She knew she recognized the number, and she definitely recognized Wayne's drawl—it was an interesting mix of the American South and the American West. Georgia meets Texas.

"Now, why'd you go and hang up on me?"

"Did I?" she asked sincerely. "I promise I didn't mean to be rude. I'm just…"

She paused, and she could tell he was listening intently to her. She started over. "A lot has happened since you came here looking for work. I now actually have more work than you might've been looking for in the first place."

"Okay," Wayne said. "Tell me about it."

"Well, my mother passed away…" She regretted telling him the minute she said it. Something about his voice had made her feel relaxed, like the calm feeling she would get after drinking a cup of chamomile tea.

"I'm sorry to hear that."

"Thank you. I appreciate that. It's been really tough." For a moment, she lost her train of thought.

After a rather long pause, Wayne prompted her. "What sort of help do you need?"

Charlotte squeezed her eyes shut for a second, struck by how the simplest things seemed to be challenging after losing her mother.

"Yes. Sorry. The work." She opened her eyes, reached for the legal pad of notes and then continued. "My sisters and I are going to make this ranch into a short-term rental."

"All right," he said.

"As you can imagine, since you've already gotten a look at the place, I've got a long way to go before I could bring horses back onto the property. And trail rides will be a big part of this new venture, so fixing the infrastructure is way high up there on the priority list."

When she finished, she waited for Wayne to respond. When he didn't, she asked, "Are you still there?"

"I'm still here. Just thinking some things through."

After a second pause, Charlotte said, "I really appreciate you hearing me out, I really do. But, I would need you to start like *yesterday*, and I know you've already committed yourself—"

"Pull back on them reins, cowgirl."

That made her laugh. "Okay."

"I'm week-to-week down here in Bozeman. I could get started at your place, say as soon as this coming Monday."

Charlotte's eyes widened, and she actually felt so elated that she stood up to ask, "Are you serious?"

"I'm always serious about work," Wayne said. "So how does Monday sound to you?"

"It sounds perfect, Wayne. Thank you." She sat back down. "And thank you for calling me back."

"My pleasure," the cowboy said politely. "Do you have a lead on those horses you're talking about?"

"No. I haven't even begun that search yet."

"Well, I'm down here at Sugar Creek, and they have some quarter horses that are better bred than most I've seen, and I've seen a lot."

"I've heard of Sugar Creek."

"I figured you had. I actually thought they might be your kin. Same last name."

"Distant cousins, I think. Not really sure."

"Why don't you come down here and take a look at their sale barn? I can already think of a couple geldings that I'd load up right now if you had a place to put 'em."

Wayne shot Jessie Brand, one of the Bozeman Brands, a text to ask if Charlotte could come to the ranch to trial some horses. Once he got the thumbs-up from Jessie, they made a plan for her to come down the next day, and after checking out the horses, they were going to take a moment to drill down on the most critical infrastructure repairs as well as the matter of his fee.

"I'll look forward to seeing you tomorrow afternoon, Wayne. Thank you," she said, and the next thing she wanted to say flew right out of her mind, so she added, "Just thank you."

Charlotte hung up the phone feeling a bit dazed. This morning she hadn't had a lead on anyone who could help her with the horse side of the new venture, and now, thanks to Wayne, she had the man *and* she would be looking at horses the next day.

Bowie putting his paw on her leg snapped her out of her reverie. She smiled at her good boy, got out of the chair and knelt down beside him so she could scratch him behind his ears.

"I feel like I just caught a tiger by its tail," she said to Bowie. "Good thing he didn't hold a grudge over the whole threatening-to-shoot-him thing."

Bowie licked her on the face, his mouth smiling. "I know, I know. You liked him right from the start."

"Or," she said as she walked to the door so they could both go outside and catch the warmth of the afternoon sun, "maybe I should start believing in divine intervention after all."

"Okay," Charlotte said to her sisters, "I'm here."

"Text us as soon as you can!" Rayna and Danica said on the three-way call.

Even though they had never been interested in contact with any possible distant relatives, after they had lost both parents all three of them had developed an innate curiosity about any extended family they might have.

"I will, I will. I promise," she said as she turned onto a gravel drive.

Charlotte drove slowly up the drive, feeling excited to be taking this first step toward bringing a herd back to the ranch: it had broken her heart to sell their horses. It had been necessary but so painful.

And if she were being completely honest, she was actually looking forward to speaking with Wayne. At first she had dismissed him as just another cowboy down on his luck. But, like fine wine, and after their phone call, the thought of Wayne had improved with some age.

"You found us!" A young woman, tall, slender, and wearing a cowgirl hat, jeans and boots, waved as Charlotte found a spot to park.

Charlotte got out of her Chevy with a smile on her face. She had to bump the door with her butt several times before it finally agreed to shut.

"Hi!" The woman met her halfway. "You must be Charlotte."

"I am." Charlotte held out her hand in greeting. "Charlie for short."

"I'm Jessie." The woman shook her hand with a broad smile on her face. "I hear we might be related."

"My dad always said that all Brands in Montana are related."

"Same." Jessie nodded. "Same."

"It's nice to meet you."

"Yeah, same here," Jessie said. "Welcome to Sugar Creek!"

"I'm glad to be here. I'm excited to see what you've got in your sale barn."

"I can drive us if you want. My Jeep's right over there."

"Sure."

Jessie walked with a long stride, her thick brown-black braid swinging as she moved, and Charlotte had to walk at double time to keep up with the young woman.

After they climbed into the Jeep, Jessie cranked the engine and shifted into gear. "I have to warn you, though. I was in charge of the quarter-horse breeding program here at Sugar Creek, and the horses you're going to see are my babies, born and bred. So if you don't like them, I invite you not to tell me!"

Jessie softened her words with a quick wink.

"I will only say wonderful things, I promise," Charlotte said. "You aren't in charge now?"

"No," Jessie said as she pulled onto a road that seemed to be part of a larger system of back roads on the ranch. "I moved to Australia with my husband."

"Australia? Really? That's a hike."

"It's a huge hike! But true love is true love." Jessie's aqua-blue eyes sparkled when she spoke about her husband. "I married an Aussie cowboy."

"The accent."

Jessie laughed. "Totally the accent! He had me quite literally at *hello*. But I have to admit that it took me a sec to adjust to the Australian outback. It just seemed so wild and untamed."

"I would love to see it one day."

Not missing a beat, Jessie said, "You'll have to come visit me there sometime."

"I didn't mean to invite myself…"

"You didn't. I just think, why not? We're family, after all. No way we aren't."

Charlotte took a quick liking to Jessie: she was wide-open and willing to make a friend.

"It must've been hard."

"What?"

"Moving to the outback."

"It was crazy hard. My husband inherited a million acres. A million! The enormity of Daintree Downs still kind of blows my mind. But once I got settled in, I honestly don't know how I ever lived anywhere else. My husband, Hawk, he likes to remind me that I am the outback personified—wild, beautiful and untamed." Jessie flashed her a toothy, brilliant-white smile. "Of course, he has to tell me I'm beautiful because he married me. Totally subjective. I'm going to start adopting some brumbies, though. Horses always make me feel more at home wherever I am."

"Brumbies? Australian wild horses?"

Jessie nodded, rounded a corner and caught a bump, which made her laugh, and then a large barn with a pasture full of quarter horses came into view.

"Will you look at that?" Charlotte felt mesmerized by the sight of the herd before her.

Jessie was smiling broadly at her. "We definitely have to be related. I feel the same way every time I see them too."

"It must have broken your heart to leave them."

Jessie pulled the keys out of the ignition and said, "Still bleeding on the inside."

Once Charlotte caught sight of the quarter horses, her mind mapped the quickest route to the pasture so she could get a closer look.

"Do you want to go in?" Jessie asked her. "Meet them?"

"That would be a *hell yes*."

Laughing, Jessie quickly climbed up the Kentucky three-rail fencing, swung her legs over easily and then hopped down. Oh, the ease of youth, Charlotte thought, climbing up the fence a bit more slowly, hoisting her leg over and then landing on both feet in a way that rattled her cage a bit. Yes, she was now in her fifth decade, but when the animals left the ranch, she had gotten a little soft, gained a couple of winter pounds. She was still a bit stove-up from the hike to the bluff. She was actually looking forward to the workout she was going to get while she put some sweat equity into the ranch.

Jessie, who seemed to have a deep spiritual connection with each of the quarter horses, introduced her to each horse, greeting them one by one with kind words and a gentle touch.

"I heard that Wayne is heading to your ranch this coming Monday?"

Charlotte felt her body gravitating toward one blue roan gelding in particular. "What's your opinion of him?"

"Of Wayne?" Jessie asked. "From what I know of him, I like him. Daddy really likes him, so for me, that's a gold stamp of approval."

"Good to know."

Jessie ran her hand down the blue roan's face. "This is Bet Your Bottom Dollar, or Cash for short."

"He's incredible." Charlotte's heart was racing at the connection she was having with this gelding. "He speaks to my heart."

Jessie looked at her, a bit more examining than before. "That's how it should be. A soul-to-soul connection.

"There's Daddy and Wayne!" Jessie seemed to understand that she didn't want to leave Cash now that she had found him, because she added, "You'll have more time with Cash, I promise. But come meet Daddy."

Jock Brand was driving a giant excavator, and Wayne was catching a ride in the oversize bucket. Jock shut the vehicle off and swung down to the ground while Wayne jumped out of the bucket.

"Daddy, I want you to meet one of our long-lost relatives." She gestured to Charlotte. "This is Charlie Brand. Charlie, this is Jock Brand, my dad."

"Nice to meet you, Charlie." Jock shook her hand with a tight grip, his deep-set blue eyes the exact same color as Butch's.

"I'm glad to meet you, sir."

"Every Brand in Montana is related some ways or another," Jock said.

"That's what my dad always said," Charlotte said. "My grandfather told me that one of our ancestors had a secret family. That's the lore, anyway."

"I love a good, seedy family secret," Jessie said with a charming laugh. "And obviously you know Wayne because you are going to steal him right from under us."

"Nice to see you again—" there was a smile in Wayne's eyes as he shook her hand for the first time "—Charlie Brand."

Chapter Three

"I'll leave you in good hands. It was real nice to meet you, Charlie. Don't be a stranger," Jock said and then as an afterthought, he pointed at her and said, "and don't be poaching any more of my men."

"Thank you, sir," she said. "I won't. Just this one, I promise."

"Now, let's get to the real reason you came to Sugar Creek." Jessie's pretty face was alight with joy. "My beautiful horses."

Charlotte knew she was looking for more than one horse, but at the moment, she only had eyes for one: Cash.

Jessie put a halter on the blue roan and led him to the small arena in front of the barn. She handed the lead rope to Charlotte and then trotted off to the barn to get some grooming tools. A few minutes later, Jessie reappeared with Wayne, who was carrying a dark brown Western saddle and a bridle. He threw the saddle over the top rail of the arena fence, then put one booted foot on the bottom railing and leaned his arms on the top one.

"Do you want to groom him?" Jessie asked. "Get a feel for how he responds to a new person?"

"Yes. Thank you." Charlotte knew in her gut that Cash was her horse. She was in the market to bring five or six horses total onto the ranch; Cash, if he made it through the trial and the prepurchase exam, would be the horse she rode when she took groups of guests on a trail ride.

Charlotte started with a currycomb to knock off any bigger clumps of dirt and bring finer grains of sand up from his coat. Then she brushed away the dirt, talking to the horse as she worked. Cash was a gentleman, lifting his hooves without resistance so she could clean them and check them before she rode him. She ran a brush quickly through his mane and tail; he didn't get antsy or frustrated, and he hadn't reacted negatively to having a new person handling him.

"He's a lovebug," Jessie said proudly.

"He's perfect," Charlotte said. "Did you train him?"

"I picked out his sire and his dam, I bred them, I was there when he was born, and I have trained him every step of the way."

For someone as young as Jessie, her breeding acumen and her ability to take a horse from halter training to standing stock-still while he was being groomed was beyond impressive.

"When did you start breeding horses?"

"When I was fifteen," Jessie recalled. "I think Daddy was the one who spotted my talent for it early on. It didn't matter to him that I was only a teenager. He trusted my ability and fostered it. His confidence in me helped me build confidence in my own abilities."

"Well, it's impressive." Charlotte sprayed Cash with fly spray. "You're a prodigy."

Jessie wore a pleased expression on her face. "I like you so much already, Charlie. I would love for you to give some of my beloveds a home."

"Honestly, I can't imagine leaving here without putting deposits on four or five of your horses," Charlotte said.

"Such great news." Jessie seemed to get emotional, and unshed tears made her eyes change to a deeper, more intense shade of blue. Without asking, Charlotte knew the place where this emotion had sprung from. Like her, Jessie cherished her animals—they were family to her, precious. Charlotte shared that viewpoint. And she had been in similar shoes to Jessie when she'd had to find new homes for her cattle and horses because she couldn't afford to keep them any longer. Charlotte could still feel the pain of the loss of her animals in a tangible way; it was tethered to her inner core, and it had never gone away with time.

"Ready to ride?" Wayne called out to them.

Charlotte gave him a thumbs-up and he brought the saddle, saddle pad and bridle over to Cash. As good as he was during grooming, Cash did not disappoint while he was being tacked up. Wayne put the saddle pad on first and then swung the saddle onto the gelding's back; he tented the pad so it wouldn't bind the horse's withers before reaching under the horse's belly to grab the rope girth. Wayne was a pro when it came to horses as evidenced by how adroitly he saddled Cash and how kind he was when he was tightening the girth. Most horses liked to blow up their bellies when the girth is tightened and hold on to it. Then, when they let the air out a couple minutes later, the girth would be too loose to ride.

Wayne didn't overcinch Cash: he would tighten it right before she got into the saddle.

Cash accepted the bit without issue. Wayne tightened the girth, and then he gave Charlotte a leg up into the saddle.

"How're the stirrups?" Wayne asked.

"Good," she said, suddenly feeling more anxious and self-conscious than excited now that she was back in the saddle astride a dream horse. "I haven't ridden in a couple of years, so…"

She heard the insecurity in her own voice and was frustrated by it.

"Just like riding a bicycle." Wayne checked the girth. "Tap into your muscle memory, and you'll do fine."

"Cash will take care of you," Jessie added.

The fact that both Wayne and Jessie wanted to help settle her nerves and increase her comfort made her feel more confident as she gave Cash a little leg and asked him to move forward.

Jessie and Wayne watched from their perch on the fence's top railing. Charlotte did her best to focus on the feel of Cash as he moved, giving a bit more leg to give her a more animated walk. To her surprise, it didn't take long for her to settle into the saddle, drawing on her decades of riding experience and focusing all of her attention on Cash. Jessie and Wayne disappeared into the background while she put Cash through his paces, walking, trotting, cantering, halting and backing.

"How does he feel?" Jessie called out to her.

"Like a dream." Charlotte patted Cash on his neck while they walked over to where Jessie and Wayne were sitting.

"He looks like he was made just for you," Jessie said.

"I think he was," she agreed. "If I could take him home today, I would."

Charlotte swung out of the saddle onto the ground; when her feet hit dirt, she felt the stiffness in her knees and an ache in her inner thighs from being back in the saddle. She winced from the pain but did her best to hide it from her companions.

"What do you think of him, Wayne?" she asked him as he loosened the girth to remove the saddle.

"He was one of my top picks," he said simply.

Charlotte took the opportunity to study Wayne. Yes, he had some years on him, but he was still a handsome man with a strong profile and, in her mind, a wealth of experience that she was interested in tapping into.

Wayne felt her studying him, and he turned his face to look at her. Their eyes met, and Charlotte felt an undeniable spark. She felt an attraction to him—she couldn't remember the last time she had been attracted to anybody. It felt uncomfortable, so she shifted her attention back to her purpose here: horses.

"If Cash was on the top of your list," she said, "what other horses made the cut?"

Wayne felt respected by Charlotte, and it only confirmed his decision to bring his talent and resources to her ranch for the summer and, perhaps, early fall. She was sharp as a tack, quick-witted and grounded in the homestead lifestyle. And, she was real pretty to look at. She had an infectious smile and ocean-blue eyes that gave him glimpses into the depth of her soul and her character; he was attracted to her beyond the physical even though that was there too. She had a solid seat in the saddle and excellent taste in horses. Every single horse he selected for her herd she saw exactly what he saw: mentally stable, healthy, well-trained animals. It was rare to find so many to choose from, but that was the genius of Jessie Brand.

"I think we'll add this pretty little mare to our list," Charlotte said, her cheeks sun-kissed and flushed from exertion. "My mom would believe to her core that the fact that she had *Rose* in her name was a sign that I needed to buy her."

Jessie smiled as she added the mare's name to the purchase list on her phone. "Docs Delta Rose."

"That's a mighty fine choice," Wayne said. "I just have one more I'd like you to see."

He saw Charlotte try to swing her leg over the back of the stocky mare's hindquarters once; when she didn't succeed, she had to regroup and try again to swing the leg over for the dismount.

"I'm not so sure I have another ride in me," she said, and he caught her wincing and limping just a bit as she walked over to the fence.

"Do you want me to get on him for you?" Wayne offered. "I'd hate for you to miss this gelding. He's special."

"Atlas?" Jessie asked him.

Wayne nodded. If he didn't live such a nomadic lifestyle, he would buy Atlas for himself. But since he did like his freedom to move around, he'd never thought to have a chance to do much more than admire him while he was in the pasture. Yes, he could have ridden him—no doubt that Jock would have given him the green light— but he hadn't asked. No sense in it. He would be moving on; maybe tomorrow, maybe three weeks from now. That's what he did, and he had learned years ago how to keep himself from forming attachments to people, places or things.

"Tell me about him," Charlotte said to Jessie while he untacked the mare.

"Well, Atlas wasn't bred by me," Jessie said. "Daddy saw this fabulous mare at an auction, and he was so smitten with her that he outbid every single suitor and managed to pay twice what she was worth. But when I saw her, I got it. I saw what he saw. She was slender and sleek but still had that big ol' quarter caboose and sane temperament." Jessie continued to smile at the memory. "Turns out, she had a stowaway."

Charlotte asked, "She was pregnant?"

"Yes, she was," Jessie said, "and her baby daddy was a Percheron."

"Unusual breeding choice."

"Agreed. But Atlas is beautiful, beefy and so calm. Wayne's right—he is special."

"Well, now I'm intrigued," Charlotte said. "If you'll ride him, I'll check him out."

Wayne didn't even realize that he had been holding his breath a bit waiting for Charlotte to make a decision about whether she had one more trial in her. When she gave him the go-ahead, he forgot about his bad knee and the sciatic nerve that had been dogging him for two weeks and walked like a young man as he made a direct line to the barn.

Atlas had his head buried deep into the hay bin, trying his best to hoover up those last bits of alfalfa that Wayne had put in his stall. Every day since he had met Atlas, Wayne had taken to stopping by his stall and giving him some attention. Atlas was the kind of horse that thrived on human touch, and Wayne had found that he got a boost after spending just a little bit of time with him.

"Hi, my boy." Wayne grabbed his draft-size halter off the hook outside of the stall, opened the gate and entered.

Atlas lifted his massive head up from the bin and turned it to look at Wayne; he whickered softly, backed up and nuzzled Wayne's hand.

"I'm afraid I've broken my one rule with you, my friend." Wayne gave him a pat on his thickly muscled, gray-dappled neck. "I might have gotten just a touch attached to you."

Atlas put his nose into the halter and let Wayne latch it under his chin. Before leaving the stall, Wayne spoke to Atlas in a whisper. "Now, my boy, there's a really nice lady out there who is going to fall in love with you the minute she lays eyes on you. Let's give her a real show, you hear me? Let's make damn sure you're on that trailer heading to Big Sky with the rest of the cream of the crop."

Just as he had anticipated, Charlotte's eyes widened, and her lovely pink lips parted nearly imperceptibly when he walked out with Atlas by his side.

"Oh my goodness," Charlotte said. "He is *gorgeous*."

"You want to take a look under the hood?" Wayne asked her. "Kick the hooves?"

Charlotte smiled at his attempt at humor, and for him, it was odd to even *attempt* humor. Smiling, laughing and humor really weren't his top-tier strengths. He couldn't even remember the last time he'd tried to make someone laugh—or even cared if someone laughed in his company. Maybe when he was a kid...as far back as that.

Charlotte was as impressed with Atlas as he had hoped she would be. She immediately put her hands on him, running her fingers over his silvery-black dapple on his coat; his mane and tail were jet-black, and he had only one small white star between his wise brown eyes.

"I have never, in my life, seen such a beautiful horse," the pretty rancher said. "I'm in awe, really. How does he do on trails?"

"Steady as he goes," Jessie said. "No matter what is happening around him, he keeps a steady, calm head. I don't like to say *bombproof* about any horse, but he's pretty darn close."

Charlotte nodded. "Saddle him and let's take a look at him."

Wayne brushed him off quickly, picked out his heavy hooves and then tacked him up. He had never ridden Atlas so he had to figure him out on the fly. He knew that ultimately he couldn't keep this horse, but he could do his best to get him a great home. And that's what he thought Charlotte would give him on Hideaway Ranch— a comfortable home, a happy life.

Wayne silently willed his knees to cooperate long enough so he could mount Atlas. There wasn't a mounting block around, and he certainly wasn't going to ask Charlotte or Jessie to give him a hand. So he just gritted his teeth and got his boot into the stirrup, one hand on the saddle horn, the other hand barely able to reach the back of the saddle seat so he could hoist himself up with as much grace as he could muster. He groaned a tad on his way up into the saddle, but he made it, and that was what mattered most. He knew he didn't have too many of those types of mounts in him, so he was glad he managed to pull it off in front of Charlotte for the sake of Atlas.

"I'll show you the gates," Wayne told Charlotte.

Charlotte had her eyes focused on him, and it made

him sit taller in the saddle. It had been a while since he wanted to impress a lovely lady with his riding skills.

When he asked Atlas to trot, it took a heck of a lot more leg than most horses. He had to squeeze real tight with his thighs and even give a nudge with the heels of his boots, but once the quarter-draft mix shifted it into gear, he was forward-moving. He trotted Atlas both ways, right then left, then he asked for the canter. He tried for a flying lead change, which was really just showing off, but Atlas seemed to understand his role, and the horse performed a beautiful lead change without any effort at all. Wayne snuck several glances at Charlotte, and she was hooked. Line and sinker.

Wayne gave Atlas a big pat on his neck as they walked over to where Jessie and Charlotte had been watching.

"What's the verdict?" Wayne asked Charlotte directly.

Charlotte's eyes traveled the length of Atlas's muscular body while she gave just a slight shake of her head. He had the feeling she was crunching numbers and that her head and her heart were in a tug-of-war. Damn if his gut didn't twist while he waited for the verdict.

Finally, after what seemed like a long time to him, Charlotte said to Jessie, "Please add Atlas to my tab."

Charlotte felt exhausted and sore in several parts of her body, and yet her outlook, which had been rather bleak as far back as the beginning of the COVID-19 pandemic to as recent as her mother's passing, had been buoyed. The exercise, the change of scenery, becoming instant friends with Jessie, and talking about one of her passions with a man like Wayne who had such a vast knowledge about these extraordinary creatures had turned up the volume in her life in the best of ways.

"Can I hug you?" Charlotte asked Jessie when it was time to part ways.

"I'd be offended if you didn't!"

They hugged each other tightly after they had exchanged cell numbers and followed each other on every social-media platform, with a promise to stay in touch.

"I have your deposit." Jessie folded the check and put it in her front pocket. "I will give this to my brother Bruce today."

"Thank you."

"My brother Liam is a large-animal vet, so I'll ask him to text you some names of the other vets in the area for the prepurchase vet checks."

"I appreciate that."

"And, if you want, if the sales go through, I can text you my brother Gabe's number—he hauls horses for a living."

After giving Jessie one more hug, Charlotte walked alongside Wayne to his truck. "I am really grateful for *everything* you did today."

"My pleasure." Wayne opened the passenger-side door for her. Once she was situated, he got behind the wheel of his truck and cranked the engine.

They drove in what felt to her like a rather comfortable silence. Before she headed back to Big Sky, she was going to sit down with Wayne to discuss some of the finer details of his employment as well as an overview of the list of priorities. They wound up back at Little Sugar Creek where she had left her truck. Wayne pulled up to a small trailer that was parked nearby a quaint log cabin.

"Is this home?" she asked after they both got out of his truck.

"Pretty much," the cowboy said as he opened the door to the Winnebago Micro Minnie camper, gestured for her to walk in ahead of him and then followed behind. She was greeted by a black Lab, his muzzle gray and white from old age.

"That's Mick right there," Wayne said. "One of the world's greatest dogs."

"Hi, Mick." She reached down to pet the dog's head.

"And that's Hitch." Wayne nodded toward the large brown tabby lounging happily on the dining table. "He was a stowaway too—I think we picked him up somewhere in between Lubbock and Amarillo. He didn't seem to be harming nobody, so Mick and I had a talk about it, and we decided to keep him."

The story made Charlotte smile: it showed what a good heart Wayne had for animals.

"You can have a seat right there." Wayne pointed to one of the bench seats.

"Okay. Thank you."

"Water? Coffee?"

"Water would be great," Charlotte said, petting Hitch. The cat rolled over so he was facing her; he curled his paws under and purred for her.

"Here ya go." Wayne handed her a bottle of water.

"Thank you."

"No problem," he said, taking a seat across the table from her.

Mick jumped up on the bench seat next to her and pawed her arm for attention.

"He likes Hitch just fine, but he'd still rather get all of the attention." Wayne took his hat off and hung it on a hook next to the table.

"Well, I can multitask," Charlotte said, petting the dog and the cat at the same time.

"So fill me in on this project of yours," Wayne said

after he gulped his entire bottle of water down in one long draw.

Charlotte took a break from her animal-petting service to take out her phone to pull up a picture of the list she had begun on her legal pad. "This is a preliminary list."

Wayne looked it over; he pushed his collar-length salt-and-pepper hair back from his face several times, then rubbed his hand over his unruly goatee. Charlotte tried to read his face but failed.

After a minute or two, Wayne handed the phone back to her.

"I hope I didn't scare you off," she said, feeling a wave of crankiness beginning to metastasize in her body from the fatigue, hunger and muscle soreness. She had to work pretty hard not to let it manifest in her tone of voice.

"No, ma'am, you didn't. I don't scare easy." Wayne rubbed his hand over his goatee again, and Charlotte figured it was a habit when he was mulling something over. "But that's a mighty big list—I think you know that."

"I do."

"We'll need a crew."

She nodded.

"I think I could ask Bruce or Jock to help us with that," Wayne said thoughtfully. "I know they keep a crew on payroll even if there isn't work so they always have hands when they need 'em. We'll need equipment. Excavator, skid steer, backhoe." Wayne kept on with his train of thought. "I'd like to bring my brothers on board. I trust 'em, I know their quality of work and they've helped me build remote ranches in some tough spots with tight timelines."

"How many brothers do you have?"

"Three," Wayne said. "They're picking up some pocket change on a cattle ranch in Wyoming."

"Would they come?"

"The minute I call 'em, they'll pack up."

After they discussed multiple projects, they reviewed his fee, which included wages for his brothers; from her previous experience working side by side with her father, she knew Wayne's fee was fair, and she was happy to pay it.

"Well, I think we've gotten a good start here," Charlotte said. "I should get going."

She gave Hitch one last pet before she stood up. Wayne and Mick followed her out of the trailer and walked her to her truck. She tugged on the driver's door and eventually got it to creak open. Once inside, she rolled down the window so she could shake his hand.

"Thank you, Wayne, for taking me on."

"You're welcome," he said. "Happy to help."

On her way back to the highway, Charlotte took an internal inventory; this was the best day she'd had in a long while. She had found a small herd of horses that could get her started in providing trail rides to visitors; in fact, she could offer rides to people staying at the ski lodges. In a roundabout way, reconnecting with Wayne had gotten the ball rolling on her massive project. She had always been a hard worker, a woman willing and able to go toe-to-toe with any man. It felt as if she had just met a man with a similar mindset: Wayne was the type of person who made things happen. Heck, he'd even managed to light a fire under her backside in just one day of being with him. That cowboy was the real deal, no question about it. And, at this point, he was exactly the jump start she had needed.

Chapter Four

Wayne always awakened before dawn, and his last day on Sugar Creek land was no different. It'd been years, maybe a decade or two, that he couldn't sleep for more than five or six hours a night, and he was always present for the sunrise. Once he'd accepted his lot, he decided to call it a gift that he saw the sun rise and set every day. He figured the day he didn't see both would be the day that he had died.

Wayne put on a pot of coffee, got dressed and then moved to the sleeping area to his king-size bed. He'd lived in a rolling home since he was in his twenties and he hadn't discovered a reason yet to change his itinerant lifestyle and put down stakes.

"Good morning, Mick." Wayne ruffled his dog's ears, petted him on the head and then invited him to get off of the bed. When Mick declined the invitation, Wayne scooped him up in his arms, groaning a bit from the dog's hefty size, and set him down on the floor.

"I'll get your food in a minute, buddy," he told his canine companion for the last decade.

"You too, old man," Wayne said to the cat luxuriating on the bed.

Hitch stretched and rolled over, inviting Wayne to pet his belly. Wayne chuckled, did the cat's bidding, and then picked him up and put him down next to Mick. He quickly threw the bed together, fed his companions and poured a cup of black coffee. The three of them reconvened at the small eating area: Mick on one bench seat, Wayne on the other and Hitch spread out purring on the table-top, his golden eyes half-mast. For Wayne, this wasn't a lonely life—this was the best life. While he sipped his coffee, he scrolled through his texts and emails. Most of his texts were from his younger brothers: there had been four boys in the Westbrook home. He was the oldest by fifteen years; after his father, who enlisted in the army right after high school, was honorably discharged due to injuries sustained in combat, the next three boys came quickly, with only a year between them. Waylon was the second oldest, followed by Wyatt, with Wade bringing up the rear.

"Come in!" Wayne said, at a knock on the camper door.

Bruce Brand, the oldest of Jock Brand's eight children and the heir apparent to the vast Sugar Creek ranch holdings, opened the door to the camper.

"Bruce!" he greeted his fellow cowboy. "Come on in."

"Thank you." Bruce stepped in, took off his hat and set it on the small kitchenette counter before he sat down next to Mick.

"Coffee?" Wayne asked.

"Sure. If you have enough."

"I never run out of coffee." He stood up. "How do you take it?"

"Black."

"Good man." Wayne brought a cup to his guest and said, "My dad always told us boys that it would grow hair on our chests."

Bruce thanked him and took a sip of the coffee. Putting his cup down, he petted the dog and the cat and asked, "So today's the day?"

"Yes, sir," Wayne said respectfully, even though he had at least fifteen years on Bruce. "I think I'll be heading out before noon. I've got some loose ends to tie up, and then I'll hook up this trailer to the green beast."

"Well," Bruce said and took another sip of coffee, "I can't let this opportunity go by without offering you a permanent job here at Sugar Creek. You'd be a foreman. You'd have your own crew."

The Sugar Creek holdings were vast, and each quadrant had a ranch foreman with a crew. Wayne had been filling in for one of the foremen who'd had back surgery. Bruce and Jock had made the decision to bring Wayne on board because of his age and experience. The crew he had been working with was made up of mostly young, work-hard play-hard cowboys. Not one of them was ready to take on the mantle of responsibility.

Wayne used his hand to smooth the hair of his mustache and goatee. "I appreciate the offer. I really do. Means a lot coming from you and Jock. But I gave my word. I have to stand by it."

"Well, if you change your mind, the offer stands."

"Thank you." Wayne nodded with a faint smile on his face.

"I suppose I should let you get on with your day," Bruce said.

"Actually, before you go, I'd like to have a quick word about something."

"Oh, yeah?" Bruce said. "What about?"

"Cowboys and equipment." Wayne stood up and grabbed the coffeepot. "Let me top you up so we can talk about it."

A couple hours and three cups of coffee later, Wayne had gotten the camper ready for traveling and hooked it to his restored forest green 1972 Ford F350 Camper Special. The truck was considered vintage, but it was a beast that Wayne would put up next to any of the newer, flashier models. He had traveled the country with it, and he imagined the Ford had many more years left in it.

"All right, Hitch." Wayne picked up the cat and put him into a roomy cat carrier. "We've got to keep you safe."

Hitch hated the carrier, but it was for his own good. He cried mournfully while Wayne lifted his fingers to his mouth and whistled loudly. Mick lifted up his head, moved in slow motion in a semicircle and then walked stiffly over to the truck with a slight arthritic limp. Mick put his front paws on the driver's side of the bench seat so Wayne could help him get into the truck by giving his hind end a boost. Mick quickly found his spot on the passenger side, his nose already using the cracked window to take in the last scents of Sugar Creek. Hitch's carrier was placed in the middle of the seat.

After getting his four-legged family settled, Wayne cranked the truck, loving the sound of the big block 460 engine roaring like a lion. He took one last look around before he shifted into Drive and headed toward the main highway that would lead him in the direction of Hide-away Ranch. Sugar Creek was a top-notch ranch; he liked the Bozeman Brands, and they had liked him. And Bruce trusted him enough to agree to rent some of their equipment to him for the Big Sky job along with a crew of ranch hands, just as long as Charlotte agreed to cover their salaries while they were working on her ranch.

At the entrance of Sugar Creek, Wayne stopped the truck, his arms resting on the steering wheel, his eyes gazing to the left and then to the right. If he headed to the left, that would take him east to Billings, while the right turn would get him to Big Sky. He had felt mighty sure of his gut instinct from the time he woke up until this very moment. But he wasn't so sure about his gut right now.

"In all of the years I've been traveling, I've never turned back. I've never retraced my steps," he told Mick and Hitch. "I've always moved forward. I've always moved on."

He'd actually become a bit superstitious about this life pattern, believing if he never looked back, if he never *went* back, the kinks in his life would just work themselves out. Of course, there had been temptations over the years. He'd had encounters with beautiful, soft, sweet women who were all fond memories for him. When he was alone on a long stretch of highway, he would bring them up from the photo album in the back of his mind. In those few moments when he did feel lonely or he started kicking around thoughts of giving up the road for good, mulling over memories of the women whose company, however brief, he had enjoyed always seemed to get him through the tough times.

This magnetic pull he felt for Charlotte was stronger, and therefore more troubling, than any he had experienced before. He wasn't even exactly sure what this moth-to-a-flame feeling he had for Charlotte was, and he damn sure didn't want to spend too much time trying to figure it out. He wanted to help her and he had given his word. Bottom line, he never went back on his word. Never. So even though it was probably the smarter choice to take that left, the only real option he had was to take that right. Maybe he didn't want to accept it and maybe he wanted to ignore it, but the thought of seeing Charlotte again made him feel happy at the core. There was something about her that made him feel better inside when he was around her.

"I know what you're thinking," he said to his companions. *"Stop overthinking it, turn up the music and drive."*

Wayne rolled down his window, turned the radio to XL Country out of Bozeman, and then he took that right—right back to Big Sky, Hideaway Ranch and Charlotte Brand.

"Didn't your mom tell you that a watched pot never boils?" Aspen asked her.

"A time or two." Charlotte turned her back to the window to focus on the ingredients her friend had assembled on the small butcher-block island that had been Butch's last handmade gift to Rose.

"Didn't he say that he would be here sometime today?"

Charlotte nodded while she bit on her cuticle. "He did."

"From what you told me, he doesn't sound like the type to go back on his word."

"No, he doesn't," Charlotte agreed.

Aspen wrapped her slender fingers around her friend's wrist and gently tugged. "Focus!"

Charlotte stopped chewing and returned to her first cooking lesson with Aspen.

"What's first?"

"First," Aspen said, "we wash our hands. And then we cook!"

This was her first class on how to make a dinner dish that would fit in perfectly with the ranch experience: Cowboy Casserole. After they washed their hands, Charlotte reviewed the recipe that Aspen had texted to her.

"There are a lot of ingredients."

"True, but it's easy to throw together, and it packs a really big flavor punch," Aspen assured her. "We can prepackage the spices and herbs so you will have some handy in the fridge when you need them. Trust me. This is going to turn into your go-to meal for your guests."

"I do trust you. I just don't trust myself in the kitchen."

"That's because you spent all your time growing up learning about the outside of the house with your dad. Now it's time to show you some tricks for the *inside* of the house."

"You're right." Charlotte had to agree. She had always been confident about her skills as a rancher; if she could operate the largest excavator when she was eleven, she should be able to conquer the kitchen with some time and effort on her part.

"All right," she said, her mind focused on the task at hand. "What's my first step?"

"Preheat the oven to 400 degrees."

"Okay. Done."

"Did your mom have a cast-iron skillet?" Aspen asked, poking around in the kitchen cabinets.

"Right here." Charlotte knelt down to search in a cabinet next to the oven.

"Perfect!" Aspen said, her greenish-blue eyes shining with excitement. "Go ahead and put that one pound of ground beef into the skillet. You're going to cook the meat with medium heat until it's no longer pink. That should only take five to seven minutes. While you do that, I'll prep the veggies."

While she used a wooden spoon to move the meat around in the skillet, she glanced over at Aspen. Her friend had been trying to teach her how to cook for years, and now that it was happening, Aspen had pep in her step and there was a glow of happiness on her face.

"You are really enjoying this, aren't you?" she asked.

"Are you kidding me? I'm in absolute heaven. Finally! You're learning how to cook."

"Well, I'm glad you're happy." Charlotte frowned at her playfully. "At least one of us is happy."

"Oh, shush! You secretly love this." Aspen peeked over at the meat and said, "It's ready. Take the skillet over to this old tin can so we can drain the fat without clogging the drain. Then, bring it back to the stove."

She used her mother's old, stained oven mitts to complete her assigned task. "What's next?"

"Next, stir in black beans, tomatoes, enchilada sauce and cumin," Aspen said. "I'll hand them to you, and you stir them in."

After doing so, Aspen had her bring the mixture up to a boil before reducing the heat so it could simmer for fifteen to twenty minutes.

"It smells amazing already," Charlotte told her friend.

"You're going to love it, and so will your guests," Aspen said, wiping her hands on a kitchen hand towel. "While that's simmering, we need to get a mixing bowl so we can combine the cheese, cilantro, beaten egg, flour and milk. When it feels like a dough, we'll spoon it over the beef."

Charlotte mixed all of the ingredients together; after she spooned the mixture over the beef, she had to admit that she was already feeling more confident in the kitchen. Maybe by the time their first guest arrived, she would be able to offer them stick-to-the-ribs, down-home cooking.

"Now we are going to put it into the oven for fifteen minutes and then we will add some more cheese to top it off and it'll be ready to serve."

Periodically through the lesson, Charlotte had filmed some content for Aspen to post to her YouTube channel, and now that they had a break, her friend was taking the time to post pictures and videos of her first cooking lesson.

The timer went off, and she had to admit that she was feeling a sense of accomplishment cooking her first meal. Her poor mother had been subjected to Crock-Pot meals, scrambled eggs and sandwiches. Rose would be so proud of her for taking on this challenge.

"It smells incredible." Charlotte held her breath for just a second while she opened the oven door and examined her creation.

"Look at that!" Aspen took a picture of the Cowboy Casserole in the oven. Then, the blogger turned her phone to video while Charlotte used oven mitts to take the casserole out and put it on the stovetop to cool.

"Look at this, my fellow foodies! In no more than forty-five minutes from prep to out of the oven, you can create a great winter dish that everyone will enjoy. Look at all of that bubbly melted cheese. Yum!"

Aspen stopped recording and asked her, "How do you feel?"

"How do I feel? Like I just built my first fence! Like I've cut a new trail through the woods!"

Aspen laughed along with her; the expression on her pretty, heart-shaped face was pure happiness for her friend.

Charlotte tilted her head up and shouted to the heavens, loudly so her Mama could hear her, "Mama! I did it!"

"You most certainly did." Aspen hugged her. "I'm so proud of you. And I know Rose is looking down at you wishing she could get a big ol' helping of this Cowboy Casserole."

"I hope it tastes as good as it smells," Charlotte said, an inkling of doubt breaking through her celebrating her accomplishment.

"I promise you, it's going to be delicious." Aspen opened the silverware drawer, took a spoon and scooped out a small amount from one of the corners of the dish.

She held up the spoon with its piping hot contents and said, "Blow."

Charlotte blew several times, and then Aspen handed her the spoon. Charlotte took the spoon, blew on it a couple more times to ensure that she didn't burn the inside of her mouth. She took the bite, slowly chewed while Aspen awaited the verdict with her arms twisted in front of her like a pretzel.

"Well?" her friend asked impatiently.

Charlotte put her friend out of her misery. "It's frickin' phenomenal, Aspen. How did you manage to get me to do this?"

Aspen had a happy blush that stained her naturally high cheekbones a rosy color. "A good recipe and a good student."

Aspen took a spoon out of the drawer and tasted the

casserole for herself. "Mmm. Delicious! Great job, my friend."

"Great job, my cooking guru."

"Honestly," Aspen said, "I actually need more. Want to have Cowboy Casserole for lunch?"

Charlotte got a couple plates out of the cabinet and handed one to Aspen as she said, "Great minds think alike."

They were just finishing up their lunch when Bowie began to bark from his afternoon sunning spot on the porch. The barking coincided with the gate alarm chiming.

"That must be him." Aspen jumped out of her seat and looked out the kitchen window. "Green truck, Winnebago trailer."

Charlotte's stomach began to flip-flop: she was nervous to see Wayne again, and she knew herself well enough to realize that she had developed a bit of a crush on the cowboy.

"Charlotte!" Aspen looked back at her over her shoulder. "He's *handsome*! Vintage Sam Elliott meets Jeff Bridges!"

Charlotte quickly put the dishes in the sink so she could greet Wayne. Charlotte recognized the look on her friend's face: it was the look Aspen and Aurora got when they were trying to push her in a romantic direction.

"Aspen—" she pointed her finger at her "—no!"

Aspen responded, "*Yes*, Charlotte. Totally *yes*."

"End of topic. Going outside now," she said in a sing-song voice as she grabbed her hat off the horseshoe hook and opened the door.

"I'll come too." Aspen fell in right behind her.

She stopped and Aspen bumped into her. "I'm serious, Aspen. I've got a short time to get this place ready for guests."

Aspen's expression immediately switched from playful to sober. "I promise, Charlotte. I was teasing you at the wrong time."

"It's okay," she said to her friend and gave her a quick hug and then turned her attention back to the job at hand.

Together they walked out onto the porch. Charlotte gave Wayne a welcoming wave as they went down the stairs.

"Where should I park her?" Wayne asked.

"Dear Lord," Charlotte said when she saw that, when Wayne opened his truck door to greet the dog, Bowie had managed to get himself onto Wayne's lap. "Bowie! Get down!"

Bowie looked at her like she was ruining all of his fun, but he did jump down so Wayne could shut his door.

"Thank you for coming, Wayne." She walked over to his truck with Aspen in tow. "If you follow me, I'll show you where you can plug in if you need power."

"Thank you kindly," the cowboy said to her. There was something in this man's voice that plucked at the pleasure center of her brain. It was, in truth, really distracting.

Aspen waited with Bowie while Charlotte led Wayne over to the equipment barn. The day after their meeting at Sugar Creek, she had begun searching for electrical outlets still in working order and had managed to find a good spot for Wayne to park his rig.

"If you back it in right here, there's an outlet just inside of this pole barn," Charlotte said.

Wayne nodded his head, and she watched while he pulled forward and then backed slowly into the space next to the barn. He shut off his engine and got out of the truck with a cat carrier in his hand.

"Nice to see you again." He held out his hand for her to shake.

"Thank you," she said. "Welcome."

"I'm just going to let him out in the camper," Wayne said, shutting the driver's door behind him.

She nodded. "Poor baby. Change is so hard for them."

Once Hitch was taken care of, Wayne returned to where she was standing. "Is Bowie good with other dogs?"

"He's great with other dogs. He's also really good with cats because my mom had one when we first brought him home as a puppy. So he should be fine with Hitch as well."

"Come on, old man." Wayne called for Mick to walk over the bench seat so he could put the elderly dog on the ground.

Bowie ran over and greeted Mick with a wagging tail and excited barks. They sniffed each other, fronts and backs, and seemed to agree to be friends.

"Hi." Aspen came over to where they were standing. "I'm Aspen."

He offered her his hand. "Wayne Westbrook."

"Strong handshake," Aspen said to Wayne. "I like that."

Aspen and Aurora had always been flirty with men; even though it didn't come naturally to Charlotte, she accepted her friends as they were. Aurora was a married woman with children, so as soon as she said *I do*, she stopped flirting cold turkey. Aspen was still single, and her bubbly personality and flirtatiousness had gotten her a large following on Instagram, and her YouTube channel had taken off.

"Aspen is helping me with a menu so I can cook for

my guests," Charlotte said to fill in an awkward silence. Wayne not only seemed impervious to Aurora's flirting, he actually looked a bit puzzled.

"I do have to go," Aspen said with a bright smile. "It was a pleasure to meet you, and I'm sure I'll see you around."

"Yes, ma'am." Wayne tipped his hat to her. "Likewise."

Charlotte actually felt pretty good about Aspen's meeting with Wayne: as promised, her friend had kept it mainly professional.

Aspen walked away from them with a bounce in her step. Charlotte looked over at Wayne to see if he was watching the pretty blonde walk away, but he had already switched gears back to getting set up. Halfway to her car, Aspen turned around and came right back.

Her friend had a mischievous sparkle in her eyes and a lovely smile on her lips when she said, "By the way, Wayne?"

Wayne turned back to Aspen.

"Charlotte just made the most *amazing* casserole," Aspen said. "If you taste it, I promise you will fall in love. There's plenty left to have a nice dinner for two."

Chapter Five

"Does it work?" Charlotte asked after Wayne had plugged his camper into her father's old RV 30 amp outlet.

"Let me check on it." He disappeared into his camper for a minute before he reappeared, giving her a thumbs-up. "It's good to go."

"I'm glad. Dad had an RV parked here for years, actually. He loved getting out on the road with Mama."

"It's a good spot." Wayne took a look around. "Direct sunlight to charge my batteries and an outlet for a backup system."

She shielded her eyes as she looked up at the top of his camper. "I saw the solar panels. Can you run this just off of solar?"

"You really can. But in my mind, it's never a bad idea to have a contingency plan."

She nodded her agreement, and they fell into a silence

before he asked, "Are you free to show me around the place?"

"Absolutely," she said, looking forward to making a plan with him. "We can start right here. This was Dad's Everything Building because he stored just about everything in it."

She detected a small smile mostly hidden behind Wayne's unruly facial hair. She pushed open the large metal sliding door to reveal her father's Ford tractor, the bush hog and piles of rusty gold in just about every corner of the building.

"My father was a bit of a collector," she told him, slowly walking into the building that smelled of oil, must, gasoline and rubber tires.

"My mom called him a hoarder." She ran her finger through the thick black dirt on the hood of the tractor, leaving a trail behind. "They had a really amicable, peaceful marriage just as long as he kept his collection behind these doors."

Wayne didn't say anything in response; he appeared to be taking a mental inventory of all of the nuts, bolts, hammers, saws and tractor-compatible parts. He circled back to the tractor and began to look it over.

"When's the last time this was in working order?"

Her arms crossed in front of her body, Charlotte gave the question some thought. "It has to be two or three years now."

She had linked the last time she used this tractor with the advent of her mother's diagnosis of emphysema and subsequent downturn in her health.

"Can you get your hands on the key for it?" Wayne asked. "I'd like to see if we could turn her over."

"I think I know where they are," she said. "I'll check after the tour."

"I'd appreciate it." He nodded. "Your father really knew what to buy and what to save."

Charlotte's eyes darted to Wayne's face to see if he was just being polite or if he really meant those words. Even though she didn't know him at all, she didn't read any social politeness in his expression, and on deeper reflection, he really didn't seem the type of man to spend a whole lot of time on pleasantries.

"Thank you for saying that. I always thought he did."

"There's so many usable materials in here. Just the contents of this building alone will save you a ton of money on the front end of the job."

"I agree," she said. "It's not the most organized, but—"

"We can get that taken care of."

"But there wasn't a job on this place that he didn't have a tool for right here in his domain."

"Well, this is a great start." Wayne had his hands resting on his hips, his eyes still darting from one cool thing to the next.

It endeared Wayne to her that he so appreciated her father's collection; it was no different than Aspen losing her marbles over Rose's recipe box today. All she ever wanted was to honor her parents by carrying on this legacy. It touched her that her parents' individual passions were being appreciated on the same day by people whose opinions she respected.

"I'll show you the bunkhouse next," she said. Wayne fell in behind her as she wove her way through her father's equipment storage and workshop through a door that led to a large, open area with double-size bunk beds along the walls.

"You had a decent-size crew here at one time." Wayne looked around, taking in the lockers, rusty and dusty from years of neglect.

"We did," she said. "We ran large herds of cattle here for most of my life."

"Did you wrangle?"

"Ever since I was old enough to stay in the saddle at a full gallop."

"And what age was that?"

"Seven," she said, pride thick in her voice, remembering the very moment her father had said she could come along to wrangle the herd. "I was seven."

"Impressive," the cowboy said, and his words were reflected in his deep-set ice-blue eyes.

"I think with a little bit of elbow grease and some repairs to infrastructure, this could be usable space."

Wayne nodded, taking one last look around before he followed her out of the bunkhouse and to the barn, constructed out of wood with a metal roof that had seen better days.

"My father built this barn with his father and grandfather," she said, trying to push the sliding door open. She put her full weight behind it, annoyed that it wouldn't budge. Wayne stepped up, placed his hands on the side of the door and pushed while she pulled. That did the trick: the door finally came unstuck, and she was able to slide it far enough back so they could get through the opening.

"This was the horse barn," she said, her eyes adjusting to the low light. "There's another barn, the same size as this one, that was used for housing other animals—calves, chickens, sheep—that might be easy pickings for predators."

They walked through the horse barn and had to use

teamwork to get the other barn's door open as well. "It always amazes me how quickly buildings deteriorate if you don't use them. It's only been a couple of years since we had horses here."

Wayne nodded his agreement, but he was also seemingly racking up jobs in his mind: when they passed a light switch, a faucet or an automatic watering system, he tried it to see if it was in working order. With each failed trial of the infrastructure, Charlotte felt her anxiety skyrocket while her overall mood tanked. How in the world would they be able to get this place ready in time for the first snow? How? It would take a small army of men, and all she had now, in truth, was an army of one.

She took him on the basic tour of the ranch's pastures that were pushing up weeds more than anything. Once she had the pressure of a herd of horses coming to the property sooner than later, she had already begun hauling planks of wood from her father's pile over to the closest fence line to start repairs.

"I've started fixing, but I know there's a whole lot left to do before we bring the horses here."

He looked at her with an expression of respect. Like most old-fashioned cowboys and homesteaders, he truly appreciated women who could hold their own in wild and often inhospitable parts of the country.

"You're closer than you think," he said, resting his arms on the top rail of the fence and surveying the land in front of him.

"Maybe I'm not seeing the forest for the trees," she said, mirroring his pose.

"That's what's helpful about a fresh set of eyes."

Her anxiety subsided a little, and she believed it was directly tied to the fact that Wayne hadn't seemed particularly overwhelmed by the dilapidated buildings and infrastructure.

"If you've got a healthy budget, we can get it done," he said. "Not all of it, but enough to get those first guests on the property. And the weathered wood, the rust, that's what people want. They want authenticity. They want to experience, firsthand, the romance and the mystique of the old West for themselves."

"That was as well put as I've ever heard it. I like the way you see the world, Wayne," she said. "On that note, there's one more thing I'd like to show you."

He took his hat off and smoothed his wavy hair back off his face, and then the Stetson went back to its place.

"Lead the way," he said.

What she wanted to show him was secluded and nearly hidden by a forest that had begun to assimilate the structure into its DNA. Charlotte ducked under low-hanging branches and pushed through vines and spiderwebs, careful where she stepped, certain there were any number of reptiles taking cover in the thick brush.

"Would you look at that?" Wayne stepped into a small section of clearing just in front of the hundred-year-old log cabin.

Charlotte had been fascinated with this cabin as far back as she could remember. She felt tied to it, tethered inexplicably with this tiny building that had once given her grandparents, three times removed, shelter from the long, harsh Montana winters.

"My ancestors lived in this cabin," she told Wayne. He looked genuinely surprised to hear that.

"This land has been in your family for a century?"

She nodded. "That's why I have to change with the times, infuse this ranch with corporate dollars."

Wayne caught her eyes when he said, "I hope you don't take offense to this, Charlotte. But how close are you to losing this land?"

"Too close."

Wayne breathed in deeply, and she could almost see the wheels turning in his head. She seemed to be able to read him like a familiar book, even though she hadn't yet spent a full day with the man.

"You didn't bring me here for no reason." Wayne smoothed his hand over his goatee. "What's your plan for this cabin?"

"Move it, or clear the land from around it and turn it into my abode while I have guests. I'll need someplace to hang up my hat."

Wayne seemed to be mulling over her plan: he examined the logs, walking around the building, smashing down foliage in his path until he met her back where she stood.

"I love these old log cabins. They were built to last. The fact that it's still standing is a testament to the craftsmanship of your ancestors."

"But?" she asked, since he was smoothing his goatee again.

"But I don't know if it will withstand a move. I think it may even be a stretch to make this livable. How set are you on this idea?"

"Super set," she told him. This had been an idea that she had been kicking around since she was a kid. She had spent countless hours in the cabin as a young girl. Now, as a woman, she wanted to breathe life back into the structure and give it a new lease on life. Her ancestors deserved that; this cabin had survived for a hundred years, and it would be a travesty to let it continue to decline and be engulfed by the encroaching forest surrounding it. Yes, many of the logs were rotten; yes, the roof was partially collapsed from a fallen tree; but that didn't make the cabin any less valuable to her. She had always wanted to claw the structure back from the fate of decay. In her gut as well as her heart, Charlotte knew that this was the time. Now or never, she thought, now or never.

"Well," Wayne said and adjusted his hat while he continued to size up the building, "I don't think we should move it. But you're going to need a defensible barrier to protect all of your buildings from fires."

Charlotte had to agree with that assessment. Montana had nine months of winter and three months of summer. Even though she was high enough in the mountains to see a freeze during the summer months, summer fires could also threaten them.

"I like that idea. Take all of this overgrowth away from the cabin, expose it to the sunlight and then use solar panels to power it. It isn't much bigger than your camper—you'll see once we get inside. So hopefully I could use similar-size batteries to get electricity to the cabin."

"I can't guarantee anything," he told her on the way back to open land, "except that I'll give it my best shot."

After the cursory tour of the ranch, Charlotte felt oddly overwhelmed and needed to take a moment to reflect on the amount of work to bring the place back to working order. It seemed insurmountable to her, but she had Wayne now. And he seemed to be a man cut from the same cloth as her father: a doer, not a talker. Bowie had followed her into the house. Perhaps he was overwhelmed with the appearance of another dog in his territory. Either way, she was grateful to have him by her side. She curled up on the couch, trying to position her body in a way that avoided the popped springs. When she finally got herself in exactly the correct position, Bowie curled up next to her so they could spoon. This was something that they had been doing together since his puppyhood, and it was both comforting and satisfying. She must have been so comfortable that she fell asleep, which was rare for her. Her phone ringing and vibrating on the wooden coffee table woke her.

She grabbed her phone, squinted at the incoming number through sleepy eyes and then groaned as she answered the video call.

"Hi, Aspen," she moaned.

"And Aurora." Her twin sister scooted closer to Aspen in order for Charlotte to see her.

"Hi." Charlotte rubbed her eyes for several seconds, trying to clear up the blurriness.

Her twin friends were full of energy—they were smiling, their cheeks flushed, and she could tell that they were nearly beside themselves that Wayne Westbrook had just fallen into her lap.

"Why are you guys so cheerful?" Charlotte pushed herself upright, trying to maneuver in a way that wouldn't disturb Bowie.

"You know why." Aspen's smile broadened. "He's so handsome."

"Aspen said your cowboy—"

"He's not *my* cowboy," she grumbled the correction, feeling oddly even more tired after her nap.

"A totally age-appropriate Sam Elliott look-alike cowboy just falls right into your lap—" Aspen said.

Aurora added, "It's like the universe is your own personal dating app."

"It's so exciting," Aspen said to her twin.

"It is really exciting," Aurora agreed.

"We've been wanting this for you," they said in unison.

Finally feeling awake enough to deal with the Hernandez twins in stereo, Charlotte said, "But *I* don't want it for myself right now."

"Why not?" her friends asked.

"Because my ranch is on the line. I am on the verge of losing everything."

That stark statement visibly deflated her friends.

"Look," she said, "I'm not saying *never* to romance. I'm just saying not right now."

"We just hate to see you lonely," Aspen said.

"We really do," Aurora affirmed.

"I know you do. And I hate to be lonely. I want to find the right man, settle down, I don't know, maybe even adopt some kids. But if I lose this ranch, the life I dream about building for myself will be gone. So just chill out on the matchmaking, okay? Wayne is here to help me. It's a business relationship. Period. End of story. I'm not going to sacrifice the ranch for a summer fling."

"Well, I'm sorry," Aspen said. "I know I overstepped. There's just so much chemistry between the two of you. Maybe you didn't feel it, but I saw sparks flying every which way. It was like a Fourth of July fireworks show."

Charlotte did feel the chemistry with Wayne—absolutely she did. He was objectively handsome, he had a quiet confidence that she responded to, and they both shared a passion for horses and ranch life in general.

"Do I think he's handsome? Yes. Is Wayne my type? Yes. Would I date him if the timing were right? Yes, I would."

"But you're not ready," Aurora said.

"Actually, that's not true. I *am* ready. I want to find

someone to share my life with. Of course I do. I get lonely just like the next person, but I don't need the distraction of a new relationship now," she said and then added, "And, just for the record, Wayne lives out of a camper. That doesn't exactly scream *permanent-relationship material*."

"Point taken," Aspen said.

"Valid." Aurora nodded.

"So please—"

"Back off."

"Yes," Charlotte said. "Please just focus on helping me get this ranch up to par for guests. That's the only thing that matters to me."

Before they ended the video chat, their conversation turned to the renovation of the main house and the menu. Aurora had scheduled a contractor to meet her out at the ranch on the following Monday to discuss renovations, cost and timeline.

"I appreciate you setting that up for me," Charlotte said to Aurora. "Please just CC Danica and Rayna on any email chains or text messages. Since this is a triplet project, I want to make sure they are always in the loop."

"Absolutely," Aurora said, "will do. And, I will get the final renderings of materials and fixtures for all of you to review by midweek."

"Thank you," Charlotte said. "I know you put a rush on it for us."

"Of course," Aurora said. "You're my friend first, client second."

Aspen looked at her schedule and set up the next several cooking lessons.

"I actually enjoyed our first lesson," Charlotte said. "It was a shock to me to discover that about myself, but it's true."

"I love that." Aspen smiled at her. "I'm looking forward to our next. I'll send you an ingredients list."

"Sounds good."

Charlotte said goodbye to her friends, yawned and stretched her arms over her head before she stood up and then stretched again. Bowie opened his eyes and wagged his tail at her. Even though she hadn't liked Aspen inviting Wayne to have dinner with her, it was a big casserole, and she couldn't eat it all herself. It made sense to share it with Wayne: it would be nice to have the company, and getting feedback about the dish would be helpful.

"Outside?" she asked Bowie.

The dog sprung upright, jumped down off the couch and raced over to the front door where he waited impatiently for her to catch up. Charlotte opened the junk drawer in the kitchen, fished around under stacks of papers and an assortment of miscellaneous objects. At the very back of the drawer, Charlotte found what she was searching for: the keys to the tractor.

She opened the door for Bowie, and he went bounding down the steps from the porch and ran full tilt over to Wayne's camper and pawed at the door and barked.

A moment later, Wayne opened the door to the camper and had to stop Bowie from squeezing past him so he could go into the camper.

"Hey, Bowie." Wayne sat down on the camper steps and gave the dog the attention he wanted.

"Getting settled in okay?" she asked when she reached the camper.

Wayne had already unhitched his trailer from the truck, popped out the part of the trailer that gave him extra room around the dining table and pulled out an awning that would give him some shade when he was sitting outside.

"I'm good to go," he said, still petting Bowie.

"I found the key to the tractor," Charlotte said.

"Perfect. Let's see if we can get it started first thing tomorrow."

"Sure," she said.

"I'd like to start organizing some of the tools and materials in your dad's shop. But I don't want to overstep."

"I'd actually appreciate it," she said. "And I'll help. It's always felt overwhelming for me to tackle it on my own."

After a pause in the conversation, and with her heart beating faster, making her voice waver the tiniest bit, Charlotte asked, "Would you like to join me for dinner?"

Wayne looked up at her. Their eyes met and held, and every little thing she had just told her friends and herself about the cowboy temporarily disappeared. A split second later, Wayne said, "I never turn down a meal."

She smiled at him, feeling a wave of relief that he hadn't declined her invitation, which made her nervousness subside. She had, in a small way, put herself out there with the friendly invitation, and it turned out just fine. "Okay. Good. Around six?"

"If that works for you," he said, standing up. "Okay if I get a start on sorting through your father's equipment?"

"Of course. I want you to feel at home while you're here," she said, feeling a twinge of sadness that had lingered for years after Butch had passed on. She was so happy that Wayne appreciated the stockpile of tools and equipment and materials. She really was. But she had realized with her father's passing that the pain of that loss never truly heals. She had learned to live with it, and the pain wasn't as acute as it had been, true. But she still missed her father every single day, and now she missed her mother too.

Before she headed back to the house, she said, "And if Bowie gets to be too much of a nuisance, just let me know."

"He's fine." Wayne turned to go. "I like the company."

She nodded, her hands tucked into the back pocket of her jeans. "So I'll see you at the main house at six o'clock."

"Yes, ma'am." Wayne nodded. "You can count on it."

Chapter Six

Charlotte had the casserole in the oven to heat it up; she added another layer of cheese and checked on it periodically. She wanted the dish to be hot and the cheese to be melted. While she waited for the casserole, she set the table for two and then quickly checked her appearance in the bathroom mirror.

"Lord," she said when she got a load of her reflection. Her hair was fuzzy with half escaping from her ponytail. She tugged her long hair free from the tie, brushed through it, encountering some tangles along the way, and then pulled it up into a neater ponytail.

"That's as good as it's gonna get," she said. It's not like this was a date—because it wasn't—but that didn't mean she shouldn't at least attempt to be presentable for a dinner guest.

She changed into a clean T-shirt, one that didn't smell like dog and sweat, and then got back to the oven just in time to pull out the casserole before the cheese started to burn at the edges.

"That does look really good, Charlie." She admired her first-ever casserole. "Good job."

One minute to six, Wayne arrived at her door. He had on a fresh shirt and clean jeans, and she could tell that he had recently showered, combed his hair and his goatee. His effort resonated with her; he was being respectful and thoughtful, and she liked that about him.

She greeted him and welcomed him into her home.

"Okay if Mick comes inside?" he asked.

"Sure," she said, "no problem. You can hang your hat right there next to mine."

Wayne took off his hat, hung it up and then smoothed his damp hair back from his face.

"You can have a seat right there," she said and pointed to the table. "What can I get you to drink?"

"Water's fine, thank you."

Charlotte got Wayne a glass of water and then uncovered the casserole. "How hungry are you?"

"I'll eat as much as you have to spare."

She found herself smiling at Wayne again. It was undeniable that she, thus far, really enjoyed his company. It felt *natural* to be around him, and for her that meant it would be easy to work with him on the laundry list of projects on the ranch.

She delivered a heaping helping of the Cowboy Casserole to him, feeling a sense of accomplishment and pride when his first reaction to the dish was completely positive.

"This smells as good as it looks," he said with a ring of sincerity in his voice.

"Go ahead and get started," she told him when she noticed that he was waiting for her to join him.

"I can't do it," Wayne told her simply. "I wish I could, but I can't."

"We had the same mother."

Rose would be horrified if she'd started to eat before the cook sat down at the table. She quickly put some of the casserole on her plate, grabbed a glass of water for herself and then joined Wayne.

"I hope you like it."

"I bet I will." Wayne loaded his fork with his first bite, and she held her breath for just a second waiting for the verdict.

"Mmm." He looked up at her and nodded. And that was the only feedback he gave her because he was too busy eating.

It was a quiet dinner—more quiet than she had hoped. She had been concerned that maybe they wouldn't find things to talk about but, as it turned out, Wayne's attention was focused entirely on eating. He worked his way through the massive helping she had given to him, and when his plate was clear, he gulped down the entire glass of water.

"You made short work of that."

"It's been a while between home-cooked meals."

"Would you like seconds?" she asked, still working on her first helping.

"If you've got more to spare," he said.

"Of course." She put down her fork. "There's plenty."

"I can serve myself if you don't mind."

"I don't."

Wayne filled his water glass, drank it down while he was standing next to the sink, then refilled it, brought it over to the table before he took his plate over to the stove and served up another healthy portion of casserole.

"This is the best damn casserole I've ever had," he said, eating the second helping more slowly.

"I'm so glad you like it," she said. "I've never been much of a cook."

"You wouldn't know it."

She beamed from the inside out: one dish down, and many more to go. But it bolstered her confidence to have a success right out of the gate.

"Did you get in touch with your brothers?" she asked, feeling full.

He nodded, swallowed his bite and then said, "They'll be here first of next week."

He put his silverware across his empty plate, wiped his mouth off with a napkin before adding, "And, Sugar Creek has agreed to loan us a crew and some equipment."

"Are you serious?" She couldn't hide her shock.

Wayne sat back with a content expression on his face. "It's a best-case scenario, that's the bottom line."

For a moment, Charlotte felt as if she had been holding her breath for months and now she could finally sigh with relief. She felt her eyes begin to tear up from sheer relief that the crew of men they needed had materialized.

Her shock rendered her temporarily speechless; eventually she said, "Thank you. I know that they agreed because of their relationship with you."

A brief smile drifted across his face. "I'm glad I could. Bruce—he's Jock's oldest son—said that he'd get a rental estimate for the equipment by the end of this week. Now, you'll have to cover the cost of the crew's salaries for the time that they'll be working with us. So you'll have to see if the numbers work for you."

Charlotte did have to wait to see the numbers, and of course she would have to meet with her sisters to review the budget, particularly when the cost of the horses, the renovation of the main house and the crew could easily chew right through their hefty budget. They cleared the table, and Charlotte liked the fact that Wayne offered to help wash the dishes. He didn't seem like the type that necessarily would.

"I've got this," she said. "Would you like coffee?"

"Why don't I make us a pot?" he offered.

"Okay."

"I make it strong," he warned her.

"Just the way I like it."

He walked to the door, but he hesitated before saying, "I noticed that firepit."

She put some water and soap on the dishes to soak and then leaned back against the counter while she waited for him to finish his thought.

"Any objection to me starting a fire?"

"Not a bit," she said easily. "It's a perfect night for a fire."

They agreed to meet at dusk for a cup of coffee around the campfire. When Wayne and Mick left, Charlotte's legs suddenly felt like Jell-O. They were wobbly, and she felt light-headed so she slumped down into a chair at the dining table. Bowie noticed the change in her and, concerned, came over to sit by her side and rested his head on her knee.

"I'm okay," she said to him. "Don't worry."

Bowie stayed by her side while she took comfort in petting his large head. It felt like she had been struck by a bolt of lightning—dazed, surprised and completely caught off guard.

She looked into Bowie's unusual eyes. "I think…" After a moment, she said, "I think that I may have as big a crush on that cowboy as you do."

It felt so odd to admit that out loud, but it also felt good to confess the sudden revelation to someone, even if it was her canine companion.

"I've really got to guard my heart," she told Bowie. "God help me, I hope I don't start tagging along behind him like you do or pawing at his camper door for attention."

Bowie wagged his tail and barked once. She leaned over, hugged him and kissed him on his head.

"You're a good boy, Bowie. I know that I can trust you with all of my secrets."

Wayne left the main house at Hideaway Ranch feeling like one of those cartoons that was hit over the head, stumbling around with stars circling above him. From their first encounter to this friendly dinner, Wayne had a strange feeling in his body that he couldn't shake. He and Charlotte just clicked—natural, undeniable chemistry—and it had been several decades since he'd felt that electricity in his body. It felt exciting with a good dose of irritating. He'd lived his life just fine without getting attached—he'd always cut and run before he ever got that far with any woman. He didn't love 'em and leave 'em, because he never loved them in the first place. He'd offered to build them a fire because he wanted more time with Charlotte, and he believed a campfire on a chilly night would tempt her to join him. And it had.

When he got back to his camper, he checked on Hitch to make sure he had settled in: his feline friend always took an hour or two to adjust back to stationary life in the camper. Hitch was lounging on the bed; the cat lifted up his head when Wayne and Mick arrived, then he curled his paws in greeting along with a half purr, half meow. Wayne petted the tabby, glad to see that he had eaten and seemed to be quickly settling in.

"Hey, buddy." Wayne stroked the cat until he was purring loudly, his eyes at half-mast. The trip had been short for Hitch in the cat carrier, and that seemed to have significantly reduced his adjustment time. It did Wayne's heart good to see him doing so well so soon after a move.

Wayne filled up a blue speckled ceramic coffeepot, filled it three-quarters of the way with water, grabbed a bag of his favorite coffee and two tin coffee mugs, and then waited patiently for Mick to make his way down the steps. He closed the camper door behind Mick and then took the pot, mugs and coffee to the firepit.

He headed back to the camper to get some campfire tools from his front storage bin. Mick settled himself near a log that was turned over on its side to provide some country seating around the fire, while Wayne went in search of a couple more large rocks to fill in some of the campfire circle. Once he built up the sides, he went into Butch's Everything Building and found wood that he could use for the fire. Next he hunted for smaller twigs and dried leaves to work as kindling. He'd loved to build campfires since he was a teenager. His father was often deployed for months at a time, and he didn't have much of a connection with the elder Westbrook. But, when his father received a medical discharge, they managed to bond over his father's love of camping.

Back at the pit, Wayne placed the kindling in the center, arranging the twigs in a cone shape over the dry leaves. He added some pinewood fire starters to the cone and then used a lighter on the pinewood. After he got the fire started, he stacked the logs in a way that allowed the flames to build without smothering it.

Once it was blazing, Wayne put the coffeepot filled with water directly onto the hot embers and waited for it to boil.

He kept looking over to the main house, wondering if maybe she had changed her mind about joining him for an evening by the fire. When the front door opened and Bowie came bounding out, leaping from the porch to the ground without touching a step, Wayne ducked his head and smiled to himself. Bowie barreled over to him for a hug.

Charlotte came down the steps and headed over.

"Nice fire," she said, sitting down on an adjacent log. "I can't remember the last time I had coffee made on an open flame."

"It's the best way to drink it," he said.

"Absolutely." She nodded. "I think you must be reading my mind."

Wayne slipped on a work glove, took the boiling water off the flame, put in the coffee grounds and let it percolate.

"I'll be back," Wayne said. "Don't go anywhere."

Charlotte laughed; she had such a sweet, joyous laugh that seemed to naturally lift his spirits. Wayne brought a cup of cold water back with him and sat down on the log seat to wait for the coffee to steep.

Wayne stoked the fire so it would warm them both as the temperature dropped. Charlotte was staring into the fire quietly, but he felt as if her mind was running a mile a minute. Wanting to draw her out, he asked, "Did you say your kin has been on this land four generations?"

"Five," she said, "and I feel it, the connection to this land, and that's why I'm fighting so hard to keep it."

"I hear that." He sat back on the log. "Have you considered getting back into cattle?"

"I have." She shrugged. "But for now, it's really just me out here. I need to be able to handle the place on my own."

Wayne checked on the coffee; it smelled great and was ready to enjoy. He lifted the top off the pot, added a cup of cold water to the coffee and then poured a cup for Charlotte before he poured one for himself.

Charlotte thanked him and blew on the coffee and took a sip. "Mmm. Wow. No coffee grounds! What sort of cowboy sorcerer are you?"

Wayne cracked a smile, enjoying the taste of a strong cup of coffee made on the open flame and the company of a good woman. "The trick is the cold water. I don't much care to know the science behind it. It works so I do it."

"This is the first time I won't have to pick grounds out of my teeth." She laughed, holding the mug with both hands, no doubt to keep warm.

"So, Wayne..." Charlotte restarted the conversation after a short lull. "Tell me about yourself."

He offered her a top-up of her coffee, which she accepted. He filled his mug up to the rim and then said, "What do you want to know?"

She shook her head with a small shrug. "I don't know. Whatever you want to share, I guess. I know you have three younger brothers. You know horses and homesteading." She met his gaze. "You live your life on the road."

"Well, now, see there?" he said. "You already know more about me than most folks."

He finished his coffee, then smoothed his goatee with his hand. "I was an army brat."

His history wasn't something he readily shared, but he wanted Charlotte to feel comfortable with him. She was putting a lot of trust in him without knowing much about him. She was desperate for help, and he knew that if she hadn't been desperate to save her ranch, most likely he wouldn't be sitting here enjoying this fire.

"I suppose that's the reason I move on." He leaned his arms on his bent knees.

"It's what you knew."

For a second, Wayne was distracted by Charlotte tucking wayward strands of hair behind her ear, the light from the fire giving her a lovely glow on her pretty face.

"I guess that's right," he agreed.

"Where did you learn horses?" she asked.

Wayne leaned in and stoked the fire again. He wanted to open up to Charlotte, but there were many memories he wanted to keep locked behind a door in his mind. If he let one or two memories through that door, how many others would break free?

"Texas," he told her, his eyes watching the flames send sparks of red and orange that lived for a fleeting time above the flames before dying.

He could feel her eyes on him, waiting for him to continue. He hadn't discussed his childhood with anyone other than his brothers for decades.

"My father retired from the military when I was thirteen or fourteen, somewhere around that time. We were in Texas at the time, so that's where we settled."

"Horse country."

Wayne glanced over at her, but he found it easier to remember if his eyes were set on the fire.

"Horse country," he echoed. "Cowboy country."

She was listening intently to him, and her body language, the way she was leaning ever so slightly in his direction, gave him the prod he needed to continue.

"My parents divorced almost the minute my dad was honorably discharged. They'd lived so many years apart, they couldn't quite figure out how to be married under the same roof."

"I'm sorry."

"Don't be," Wayne said. "It may as well have been a different lifetime. And if they hadn't gone their separate ways, I doubt I would be sitting here with you now."

"Why not?"

Wayne stretched his legs out and crossed them at the ankles. "The same year my mom divorced my dad, he married a native Texan. Beverly. She came from Dallas royalty—big cattle money. She had a ranch, we moved there…"

"And the rest is history."

"That's about right," he said. "I'd never ridden a horse. Never *wanted* to ride one. To me—and of course I thought I knew everything there was to know about life at that age—it was a real stupid idea to get on the back of a large animal that could be startled by a leaf and take it for a ride."

"What changed your mind?"

"Oddly enough, my early failures hooked me," Wayne told her. "My stepmom had this big old black Percheron. He was a giant by the name of His Royal Highness. I figured why not start with the biggest horse on the lot. So I got on him, and that first time, he bucked me off about ten minutes in, I broke a fence with my body, and you would have thought that would have deterred me."

"But it didn't."

"Nope, it sure didn't. In fact, it was that moment, while I was still trying to stand up and every bone in my body felt like it had been fractured, that I decided I wanted to make horses my life."

"So it turns out that you are just as crazy as the rest of us." Charlotte laughed, and he felt gratified. Whenever this woman laughed, it made him feel lighter inside, cleared away some of the darkness that lurked in the corners of his mind.

"Absolutely." He smiled the smallest of smiles remembering his first ride. "I was picking splinters out of my skin for nearly a week. But I got back in that saddle, and with some lessons from my stepmom, I managed to learn how to ride."

After several moments of silence, Charlotte asked him, "Have you ever been married?"

The question felt like a gut punch, but he refused to let her see him rattled. "No. You?"

"No. I don't get to town much." She shook her head with a small, self-effacing smile. "And I don't mean to sound like I dated around or anything, but it's a small pool around here."

Her humor eased the twist in his gut. "I thought Charlie Brand was your husband."

That made her laugh again, her head titled back, her smile lighting up her face in the most lovely way.

"No. Not my husband," she said after she stopped laughing. "I am one of three sisters. Triplets, actually."

"Triplets?"

"I know, right? My poor mom." Charlotte reached down to pet Mick's head when he walked over to sit next to her. "My dad had hoped for boys so he gave us all boy nicknames, which made my mom nuts. But it was a battle with Dad she didn't win. I was Charlie, my sister Danica is Danny, and Rayna is Ray."

She continued, "I think he wanted boys because of the ranch, really. Back in my father's day, women's work was in the house."

"But you proved him wrong."

"I did, I suppose. I just always wanted to be with him. I loved everything about this ranch. I can't imagine living anywhere else."

"I can see why." From the moment he first drove onto Hideaway Ranch, Wayne had thought that there was something mighty special about this land.

She looked over at him with a faint smile. "You can call me Charlie if you want."

"No," he said in a quiet voice. "When I think of you, I think *Charlotte*."

Wayne let the fire die down, knowing that tomorrow they had a long day of hard work ahead of them. But he sensed that Charlotte wasn't ready to leave the fire, and neither was he. In the firelight, Wayne was struck by Charlotte's natural, unassuming beauty. There was something about her face, the kindness he saw in her eyes, the freckles scattered across her nose and cheeks, and the strength he saw in her character. In his mind, she was the best kind of woman: hardworking, kind, sweet. A rare find.

Wayne pulled a harmonica out of his shirt pocket and held it up for his companion to see. "Do you mind?"

"Not at all."

Wayne began to play, something he had been doing since he was a young kid of five or six. It had belonged to his mother's father, who had lived with them briefly at the end of his life. After he died, his mother was cleaning out his drawers, and she had tossed the harmonica in the trash. Wayne had rescued it and had played and played until he could produce something akin to a tune. It drove his mother crazy, but she didn't take it away from him. His mother's family had always been musical, and she could sing like an angel. But somewhere along the line, she had stopped singing, and to this day he hadn't heard her sing a note.

"That's beautiful." Charlotte wrapped her arms around her bent legs and rested her chin on her knees.

As the flames died down further, Wayne could feel the chill in the night air, and as he played mournful tunes, the stars overhead became vibrant in the velvety-black night sky. He played until there were only orange and white ashes in the firepit. He now had a chill in his bones that made him worry about Charlotte's comfort.

"Well, I think it's time to call it a night." Wayne tucked his harmonica into his shirt pocket.

He doused the fire with some water and then offered his hand to Charlotte, which she accepted even though she clearly didn't need it. Some women took offense to his gentlemanly ways. So far, Charlotte had embraced them.

"Thank you for a lovely evening, Wayne," Charlotte said. "I enjoyed the company and the harmonica."

"Likewise."

"Good night, then," she said with a small wave.

"Good night," he said before adding, "I'll be up at dawn."

She paused to answer. "Same. I can put on a pot if you want to come to the main."

"Sure." He gave a quick nod. "If you've got eggs, I can fry 'em up for us."

They agreed on breakfast, and she continued on her way but had to stop again when she realized that Mick had followed her while Bowie had stayed by the pit with Wayne. She walked back with Mick and then patted her leg for Bowie to come with her.

On the way back to her house she said, "I know you like him. I do too, but I draw the line at you sleeping in his bed."

Bowie always filled up the empty space on her queen-size bed, and his presence had made her feel less alone after her mother's death.

Charlotte opened the door for Bowie to go in. "I don't mind sharing you, but that is a bridge too far."

Chapter Seven

During the first week Wayne spent on the ranch, Charlotte was already seeing changes. The man was as focused as a laser beam on his work, at times coming off as terse, but he got results. They were both alpha control freaks, and for her, that meant there would be conflict between them eventually.

"Can you move the tractor to the next post?" Wayne asked, his T-shirt soaked with sweat, his arms coated in a fine layer of dirt.

"Sure." She hopped onto her father's tractor, thrilled that Wayne had managed to get it started with the purchase of a few minor parts.

She moved it down the fence line, pulling a trailer of pressure-treated wooden poles and various tools to repair a significant number of rotted poles. They had been mending pasture fences for several days in advance of the horses arriving on the property. Before heading back to

Australia, Jessie Brand had sent her contact cards for two large-animal veterinarians. After doing some research, she decided to hire Dr. Tonia Vislosky. Charlotte liked her website as well as her holistic approach to veterinary medicine. And the majority of her reviews were five-star.

She parked the tractor, jumped down and picked up the top railing pole off the pile and dragged it over to where Wayne was working. They had developed a system pretty quickly, and now that she knew Wayne wasn't much of a talker when he worked, she had stopped trying to make small talk. He lifted the railing into place, she held the far end while he used a nail gun to secure it to the post, and then he moved down to her end of the plank.

Wayne walked over to the trailer, grabbed a jug of water, took off his hat, and doused his head and face with the cool water to rinse the sweat off his face and neck. He put his hat back on and then brought her a bottle of water.

"Thank you." She unscrewed the cap. "We're making some good progress."

Wayne chugged down a bottle of water, put the cap back on and tossed it on the trailer. He surveyed the work that they had done and that was left.

"This pasture is big enough for your herd as is," he said. "Once we get this pasture fence fixed, we can bring them home."

"I usually don't leave them out overnight," she said, pointing to the back portion of the pasture. "Too many predators just beyond that tree line."

"My brothers will be here in the next day or two. I'll get them started on the barn."

Wayne had managed to get the shower in the bunkhouse working. His brothers and the crew coming from Sugar Creek could set up tents if they preferred to camp under the stars or they could sleep in the bunkhouse as well as use it as a spot to get out of the heat.

Her phone dinged, and it reminded her of her upcoming cooking lesson. "I've got to meet with Aspen."

Wayne gave a nod so she knew that he heard her, but he was already climbing onto the tractor to move it up the line. She put her phone back into her pocket and began to walk toward the house.

"Hey!" Wayne had started to drive away, but he had stopped.

She turned back, and he asked, "What are you making?"

Darn if her heart didn't do a happy cartwheel. "Oven-fried ranch steak. Are you willing to be my taster?"

"Yep."

That was his way: if he could get away with all one-word answers, she was certain he would be just fine with that. Charlotte had a big smile on her face when she walked back to the main house. Bowie usually chose to stay behind with Wayne, and she had learned to accept that. Wayne treated him as if he were his own so she never worried about her dog's safety. On the other hand, Mick had taken a liking to her.

"Are you coming with?" She heard Mick's paws hitting the dusty ground behind her. She stopped and waited for the older dog to catch up with her.

"I have Mick!" she called out to Wayne, and he gave her a thumbs-up to let her know that he had heard.

"Come on, sweet boy." She reached down to pet Mick's black-and-silver head. "The call of climate control."

She walked more slowly so Mick could keep up; when they reached the steps of the porch, she gave him a boost when he seemed to tire out. He followed her inside, and he went right to the spot he had carved out for himself in the main house, right next to the kitchen floor vent.

"Smart boy," she said to her companion. "That's the coolest spot in the house."

Charlotte looked at the recipe and started the process of gathering the ingredients and utensils needed to make this new recipe. Wayne had been a willing guinea pig for the last several recipes she had tried; he seemed to really enjoy her cooking and he always cleaned his plate. Wayne was a gentleman and had been raised with good manners, but he was also direct, and there were a couple of breakfast recipes he hadn't been so keen on.

"Hey!" Aspen waved at her when she called her on video chat.

"Hi," she said, turning the camera so Aspen could see all of her ingredients, bowls, baking pans and utensils.

"Look at you! Ready to cook!"

"I have to tell you, the more I cook, the more I want to cook. I *never* thought this would be me."

She didn't share with Aspen that part of her enthusiasm for cooking was grounded in her growing attraction for Wayne. They were becoming friends: she liked his company and cooking meals that he would enjoy after putting in a full day's work on the ranch. It was a pleasure to cook for such a man. She remembered that Rose had said that it was her honor to cook for her husband; Charlotte had always thought that was fossil thinking, but now she understood what her mother meant. Nourishing the man she loved brought her mom joy.

Aspen clapped her hands together, her face filled with so much happiness and pride. "I'm so glad. So glad! Did you marinate the meat?"

"Sure did." Charlotte took the pan with the marinated meat out of the refrigerator. "And I already drained it."

"Look at you! You aren't going to need me anymore." Aspen gave her a teasing pout.

"I will always need you. Maybe not just to follow a recipe," she said.

"Well, then, why don't you just do your thing while I keep you company?"

"Is that a challenge?" Charlotte teased her friend in return.

Aspen tilted her head, shrugged one shoulder and lifted up her eyebrows. "I don't know. Are you ready for it?"

"Am I ready?" Charlotte said, feeling rather cocky about her newly discovered cooking abilities. "I was *born* ready."

Later that evening, Wayne was washed up and sitting at her dining-room table. His hat hung up next to hers brought her a sense of comfort, even though she knew that this comfort was temporary. She also knew that she couldn't stop herself from getting attached to this cowboy and his four-legged family. When he moved on—and she was certain that he *would* move on—it was going to hurt. For now, she did her best not to think about it and, as much as was possible, guard her heart.

"So next week is jam-packed," Wayne said after his second sizable portion of the oven-fried steak.

He sat back with that satisfied look on his face that she already knew so well. This man worked hard, just about harder than anyone she had known, if her father was taken out of the equation, and he loved to reward himself with a hearty dinner.

"It is." She wiped her mouth off with a napkin. "We

have prepurchase vet checks at Sugar Creek with Dr. Tonia Vislosky. Are you coming for that?"

"I can," Wayne said, smoothing down his goatee, "if you'd like."

"I would really appreciate it, actually. I've never bought this many horses at one time. I'd like to have a second pair of eyes."

The cowboy nodded his head, his eyes taking in the kitchen and the living room. "And you said the contractor will be here next week?"

"Yes. My sister is going to fly in for the walk-through with the contractor and the decorator. I'm happy to hand over the renovation to her."

"Make sure he knows that we are going to need a permit pulled for a solar system on the cabin, and if you want running water in the cabin we've got to get a permit for a septic tank as well."

"I absolutely want running water. And a small bathroom with a shower," she said. "I've used plenty of outhouses in my day. I've paid my dues."

He smiled at her behind his facial hair, the expression in his eyes appreciative. Wayne always made her feel like an attractive woman in a way that didn't make her feel uncomfortable. He found her attractive on all levels, not just the physical, and it had been years since a man had made her feel special in the way he did. And she was certain that her attraction to him showed in her eyes; she didn't try to hide it. Why should she? They were adults, and they both knew their boundaries.

"Duly noted," he said. "The crew and equipment will be on site midweek."

She picked up their plates and took them to the sink to

soak. "That's unbelievable. Everything is going so fast all of a sudden."

"Does that bother you?"

She rejoined him at the table. "Yes and no. It's been such a long time since we needed so many people on the ranch. I'm used to the quiet, I guess."

He nodded. "I have enjoyed the quiet here, and I've…"

He seemed to have something else to add but when he didn't, she didn't push the issue. The fact was, she was keeping some of her feelings close to the vest: she hadn't said how much she would miss *their* time alone on the ranch. Their dynamic would change—it had to, with so many people and animals coming on board. And yet, in a short amount of time, she had come to love their dinners, and their nearly nightly fires and the conversations they had. Wayne not only challenged her to tap into her homesteading roots, he also excited her mind. Hopefully, they would be able to find some alone time after the cavalry arrived.

"Meet you at the firepit?" he asked.

"Are you making cowboy coffee?" she said and smiled at him. It was a smile that had started deep inside of her before it reached her lips.

He smiled back at her broadly enough that she saw his teeth, a rare occurrence indeed. "If you're requesting, I'm making."

"I'm definitely requesting."

He rubbed his hands several times over his jeans. She had seen him do this many times when something was so exciting for him his mind was churning with good ideas.

"Then, I'm definitely making." He stood up and tapped the table several times with one finger. "See you in a bit." He took his hat off of the horseshoe hook and called to Mick, who stayed put while Bowie raced over to Wayne.

"I think resisting them is futile," she said.

"I'm seeing that."

"I'm okay if you're okay. I'll bring the old man with me to the fire."

"Sounds like a plan."

Charlotte hurried with the cleanup of their meal, watching Wayne through the kitchen window. It was possible that her feelings were developing past a crush on this big sky cowboy. There wasn't any way for her to wall off those feelings completely; he had so many qualities that she had always hoped for in a partner, with one major drawback: Wayne wasn't the settling kind. And she knew that right out of the gate. She didn't have any illusions that she would be the one woman who could change him. But her heart didn't much care about what her head had to say. Falling in love didn't have anything to do with practicality; it had everything to do with a heart-to-heart, soul-to-soul connection. She had that with Wayne.

"Wading in too deep," Charlotte said as she dried her hands off on the dish towel. "I've waded in too deep."

Charlotte grabbed her hat and waited for Mick to walk over to the door. This would be one of her last evenings alone with Wayne; she needed to push aside any reservations about her growing feelings for the cowboy and embrace the moment. At the end of summer, when the bulk of the job was done, she would have to watch him drive away. Would she be brokenhearted when he left? Yes. Deeply. But Rose had always encouraged her to enjoy the present without worrying about the unknown future. In honor of her mother, she was going to throw caution to the wind and squeeze every bit of enjoyment out of her time with Wayne.

"Come on, my good boy." She petted Mick's head. "Let's go enjoy Papa's fire."

The next morning, Wayne awakened feeling groggy and out of sorts. He hadn't been able to sleep much the night before, and that was rare. Usually when he put his head on the pillow, he fell asleep moments later. But then again, he hadn't yet met Charlotte Brand. Thoughts of her had kept him wide awake, staring up at the ceiling, listening to Hitch purring happily beside him. Images of Charlotte's face when she laughed and the way her blue eyes sparkled with affection when she looked at him. He appreciated her homesteader's heart, her natural kindness and her strength. Whatever the task in front of her, Charlotte leaped in feetfirst: her father had given her a solid education in the skills needed to keep a ranch going. Wayne knew that he was developing strong feelings for Charlotte, and he hadn't felt that falling-without-a-parachute feeling in decades. And that knowledge, that self-awareness of his connection to Charlotte, had kept him up nearly all night. If he had to describe what he was experiencing, the only word that came to mind was *love*. He was falling in love with Charlotte. It was unexpected, exhilarating and downright terrifying. Would he be able to leave her at the end of summer? Could he finally put down stakes and give up his rolling-stone life? Answers to those questions eluded him even after a night of thinking. The only thing that made sense to him was to throw himself into the work and push his feelings, as best he could, back into the recesses of his mind.

Wayne gave Hitch a kiss on the top of his head and

then raised the blinds so the cat could enjoy the warmth of the afternoon sun later on in the day. He opened the door to his trailer and waited patiently for Mick to make his way down the steps. Together, in the early-morning darkness, they walked the short distance to the main house, the light from the kitchen guiding their path.

He knocked on the door and then opened it. The smell of coffee and scrambled eggs met them at the door.

"Good morning," Charlotte greeted him, looking refreshed. Her hair was wet and slicked back into a ponytail, and her face, devoid of makeup, was so appealing to him. He appreciated the fine laugh lines around her eyes, the creases in her forehead that spoke of a life well-lived and the silver strands in her mahogany hair. He liked the way her Wrangler jeans hugged her curvy hips and thick, muscular thighs from years in the saddle.

"Morning." Wayne hung up his hat and then greeted Bowie too. "It smells good in here."

She smiled at him as she brought him a mug of black coffee. "I made your scrambled eggs."

He had taught her how he made scrambled eggs: sharp cheddar, minced tomatoes and onions, mushrooms, and salt and pepper.

She brought him a plate with a sizable portion and then joined him with her own coffee and eggs.

She watched him when he took his first bite, and he gave her a thumbs-up, which made her smile broaden. He washed the first bite down with coffee and then said, "Perfect."

After she got his verdict, she took her own first bite. "Mmm. I did get it right."

He cleaned his plate first: he was used to eating on

the go. He topped up his coffee and brought the pot over to her when she said she'd like more.

"So," he said, sitting back down, "today is a big day."

"I know. I feel excited and sick to my stomach." She explained, "My sister, Danica, is funding this upgrade, and she doesn't understand why I'm buying horses when there is so much left undone."

"I can see that from an outsider's perspective…"

"So can I."

"But when you're in the market for a well-bred, well-trained horse, with a solid personality suitable for novice riders, those are nearly impossible to find," he said. "And the fact that you found six, that's damn near a miracle."

"You're right," she said, putting her fork down on her empty plate. "I would be crazy to let this opportunity go by."

They cleaned up the kitchen together, put Mick and Bowie in a sizable outdoor kennel, making sure there was plenty of water, and then hopped into his truck.

"Ready?" he asked as he cranked the engine.

"Ready."

He shifted into gear and drove them on the long gravel drive that would take them to the highway. He switched on the radio, knowing that they both listened religiously to country. Charlotte liked to travel with the windows down. She liked the feel of the wind on her face, and he always wanted to make her happy.

Without thinking it through, he reached over and gave her hand a quick squeeze. "Today is going to be a great day."

She looked over at him. "I hope so."

"Don't hope. Know," Wayne told her.

Charlotte was no doubt feeling extra pressure because

of her sister's concern over the possibility of purchasing a herd of six horses. But from experience, he knew that they were doing the right thing. The horses needed to get used to the new environment, be fitted with equipment and acclimated to the trails that spread out all over the ranch like veins under the skin. By the time the first guests arrived, the horses would be ready for trail riding. The time to bring them onto the ranch was now, not later.

"I like this song," Charlotte said when "She's Got It All" by Kenny Chesney came on the radio.

"It's one of my favorites," he said.

"Turn it up?"

He turned up the volume, listening to the words more closely now that he had met Charlotte Brand. The next thing he said to her had come from his heart, not his head.

"I have to admit, this song reminds me of you." He glanced over at her. "You seem to have it all."

Charlotte still felt nervous energy rushing through her body, increasing her heart rate and making her hands shake. Having Wayne with her had managed to calm her as much as was possible; she did realize that this uncertainty, so uncommon for her in general, came from the desire to not waste Danny's investment. They pulled in next to a heavy-duty Ford that had a door sign with Dr. Tonia Vislosky's name and contact information. She was glad that the veterinarian was already on site.

Bruce Brand met them when they got out of the truck. After the introduction, Bruce said, "My wife, Savannah, got our DNA done a while back. We are definitely cousins. Several times removed."

"So the sordid family scandal is true," she said.

"We share a great-great-great-grandfather," Bruce

said, the blue of his eyes so similar to her own. "You and your sisters are officially invited to our next family reunion."

"Does that mean she gets a family discount?" Wayne asked.

Bruce laughed. "I suppose I should've shared that news *after* the ink was dry on the check."

The mood lightened, and they walked over to the paddock that held the six horses they had put a deposit on.

"We brought them to Little Sugar Creek. If you buy them, it will be easy for Gabe to load them up from here if you want him to haul them for you."

"Makes sense," she said. "Thank you."

"That's Dr. V right there," Bruce said, nodding his head toward a petite woman with thick blond hair pulled back into a ponytail unpacking some equipment. The veterinarian wore slender-fit jeans tucked into brown knee-high barn boots, and a long-sleeve shirt with her business logo embossed over the heart.

"Good morning." Dr. Vislosky walked toward them when she saw them heading in her direction. "I'm Dr. Vislosky, but you can call me Dr. V."

"Nice to meet you." Charlotte shook hands with her, noting the strength in the woman's handshake. "Thank you for blocking out an entire day for us."

"My pleasure," Dr. V said.

The veterinarian introduced them to her assistant and then explained her prepurchase process. "I know we've all been here before, but since this is our first time together, I want to review my steps so we are all on the same page. I'll start with the medical and performance history. Jessie already sent me a history on all of these horses—any previous lameness issues, vaccination and worming history, and previous medical concerns. This will all be included in my report along with a written identification of each horse. I will then conduct a physical exam, a movement evaluation and flexion tests to determine any soundness issues."

Charlotte took an immediate liking to Dr. V: the veterinarian appeared to be grounded in self-confidence, sincerity and honesty.

"And I believe you requested diagnostic imaging for each horse?" Dr. V asked her.

"Yes." Charlotte nodded. "I'd like images of the front feet, stifles, hocks, as well as front and hind fetlocks."

"We can do that," Dr. V said. "I think that will give you an excellent baseline on all of these horses if you decide to purchase. We should get started. We have a lot to do, and storms are in the forecast so it would be good to beat the weather. Do you have a preference which horse goes first?"

Charlotte knew exactly which horse would be first. She had searched out the blue roan, and when they met eyes, Cash whickered at her.

"First to go is that handsome blue roan right over there," Charlotte said. "His name is Cash."

Chapter Eight

The storm cloud that had formed over Bozeman during the prepurchase exams had materialized in the form of heavy rain, howling and gusty wind with frequent lightning strikes, and loud booms of thunder. Once the wind and lightning passed, the heavy rains lingered over Big Sky, dumping nearly six inches of rain in three days, which waylaid the outside jobs that they had planned to finish to get the pastures ready for horses. It wasn't that they couldn't work in the rain—both of them had in the past, and no doubt they would do again—but with only one tractor combined with large puddles of water and slippery, muddy ground conditions, they both agreed to work on indoor projects instead. Wayne had decided to expend his energy finishing up the organization of the Everything Building while she met with Danica and Rayna to discuss the updates in the main house, expanding the menu to include more healthy choices, and the most urgent projects that had to be completed prior to guests' arrival, with a secondary list of projects that could wait. Even though they were managing to keep on schedule now that they were sharing the workload, it seemed like they still had a mountain of things to get done before the first visitors would be there in October. And even that would be a stretch.

"Are you sure this is what we need to do?" Danica asked via video chat.

"Yes," she said. "One hundred percent. Dr. V was very thorough, she wrote excellent, detailed reports on the geldings. Each of the horses has some minor issues, but that's to be expected. These are sound, healthy, sane, well-bred quarter horses, and we need them. And we need them now. Wayne and I need time to work with them before we let the first guests ride them. It's a liability issue."

Danica wore a skeptical look on her perfectly made-up face. Charlotte was grateful that her sister had stepped up and was increasing her involvement in the project while still selling houses for her elite clientele in LA.

"This is your area, Charlie. If this is what you think we should do, you can write them a check out of the business account or I can wire the money over," Danica said.

"Thank you, Danny, I'd appreciate it if you would wire it," Charlotte said sincerely, pressing her fingers hard into her tear ducts to stop tears from forming. Ever since their mother had passed, Charlotte felt the urge to cry more often than she ever had. Perhaps it was as much to do with her sisters' interest in the ranch; this renewed triplet bond, this reliance on each other, was exactly what Rose had wanted. It was, in fact, the final wish Rose had shared with her only one week prior to her passing.

"I think it's the right move," Rayna added from her

home in Connecticut. It was strange to see the walls stripped bare behind her. Her husband had already moved out and had taken some of the choice paintings with him. Rayna, who lately seemed to have a flat affect, didn't seem to have the fight in her to battle with her soon-to-be ex-husband. The only time she seemed to perk up was when she discussed the menu for the ranch.

"Okay." Danica tucked her blond hair behind her ear. "I'll wire the money today. I spoke with Gabe Brand, and I have to tell you it's pretty wild to be connecting with all of these cousins."

"It is so weird." Rayna nodded.

"And pretty cool," Charlotte said.

"Gabe can bring the geldings when the Sugar Creek crew comes down with the equipment."

"So by the end of this week."

"Looks like," Danica said.

"And you're coming when?" Charlotte asked Danica.

"The earliest I can make it is middle of next week."

Danica's trip also was delayed, which Charlotte felt was for the best: the ranch was wet and mucky and un-appealing. By the middle of next week, the water would be dried up with most of the mud puddles gone. It would make a better impression on her savvy California sister.

"And you're taking over the home reno?" Rayna asked.

"Yes." Danica nodded. "It's too much for one person to handle. Charlie has her hands full with the outside projects."

Charlotte was happy to turn over the renovation of the main house to Danica, Aurora and the contractor. Just as long as permits were pulled for her cabin, she didn't really care what was done with the interior of the main house, as long as it was ready by October at the earliest and November at the latest.

Rayna was nibbling at her lip and playing with her small sapphire stud earrings.

"What are you thinking, Ray?" Charlotte asked.

"Well," her sister said hesitantly, "I was wondering if there was a bigger role I could play."

Charlotte was temporarily stunned by the thought, as was Danica, but after a quick second she said, "If you want to work with Aspen to get a solid menu together, just as long as the dishes are fairly easy to assemble, I would love to hand that over to you."

"Are you sure? I really don't want to step on your toes."

Charlotte laughed. "Are you kidding me? My toes are already out the door!"

That made Ray smile, and Charlotte was gratified to see even a small smile from her sister. Ray's complexion was pasty and her eyes puffy, no doubt from hours of crying.

"Danica just signed a contract with Aspen to set up a ranch kitchen outside to feed all of the cowboys who will be arriving soon," Charlotte said. "If you could work out those details with her—supplies needed, refrigeration, food to stockpile…"

"I believe they delivered the deep freezer yesterday?" Danica formed that sentence more as a statement than a question.

"Yes. They did. I don't know how they managed to get through that mud without getting stuck, but they did deliver it."

"They put it in the walk-out, correct?"

Charlotte nodded, while Danica continued, "Honestly, that space could also be used for a mess hall."

"Not enough ventilation to cook," Charlotte said. "But we could easily set up tables for meals."

"I think," Rayna said slowly, "that it would mean a lot for me to be more involved with the ranch. I feel so…"

"Disconnected," Charlotte and Danica said at the same time.

"Yes." Rayna nodded. "Adrift."

"This is your home, Ray." Charlotte leaned forward so that her sister could see her eyes and face more clearly. "It's more than just our financial future, it's *our* family legacy."

"You know what, Charlie?" Danica said. "I always thought this family-legacy business didn't matter to me. I actually thought that it was a bit silly, if I'm being honest, but—"

"It does," Rayna interjected. "Matter."

"It really does," Danica agreed. "And I want you to know how much it means to us that you took care of Mom and Dad and held down the fort for us."

"Yes," Rayna agreed. "Thank you, Charlie."

Now the tears were flowing onto her cheeks, and she wiped them away with her hands. "I couldn't imagine how this would turn out. I hoped, but I didn't know. This business wouldn't have gotten off the ground if the two of you hadn't come to my rescue."

"Triplet hug." Rayna reached her hands forward. Danica and Charlotte reached forward also.

"We can't celebrate just yet," practical, business-minded Danica said. "We still have to launch this sucker."

"Hi, girls!" Danica's fiancé appeared over her sister's left shoulder. Grant had a perfect, youthful super-white smile and golden spray-tanned skin. His dyed brown hair was professionally highlighted and styled, and the sleeves of his Gucci shirt were rolled up to his elbows and the top two buttons unbuttoned.

"Hi, Grant," Rayna and Charlotte greeted Danica's long-time life and business partner.

He dropped an air-kiss on Danica's cheek and put his hands on her shoulders, the diamonds on his Rolex catching the light.

"I hate to steal her away but—" he tapped the face of his watch "—we have to meet the Petrovs in thirty."

From Charlotte's perspective, the way Danica brushed Grant's hand off her shoulder and the annoyed expression, so fleeting that most people wouldn't have picked up on it, made Charlotte wonder if that relationship was as rock-solid as Danny had always portrayed.

"I have to go," Danica said. "But, before I do, I did have a thought. What would you think about rebranding the ranch now that it's having this massive makeover?"

In the background, they heard Grant calling for Danica in a singsong voice. She ignored him.

"Rebrand how?" Charlotte asked.

"Now, don't dismiss it out of hand, Charlie," Danica said, and then she moved her hands like she was creating a banner in the sky. "Three Fillies Ranch."

"Three Fillies Ranch?" Charlotte and Rayna repeated the name in sync.

Danica stood up, grabbed her purse and then got ready to log off the video chat. "Just think about it. Let the idea marinate."

"It kind of sounds like a brothel." Rayna's eyebrows were drawn together.

"That's what I thought," Charlotte agreed.

"A brothel? No! It's the three of us. Three fillies." Danica looked at them, and they looked back at her. Grant called her name again so Danica blew them each kisses. "I love you, I love you. Charlie, I'll send you my flight info, and I'll see you next week."

"It sounds like a great brothel name," Rayna said, laughing after Danica logged off, her eyes shining from unshed happy tears instead of sorrow for the first time during this conversation.

"It absolutely does," Charlotte said. "But maybe we should give it some thought. It may just be the hook we need to generate interest in this place. Three Fillies Ranch, satisfaction guaranteed."

Charlotte's mood had been lifted during the conversation with her sisters. This was the first time that she felt as if they were truly committed and *excited* about turning this ranch into a revenue stream which they would all benefit from.

"Thank goodness the sun is shining," she said to Bowie, who had decided to hang with her instead of finding Wayne outside. It was getting hotter out, and Bowie could be particular about extremes in temperature. He enjoyed more temperate weather.

They found Wayne in her dad's Everything Building, finishing up with his organizing and inventorying.

"Hey." He smiled at her when he saw her. "I was just wondering about you. Are we a go?"

She knew he was talking about the horses. She gave him two thumbs-up. "She just wired money into their account, and we should have horses back on this property soon."

"Good." He nodded. "Good. Bruce is willing to sell us some hay, but with the drought the year before, and the flooding last year and this year, it's gonna be slim pickin's."

"I'm pretty blown away by the Bozeman Brands. They're treating us like we are their real family, even though we just met them."

"They're good people." He nodded. "Salt of the earth."

Charlotte breathed in deeply at the thought of another hay shortage. "I leased that west pasture to the Danforth brothers—they seeded for alfalfa—but the crop was destroyed two years in a row, and they decided not to make the investment this year."

"Can't say that I blame them."

"Neither can I," she agreed. "I was hoping to grow a crop this year, sell some, keep some, but I think we'll have to wait until next year."

"Most likely." Wayne chugged down a bottle of water but left enough to pour into his hands and cool off his neck.

"Yesterday it was cold and rainy. Now today it's humid and scorching." She wiped the sweat off her forehead on the sleeve of her T-shirt.

It was getting hotter by the day, and Wayne was leaving more buttons of his shirt undone, and Charlotte was very attracted to his exposed dark brown and silver chest hair. She did try not to be too obvious with her admiration of the cowboy, but she was pretty certain that Wayne had caught her looking.

"I hate to tell you what's going on way back in both of those pastures." He took the red bandanna from around his neck, wiped the sweat off his face and retied it.

She didn't have to walk it to know that the heavy rain had left standing water closer to the tree line. Standing water was horrible for horses' hooves, leading to thrush and abscesses. Would the ground be less soggy by the time the horses arrived at the ranch? There was no way to really gauge it.

"I feel like we just can't catch a break," she said, kneeling down by Mick, who was lying on his side in front of one of her father's old fans.

"You'll need a good farrier," Wayne said, scratching the hair on his chin. "I think I'm gonna have to shave this off—it's getting too damn itchy."

Charlotte voiced her next question without any real thought. "Shave off your goatee? All of it?"

Wayne sent her a quizzical look that made her laugh at herself while she added, "I like the goatee, that's all. It's your face. And really not my business as your employer."

The more she talked, the worse it sounded to her ears. Wayne kept right on smiling at her with a pleased expression. He always enjoyed those moments that seemed to confirm her mostly unspoken attraction to him.

"I could just trim it back a bit."

"I shouldn't have said anything." She continued to backpedal. "Your facial hair is your business."

Now her cheeks were hot, and trying to blame it on the heat would be useless, so she jumped to a new topic, safer territory. "I can't believe what you've done with this place."

Wayne's eyes lit up. "I hope you don't take this the wrong way…"

She looked at him, curiously waiting for him to continue.

"I feel like I know your dad, after organizing this space." Wayne looked around, gesturing to the large building. "He was a master homesteader. I can tell how methodical his thinking was, why he stockpiled the materials he did and why he assembled the equipment he did in this building."

For the second time that day, Charlotte felt her eyes well up. She stared at Wayne. His apparent appreciation for her father and his collection of odds and ends made her heart swell with love for this cowboy.

"Can I hug you?" she asked him.

Now he was looking at her as if she had just asked for one of his kidneys. He crossed his arms in front of his body, cleared his throat several times, seemingly choking on the response to her question. Finally, he managed to croak out, "You want to hug me?"

"Yes, I do."

"Right now?"

Then there was another odd silence between them. They were looking at each other, which was undeniably awkward, so she said, "Is that okay?"

He grumbled something under his breath that sounded sort of like a green light to physical contact so she didn't waste time. She closed the distance between them. She unfolded his arms, stepped close to him and wrapped her arms around him. Wayne's body, head to toe, was as stiff as one of the planks of wood he was using to patch the fences. After a second or two, she patted his back, stepped away from him and refolded his arms.

"Thank you for appreciating my father and taking such good care of his things. And thank you for letting me hug you."

"'S all right," he mumbled.

"Do you feel okay?"

"I'm not sure," he said, and he did appear rather per-plexed.

"Would you like to show me some treasures that you

found?" she asked him, feeling sincerely embarrassed for crossing that professional boundary they had erected between them. Yes, there was an undeniable attraction; yes, there was an undeniable appreciation for each other's talents; and yes, they shared many of the same interests. They had shared wonderful meals together and evenings by the fire, but mainly their conversation had been at the surface level, rarely crossing over into more personal territory.

"Yes," he said, his face a bit flushed after she'd flung herself at him. "I'd like that."

To Charlotte, the arrival of the Westbrook brothers seemed like a turning point for Hideaway Ranch. On the day of what she had affectionately come to think of in her mind as the Hugging Incident, Wayne's brothers arrived in a caravan of three black heavy-duty Ford trucks, jacked up with oversize tires, blasting their horns and hauling trailers of equipment and personal belongings.

"Holy cow," Charlotte said to Aspen, who had brought food to stock the freezer in the basement. "The Westbrooks have arrived."

Aspen came over to the window. "Bring on the cowboy cavalry! Man oh man, do I love a cowboy in a big ol' truck."

Charlotte laughed. "The higher the truck, the closer to God?"

"It's the cowboy way." Aspen pulled her ponytail holder out of her hair, fluffed her blond locks and then asked, "How do I look?"

"Gorgeous," she answered truthfully.

Aspen tilted her head back with a confident, happy laugh. "Come on, Charlie. Let's go have some fun!"

Wayne came out of the Everything Building, a genuine smile on his face. He took his hat off and swung it around like a lasso while he hooted and hollered at his younger brothers. The thirtysomething cowboys parked in a line, one right next to the other, shut off their engines and jumped out of their trucks. The brothers converged in front of the vehicles, and Charlotte was fascinated by Wayne's reaction to his younger brothers. Although he was the oldest, they all had him by height. Even so, Wayne gave each brother a bear hug and picked them up off the ground as if they were light as a feather.

After making the rounds, Wayne led them over to where she was standing with Aspen; the women had wanted to give the brothers a chance to reunite without an intrusion from outsiders. As they walked toward them, Charlotte was struck by how similar the men looked. Yes, Wayne had a decade on his brothers, but Wayne was still fit, handsome and rugged. The three younger ones carried themselves in a way that matched Wayne; they had more swagger, more ego, but they also didn't have the same quiet confidence that her cowboy exuded.

The four Westbrooks lined up in formation in front of her. "Charlotte, I'd like you to meet my brothers—oldest to youngest—Waylon, Wyatt and Wade."

They all tipped their hats, ma'amed her and greeted her with the same firm handshake of Wayne's.

"It's nice to meet all of you," she said. "I'm grateful that you could come."

Then, with all eyes of the three younger brothers trained on Aspen, Charlotte introduced her friend to the newly arrived cowboys.

"I'm gonna get them settled and take them on a quick tour," Wayne said, the novelty of the reunion having worn off rather quickly for him, which wasn't much of a surprise for her. Wayne didn't like to linger on sentiment.

"We have hamburgers and hot dogs for the grill," Charlotte said.

"Count us all in!" Wyatt said with his eyes focused intently on Aspen.

Wayne, of course, noticed his brother's puppy love and playfully put his arm around Wyatt's shoulders and led him toward the work that needed to be done. Wyatt swiveled his head around and shouted, "I'll see you later, Aspen. Don't stand me up! It'll break my heart!"

After the Westbrook brothers turned their attention to unloading their trucks before the five-cent tour, Aspen seemed a bit dazed, rooted in the spot where she had first encountered Wyatt.

"You look like you just got struck by lightning," Charlotte told her friend.

"No," Aspen said in a dreamy, slightly stunned voice, "not lightning. Cupid's arrow."

Wayne helped his brothers unload their trucks and set up their tents near the firepit. They had grown up camping in tents with their father, and his brothers carried on that tradition. Once he hit the fifty mark, he traded in his tent for a camper. After they were finished setting up, Wayne showed them around the place, and his brothers didn't disappoint him. They saw the magic in this expanse of big sky country. And they were chomping at the bit to start working on the multitude of projects that needed doing. Wayne ended the tour at the bunkhouse where they could shower, shave and sleep on the new mattresses and linens that Danica had delivered for the bunk beds.

"Outside's still good for me," Wade said before answering his phone and turning away from his brothers.

Wayne lifted his eyebrow at his remaining brothers.

"Jillian," Wyatt told him in a quiet voice.

"Reconciling?" Wayne asked, the thought of Wade returning to his marriage with his high-school sweetheart twisting his gut. Wade was a romantic, a true-blue, one-woman-man kind of cowboy, and he shared a daughter, Phoenix, with Jillian, and that had tethered Wade to his wife for too many years.

"It seems to be heading in that direction." Waylon took off his hat to put his long shoulder-length hair back into a tighter ponytail. "He's hooked. Like a drug."

Wade and Jillian were oil and water: they just didn't mix. They fought, they made up, they broke up again, and the cycle went on and on until Wayne had finally convinced Wade to focus on being a great father, co-parenting and putting Phoenix first. The idea that his little girl could grow up in a war zone helped Wade make the difficult decision to separate from Jillian. But little by little, one text and phone call after another, Jillian was reeling him back in.

After the three of them mentally played possible scenarios unfolding if Wade took Jillian back, Wyatt rebooted the conversation and asked Wayne, "So—Aspen. What can you tell me about her?"

Chapter Nine

The next few weeks after his brothers arrived on Hideaway Ranch, the quiet life that he had grown accustomed to was transformed into a bustling hive of tearing down and rebuilding. Every morning, the outside crew would meet at the back of his truck for a tailgate, a meeting that set the tone, establishing goals and setting assignments for the day. At the first tailgate that Charlotte and he had with his brothers and the six ranch hands for hire from Sugar Creek, Charlotte announced that he was the foreman in charge of all outside crews.

Wade took two ranch hands to dig up and replace broken piping that would carry water to the pastures as well as dig a new pipeline that tapped into the existing one to bring running water to Charlotte's hundred-year-old log cabin. Waylon took a crew with him to fix up the stable so the horses could be put up at night; for now, the horses

were staying round the clock in the pasture but appeared
to be settling into their new home without much issue.
The remaining ranch hands were helping him clear a defensible perimeter around all of the buildings to protect
them from summer Montana fires. Prior to creating that
hundred-foot barrier, Charlotte had walked the property with him to pick out trees that could be harvested
for lumber with a portable sawmill on loan from Sugar
Creek. Once the trees were selected, Wayne used one of
Butch's chain saws to cut the trees down.

Wayne was in his element: he was at home in a bulldozer and managing crews of men. But a woman was
distracting him while he worked, and he wasn't accustomed to that. In his line of work, a lack of focus could
result in death. Ever since Charlotte had hugged him,
he'd been kicking himself for his reaction. He had been
as rigid as a corpse, and he replayed that moment a hundred times in his head, imagining a hundred different
ways he could have responded, but nothing he came up
with changed the fact that he was embarrassed about
that moment with her.

"Boss!" one of the Sugar Creek ranch hands by the
name of Flint Dawson hollered at him, waving his light
tan cowboy hat to get his attention.

Wayne cut off the bulldozer so he could hear what the
ranch hand had to say, unhappy with the interruption unless it was an emergency.

"Is someone hurt?" Wayne asked him.

"No, sir."

"Dead?"

"No, sir. I just wanted to let you know that I'm gonna
head over to the paddock." The tall, lanky cowboy hooked

his thumb over his shoulder. "See if they need some help on that project."

Wayne leaned forward, his eyebrows drawn together and pointed toward the stable. "Get back to your crew, and get back to work."

Flint put his hat back on his head and spread his arms open. "I was just trying to help."

"Help by working your post," Wayne barked at him before he switched on the monster bulldozer and began the daunting task of clearing smaller trees, rocks, boulders and brush away from the buildings. While he worked, his mind kept on circling back to that cocky kid. Flint had been like a bee to honey with Charlotte since the moment he arrived. In Wayne's mind he was still just a kid, but how could he know how Charlotte felt about Flint? He was good-looking, young and wore his infatuation for Charlotte on his sleeve. And there was the source of his distraction: instead of focusing all of his attention on his work, there was a part of his brain that wanted to run defense. Wayne imagined that Flint wouldn't turn into a wax figure if Charlotte decided to hug him—not a chance.

"Not a chance," he muttered.

It seemed like every time he saw Charlotte at the end of the workday, when everyone was gathering to eat the evening meal, Flint was buzzing around her. And the kick in the gut for him was the kid was sincere. Wayne could see it in the way Flint admired her, complimented her and did his best to charm her. Whenever Charlotte laughed at one of his jokes, it felt like someone was slicing him up on the inside, one tiny cut at a time. Wayne felt like he was losing a woman he wasn't entirely sure he had in the first place.

Wayne was still fuming on the inside when he reached the back side of the cabin. He shut off the bulldozer, grabbed Butch's power saw, and started carving his way through the vines and saplings to reveal the weathered logs that were placed by Charlotte's ancestor to build the back wall of the cabin. Wayne ripped off his sweat-drenched shirt, balled it up and tossed it toward the bulldozer to be retrieved after he accomplished his goal: he wanted to be able to bring Charlotte back to this spot after dinner. In a way, this was his love letter to Charlotte. He was rarely good with words—he didn't know how to romance a woman like Charlotte—but he felt deeply for her. And he wanted to show her how he felt by taking this first step toward making her dream come true. Once he released the cabin from its prison of vines and fallen trees and weeds, they could move forward with the first phase of converting it into a little house for Charlotte.

"Wayne!"

He saw Charlotte picking her way through the overgrowth over to where he was working. Wayne shut off the chain saw, wondering if his thinking so hard about her had actually called her to him.

"Look at this!" Charlotte had a look of wonder in her eyes when she took in his progress. "How could you have gotten this much done? You've freed it, Wayne! You freed it!"

Her unvarnished reaction made his effort worthwhile. Charlotte had always been the type of woman to appreciate a man's effort. She was kind and quick to praise.

"It's getting there," he said humbly, wishing that he had gotten even further still. The sooner he got this cabin ready for rehabilitation, the quicker he would be able to slow Flint down in his pursuit of Charlotte.

Wayne knew it hadn't been settled—heck, it hadn't even been *discussed*—but he felt that Charlotte was his girl. And, he'd begun to wonder, every now and again, if his life on the road still made sense. He began to wonder if maybe, just maybe, putting down stakes for the first time in more than three decades was the better option.

"I promise I'm not going to hug you again," she said, her eyes so full of emotion, her head shaking slightly at her surprise that he had nearly cut the cabin free. "I promise—"

"About that…"

"But Wayne—" Charlotte rested her fingertips on her lips "—you are a magician."

"No," he said, "I'm just a man."

Wayne had been at several crossroads before, and each time, he'd taken the turn that moved him away from attachment and commitment. That had been his way. And that way had suited him for quite a while. But right now, with a woman like Charlotte standing before him—a rare, rough-hewn jewel already more precious to him than any amount of money, completely vulnerable and open, making him feel more like a man than he'd ever felt—he knew that it was in his control to change the tide of his life.

"Thank you, Wayne," Charlotte said with a catch in her voice. "How can I thank you for everything you've done for me? You brought life back to this ranch. *You* did that."

They both had spent the day working outside, fighting dirt and mud and the heat; their clothing was dirty and sweaty, and it couldn't be a less romantic moment even for him, but this was the moment that had presented itself, and he would be a fool not to take it.

Wayne walked straight over to Charlotte, took her

lovely face in his hands and kissed her. He kissed her with all of the love and passion and desire he had pent up inside of him. He kissed her sweetly, tenderly, doing his best to distill every feeling he had ever had for her concentrated into that one kiss.

After the kiss, Wayne looked down into Charlotte's upturned face, loving the dreamy, surprised expression in her dark blue eyes. He held her face in his hands and asked, "Now, are you going to fire me for that?"

"Why don't you kiss me again and you'll see?" Charlotte laughed, her eyes shining with love—yes, love—for him. He kissed her again, taking full advantage of her invitation before he dropped his hands from her face, hoping to leave her with a preview of what might come to pass between them.

"I've been kicking myself ever since that hug," he told her honestly.

"I surprised you," she said, always wanting to skew things to the positive when it pertained to him.

"I wished I had kissed you then."

"No." She reached for his hand and held his fingers lightly. "I'm glad you kissed me now, in this place that means so much to me."

Wayne felt lighter in his soul than he had in more years than he could count. It wasn't that the place was magical, it was Charlotte. She was the magic.

Wayne brought her fingers up to his lips and kissed them. "Now, let me get back to work."

"Okay," she said, with her cheeks still flushed pink from his kisses. "I'll see you at chow time?"

"You can count on it," Wayne said before he picked up the heavy chain saw with a renewed sense of purpose.

He ripped the cord until the tool was growling and ready to chomp through anything in its path.

"You've still got plenty of fuel left in your tank, old man," Wayne said with a genuine smile that began in his heart and showed up unabashed on his face. "Plenty of fuel."

Evenings at Hideaway Ranch had turned into an event. After a long day's work, the cowboys liked to eat the good food prepared for them by Aspen, Aurora and Charlotte, sit around the fire telling tall tales and listen to music, whether it was on a turned-up truck radio or from the Westbrook brothers, who pulled out their guitars, drums and Wayne's harmonica. For Charlotte it felt both exhilarating and overwhelming. On the weekends, the cowboys would go off-site for drinks if that hit their fancy, but on Hideaway Ranch, the policy for now was no alcohol or drugs.

"I am shocked," Aurora said. This was the first time that Aurora was able to help Aspen in the chow tent. "I wish Dale could've made it tonight. He would love this."

Aurora's husband was a long-distance trucker, and he had just come home after a two-week stint. He wanted to stay at home to have quality time with the twins while she helped Aspen.

"It's crazy. Less than a month ago, this place was a ghost town."

"I just want Danica to get here." Aurora flipped her long blond braid over her shoulder. "Do you think she'll make it this time?"

"I do," Charlotte said. "She knows the clock is really ticking."

As Charlotte was leaving the chow tent, Wyatt with his

quirky smile and his dashingly handsome face strolled by her on his way into the tent, tipping his hat to her and then his eyes went straight back to the object of his infatuation: Aspen.

From the moment Wyatt had laid eyes on Aspen, he was determined to win her over. Charlotte smiled to herself as she left the tent: she knew what Wyatt would one day soon discover—the only key to that cookie jar was an *I do* at the altar.

"Hi!" she said when she found Wayne by the grill filling up his empty plate with hot dogs and hamburgers, no buns. "I was wondering when you were going to emerge from your lair."

He greeted her with that small smile of his, but this time it was easier to see his teeth because he had trimmed his mustache and goatee.

She naturally put her hand on his arm now that the intimacy barrier had been broken between them. "Wayne! I love it."

"I had you in mind when I trimmed it."

"Thank you for leaving it there for my enjoyment."

"My pleasure," he said with another small smile.

"You have a great smile, Wayne," she said, still happy to look at his handsome face that had some years of experience etched around his eyes, nose and forehead. She liked that about him: she had those same experience lines, and when she looked at her reflection, she had to acknowledge the passage of time had not necessarily been kind to her, but she couldn't honestly say she would take one of those lines away if the learning, growing and maturing also disappeared.

Wayne leaned his head down. "You are a beautiful woman, Charlotte."

She was full-blown blushing like a lovestruck teenager. In the light of the fire, no one would notice except for the man who paid her such a lovely compliment. She walked with Wayne toward his spot on the log that everyone kept empty as a show of respect for him. Halfway there, Flint intercepted her, swept her up into his arms and spun her around.

"Would you like to dance with me?" Flint asked, slowing down so he could hold her close.

"I think I already am," she said, feeling light-headed and a smidge nauseous. Spinning for her had ceased to be fun while she was just a teenager.

Flint was young—way too young for her. His flirtations with her were flattering to some degree, but mainly she was more interested in him focusing on his work and not so much on her.

"I'd like to take you out on a real date," Flint said seriously. She could see in his eyes that he meant it. He had a crush on her.

"Thank you, Flint," she said. "That's very sweet of you. But you are way too young for me, and I'm not a cougar."

Flint, she believed, was gearing up to state his case with her, try to persuade her with his country charm and his slow drawl. But he didn't get that chance because Wayne was by their side, tapping on Flint's shoulder.

"That means that he's cutting in," Charlotte told Flint when he looked perplexed.

Wayne physically stepped in between her and Flint. After taking her in his arms, Wayne said to the baffled Flint, "Let me show you how an old man gets this job done."

Charlotte turned her head so Flint wouldn't see her joy at being whisked away by her jealous suitor. She didn't want to hurt the young cowboy's feelings, but it was best that he realize his chances were zero-point-zero so he could move on to another available woman.

In truth, she didn't have much time to reflect on Flint's feelings because Wayne was holding her in a tight Texas two-step frame with one hand holding hers and the other hand high up on her back so he could lead her, step-by-step, around the fire.

"You know what you're doing." She laughed breathlessly, just holding on for the ride and trying not to trip over his toes.

"I do know what I'm doing," he said confidently, and he had the skills to back that sexy self-assuredness.

He whisked her away from her worries, making her very rudimentary knowledge of the steps seem like she was ready for a competition. Wayne set her up for a twirl, spinning her three times before he caught her back into his territory. She was vaguely aware that an audience had formed, just as she was vaguely aware of Wyatt and Aspen walking a few feet apart from each other, hands to themselves, as they walked along a path that would take them to a short trail in the nearby woods. The crowd was clapping their hands and cheering them on, and in that moment, in Wayne's arms, Charlotte felt something she had never in her life felt before: she felt seen, appreciated, desired, *loved* by a man who only had eyes for her. Almost every man—young, old, married, not married— did a double take when Aspen or Aurora walked into a room, and Lord help those men if the twins showed up together. But not Wayne, never Wayne. He had looked at them like they were just everyday women: no more, no less. He had been polite, gentlemanly, but she was the woman that drew his gaze time and time again.

By the time the dance ended, Charlotte felt such an interesting combination of invigoration and a heightened sense of feminine sensuality. Wayne had come at her from unexpected angles, like a mountain lion on a hunt. And it made her want to tear off the buttons of his shirt with her teeth and give herself to him, her naked body intertwined with his naked body...

"Do you want a Coke?"

This pedestrian question did not fit with the fantasy seduction she had been living in her mind, and it took her a split second to realize that the dance had ended, the music had changed, and Wayne was looking at her curiously.

"I'm sorry?" she asked.

"Can I get something for you to drink? Do you suffer from low blood sugar?"

"Low blood sugar?" she repeated, her brow creased. "No, I don't have low blood sugar."

What she had was a very vivid imagination, and just seconds ago she had stripped him down, preparing to take him out for a highly satisfying gallop.

Wayne offered her his arm so he could escort her to his designated spot on the log. "Did you enjoy our dance?"

"Every single solitary second," she said, still feeling loose and languid. "How did you learn how to dance like that?"

"My stepmother," Wayne said, his body language showing that he was proud to have her on his arm. "She said, 'Wayne, if you're going to be a true Texan, you've got to learn the two-step.'"

"She was kind to you."

"Yes, Beverly was always kind to me. She still is."

Charlotte looked up into Wayne's face—a handsome

face, one that made her want to look at this man for the rest of her life. "A good woman."

Wayne covered her hand that was resting on her arm. "A very good woman. And now I have found another."

"Wyatt," Aspen said quietly when they reached a flat boulder just beyond the grand oak tree she had sat beneath many times.

"Yes, Aspen?" Wyatt Westbrook was leaning his back against her tree, keeping a polite distance between them. He hadn't tried to hold her hand, or sneak a kiss—he had been a perfect, yet completely persistent, gentleman.

"There's something you need to know about me."

"I want to know everything about you," Wyatt said with the resonance of sincerity in his Texas drawl. "You are the most beautiful woman I have ever met."

Aspen ducked her chin down. As an adult and a social-media influencer, she regularly received compliments from men and women from all walks of life, and people always told her how beautiful she was. And she knew that she was attractive now, but when she looked in the mirror, she could still manage to pick out every single annoying flaw on her face, particularly when she had suffered from acne as a teen. So she had been on the other side, being bullied horrifically by boys, and not just from local kids. Nope, with social media, her acne had been like a shining beacon for bullies across the globe. Yet, when she looked at Aurora, she could see how beautiful her sister was and she had been told all of her life, from strangers and relatives, that Aurora was the pretty twin. Their differences were infinitesimal but gigantic enough to label her as *still pretty but less pretty* than her identical twin.

"So I'm ready. Let me have it," Wyatt said.

"What do you mean?"

"You brought me out here, away from everyone else so you could let me down easy without embarrassing me," Wyatt said. "I love that about you by the way. Beautiful and sweet."

"I didn't come here to let you down easy."

"Oh, good. So let's go out. Your choice. I'll take you anywhere you want to go."

"I'm trying to tell you something about myself, but you won't let me."

In the moonlight, she saw Wyatt pretend to take a key, lock his lips and throw that imaginary key over his shoulder. It was so unexpected that she had to fight to maintain the serious, earnest expression on her face.

"I've brought you here to tell you that I'm—" she shrugged her shoulders and dropped them "—celibate."

"Celibate?" he repeated.

"Yes."

Now came the part when most men found a way to not walk but sprint in the opposite direction. But Wyatt was still here, still leaning up against that tree.

"So you haven't…?"

She shook her head.

"Not ever?"

Another shake of her head. Aspen was in uncharted territory, because no one had ever gotten to this point after her pronouncement of celibacy.

"So not until…"

"Until death do us part," she said, dropping her hands into her lap.

Wyatt took a couple of beats of thought and then he said, "Then, let's get married."

Aspen stood up, crossed her arms in front of her body protectively and walked past him, seemingly done with the conversation.

"Wait! Aspen! Wait! What did I say? What did I *say*?"

"Really? You want to marry me just to get me in the sack?"

"Well, first, I wouldn't use the phrase *in the sack* under any circumstances, and secondly—" he held out his arm, not touching her but beseeching her to listen "—I am serious about getting married."

That made Aspen stop in her tracks. "That was a serious proposal?"

"Yes, it was," he said. "It wasn't the most romantic proposal in the history of proposals, but it was real."

"Why?" she said, her arms still crossed in front of her body. She was wondering why she was still standing in the woods with this cowboy while he tried to lay on the charm for some unknown reason other than possibly to test her resolve.

"Love at first sight." Wyatt had a slight catch in his throat, giving his smooth voice the tiniest vulnerability that resonated in her core. "Do you believe in love at first sight, Miss Hernandez?"

"Yes," she answered honestly, "I do."

"But not for someone like me?"

"From what I've heard, you just came here from a six-month stint with a one to fifty woman to man ratio, so I think you'd fall in love with a stump after that."

"And you're funny," he said. "A beautiful, funny, sweet girl."

"I need to get back," she said, having entertained this conversation much too long.

As they walked back to the group, Wyatt asked her, "So, what if it doesn't work?"

"What?"

"What if your confession doesn't scare me away?" he said. "What if I think you're more than worth the wait? What then?"

"I don't know," she threw over her shoulder, stepping into the firelight. "That's never happened before."

Wyatt grabbed his chest as if he were having a heart attack, stumbled and fell back onto the grass. He lay there for quite a while, looking up at the stars, thinking about how many ways he had already found to love Aspen Hernandez.

"What a woman," he said quietly at first, and then he shouted to the sky above, not giving a hoot who heard him, "What a woman!"

Chapter Ten

The day that Danica arrived to meet with the contractor and Aurora to go over the plans, cost and timeline for the renovation, Charlotte finally felt as if the universe had aligned in her favor: it was a sunny, big-blue-sky day, but the humidity was low and the temperature mild. Danica had booked a suite at the local resort and had hired a limousine service to pick her up at the Big Sky Airport.

Danica arrived in a black Mercedes with blacked-out windows; the chauffeur, a large muscular man in a black suit, got out, took one step to reach the passenger door and opened it.

"Is that your sister?" Aurora asked.

"Yes, it is." Charlotte smiled as she came down the steps of the main house's front porch.

"She certainly knows how to make an entrance," the decorator said with a good dose of appreciation in her tone.

"She always has," Charlotte tossed over her shoulder.

"Charlie!" Danica greeted her with a genuine smile that reached her violet-blue eyes.

Danica had accepted the hand of the chauffeur, opened her Chanel bag and slipped a tip into the man's hand before she met Charlotte halfway, seemingly defying the laws of nature by walking elegantly across gravel in a pair of black Chanel stilettos that were a perfect complement to her slim-fit pinstripe suit. Beneath her suit jacket, Danica wore a delicate lavender silk blouse and a platinum-and-diamond choker, and her icy-blond hair was blunt cut at the shoulders and tucked behind her ears to show off the two-carat round-cut diamond studs on her ears.

Charlotte hugged her sister, so happy to see her. "How was your flight?"

"Lovely." Danica hooked her arm in hers. "I worked through all of my emails and talked several high-demand clients off proverbial ledges. I've cleared the deck so I can focus all of my attention on this reno.

"And this must be Aurora!" Danica unhooked her arm and greeted the designer with a warm handshake. "I've been counting down the days!"

Charlotte could tell that Aurora was duly impressed by Danica, from her entrance to her swag to her open, friendly nature. It was telling of their recent history that Aurora and Aspen had been her friends for nearly a decade and, before embarking on this project, the sisters had only known Danica through her social-media accounts.

Danica gave Aurora a hug and linked her arm with hers as they walked up the steps of the house. She asked the decorator, "Is the contractor late, or am I early?"

"He texted me," Aurora said, a nervous, excited catch in her voice. "He's running just a smidge late."

"Well," Danica said, dropping her handbag on the kitchen table and slipping out of her jacket to hang it on the back of a chair, "it's not ideal, but I suppose we can use the time to our advantage. I'd actually hoped to do a walk-through with you prior to meeting with the contractor."

"I would *love* that!" Aurora said, having a fan-girl moment. "I have to tell you, I've admired your interior design for years. Literally years!"

"That's sweet of you." Danica smiled at Charlotte, her hands relaxed and tucked into the front pocket of her trousers. "I'm a big fan of your work too. The palette and finishes you have chosen for this house are spot-on— clean and modern while keeping it in the country-comfort style and honoring its history."

Aurora made the highest and tiniest of squeals of joy and clasped her hands together. "Thank you, Ms. Brand. That means a lot coming from you. It really does."

When there was a lull in the conversation, Danica said, "Shall we get started?"

"Yes, please!" Aurora clutched her binder full of color stories, fabrics, flooring and finishes for the bathroom, kitchen and common areas. They would be building out the attic, and adding a Jack-and-Jill bathroom, which would allow them to host four more guests. All of the furniture would be updated while still holding on to historic family pieces that would give a nod to the homesteading history of the house and the property.

"Do you guys need me?" Charlotte asked, feeling like she'd rather eat paint than discuss finishes with Aurora and Danica.

"No." Danica sent her an understanding look. "I'll text when it's time to show the contractor the cabin."

Charlotte gave her a quick thumbs-up and then raced out of the door. Now that Wayne had finished clearing a fire barrier and had stripped away the overgrowth from her future home, he was going to begin the process of fitting saddles to the horses. They had been so busy that there hadn't been much time for working the horses or riding them.

She found Wayne in the new covered paddock area that had been built from trees harvested and milled on the property, and it had been erected in a week. With Wayne in charge of the outside operation, projects were getting crossed off that list in record time without a compromise on the quality of the craftsmanship.

"Hey." Wayne winked at her with a half smile. "Perfect timing. Cash's next."

She leaned down to pet both Bowie and Mick, who were lying together in the shade provided by the green and enjoying the occasional cross-breeze, before she straightened and said, "I'll get him."

"I figured," he said with the same affection in his eyes that he used only for when he was looking at her.

"So who's the VIP?" Wayne asked, taking off his hat and wiping off his brow.

She put a halter on Cash and led him through the gate and into the paddock where Wayne was waiting for them.

"My sister Danica," she said, "in from California."

"I figured," he said offhandedly.

When she got Cash into position, Wayne ran his flat hand along the blue roan's neck down to his back and haunches.

"How long have you been fitting horses?" she asked him.

"Seems like all my life."

"Did your dad teach you?"

"No. Not him," Wayne said but didn't elaborate further.

"Did you learn from your stepmother?" She was prodding him in a way that was beginning to just be a part of their communication style. He spoke in short bursts, and she lassoed those words and pulled more out behind them.

Wayne nodded. "The trick to a good saddle fit is finding the eighth and the eighteenth thoracic vertebrae. I want to teach you so when I'm not around, you can do it for yourself."

Charlotte had to pretend that she found something fascinating out in the pasture while she reined in her emotions. They didn't talk about him leaving or staying; it was a subject they both had a silent agreement to avoid. The fact that Wayne hadn't changed his internal mind about eventually driving away from her didn't make it any easier for her to protect herself from the feelings she had for him. She wished it did.

"Feel this right here, two fingers behind the scapula," he said, pointing to a spot with his finger, "and the last rib. Your weight should be carried around the rib cage."

She forced herself to focus on his instruction. Knowing how to fit a saddle was important for the health of her horses. And maybe she could take an online course to become a saddle fitter and create a new revenue stream to help her stay afloat during any lean months. There were always lean months on a ranch.

Wayne saw Waylon walking across the yard, and he whistled loudly, getting the attention of his brother. Waylon stopped and looked over at his older brother.

"Bring me that black Billy Cook. Front storage."

Waylon gave a nod and changed his direction. Charlotte noticed that whenever Wayne whistled a certain way within earshot of one or all of his brothers—the three Ws, as Charlotte had started to think of them—they would drop what they were doing to find out what Wayne needed. A couple of minutes later, Waylon delivered the saddle to his brother.

"He's the quiet one," Charlotte said of the tallest Westbrook brother. Waylon was lanky, sort of awkward and gangly, but he was a hard worker. No one could fault him.

"That he is." Wayne put the saddle on Cash's back without a saddle pad. "Ideally, you want three fingers from neck to top of the gullet and four fingers horizontally. This is a good fit for your boy."

"This is an iconic saddle," she said, running her hands along the smooth, worn leather of the circa 1970s saddle.

"It's served its purpose," Wayne said. "Never let me down."

"Well, I would really appreciate borrowing it until I can get a new saddle for him."

"No need." He took the saddle off the roan and hoisted it onto the top fence rail. "It's yours."

She looked at him with what must have been a perplexed expression, because he shifted out of his superfocused work persona to smile at her. "It's a gift."

"I…" She gave a small shake of her head. "I can't accept that. It's too much."

"I want you to have it," he said, leaning his head closer to hers. "I really do."

She took several seconds to consider before she decided to accept the saddle. In the short time she had known this man, he didn't do things without thought. And she could see in his eyes that the gift was his way of showing her he cared.

"Thank you," she said, again caught off guard by his thoughtfulness. "I'll cherish it."

"That's what I like to hear." He took off his hat and held it in a way that would block anyone's view so he could steal a kiss.

They were just finishing fitting one of the other geldings when Danica sent her a text.

"My sister's ready for the outside tour," she said.

"I'm ready," he said, stuffing a pair of tan leather gloves into the back pocket of his Wranglers.

Wayne walked with a purpose to the front of the main house, greeting Danica, Aurora and the contractor, a man named Val Allard. Aurora had to leave for another appointment; Danica and the interior decorator hugged goodbye, and Charlotte could see that they had made a genuine connection.

Charlotte hadn't been so sure how Wayne and Danica were going to get on—polar opposites that they were. But she was glad she hadn't placed a bet against them, because the two got on like a pair of old friends.

The first project was the greenhouse that was being built in order to extend the growing season. Danica seemed enamored by the simple, elegant design and the repurposed materials they were using.

"Are these Daddy's windows?" Danica ran her fingers gently across the thick glass. "These *are* Daddy's windows, aren't they?"

Charlotte nodded and bit her lip. Seeing those windows being put to use touched her each and every time. She could see in her sister's face that they shared that tender, nostalgic feeling.

Danica stared at those windows for many minutes before she said, "That's just so special I can't put it in words."

But even though her sister had made a sincere emotional connection with the repurposed materials, she was still a professional with a business plan and a budget. When she switched to business, Charlotte felt gratified that Wayne had answers to all of Danny's questions from the materials needed to the manpower, costs, timeline and contingency plans.

"I'm impressed." Danica addressed Wayne specifically, looking him dead in the eye. "And I'm not often impressed."

They moved on to the new chicken coop, the repaired pastures and waterlines, and she was able to spend time with all of the horses, laughing as they used their lips to take carrots from her palm. The tour took them to their father's garage and workshop. The first thing that caught her sister's eye was the plaque that Wayne had hand-carved and hung above the main door in honor of their father.

"Butch's Everything Building," Danica read aloud, her hand resting lightly over her heart. "I promised myself I wasn't going to cry."

"Your father was a very smart man," Wayne said.

"Thank you for that, Wayne," her sister said. "Thank you for honoring him."

"It was my pleasure."

The tour continued to the bunkhouse, and Val chimed in to discuss any permits that needed to be pulled and inspections that needed to be made after installations. Then they walked into the barn that had been cleaned and repaired well enough to house the horses at night. At the far end of it, Danica was shocked to see their father's tractor.

"I thought that was rusting in some tractor graveyard," Danica exclaimed.

"This is a classic." Wayne had cranked up the machine,

and over the noise of the motor, he asked, "Would you ladies like a lift?"

"And you think I won't?" Danica said to him. "I was driving this tractor before I could walk."

Charlotte climbed up on one side of Wayne, and Danica in her stiletto heels and Chanel suit climbed up next to the cowboy.

"Hang on tight," Wayne said, and Charlotte thought that, flanked by two women, he looked like the cat that got the cream.

Charlotte reached behind Wayne's back to touch her sister's arm. "We saved the best for last."

Charlotte wasn't looking ahead when they rounded the corner; she was leaning slightly forward, watching the expression on Danica's face. Her sister certainly wasn't the most sentimental triplet, but this cabin was dear to all of them.

As they rounded the corner the cabin, standing on its own merit, freed from the weeds and trees and vines that had long since cut it off from the rest of the world, came into view.

Danica didn't say a word, but the tears on her cheeks spoke volumes. Wayne must have seen Danica's tears in his periphery, because he fished out a clean handkerchief from his front shirt pocket and handed it to her.

Charlotte jumped off the moment Wayne braked and shut down the tractor. He helped Danica reach the ground safely, and Charlotte linked her arm with her sister's as they walked together toward the beloved cabin.

"Charlie," Danica said. "Charlie," her sister said again, Danica's hand clutching her arm tightly in her excitement. "How did he do this?" she asked in wonder. "It's…"

"Amazing."

"Yes. Amazing. And it's still—"

"Standing," they said in unison.

"After all of these years." Danica slipped her arm free to walk even closer to the structure where they had played as children.

Charlotte was moved that her sister was touched. For many years now, Danica had become a living, breathing, glossy, flawlessly staged *Harper's Bazaar* centerfold. Her exterior was flawless, and for Charlotte, for many years, she felt that there was no real way to connect with *Danny* because *Danica* kept the real her locked tightly behind a facade. But the cabin, a tangible connection to generations past, seemed to unlock a vulnerable place in her sister.

"I wish we could go inside," Danica said quietly, almost reverently.

"I know," Charlotte agreed. "One day soon we will. Maybe even for your next visit."

Wayne and Val joined them at the site.

"This is a beautiful structure," the contractor said, and his appreciation of the cabin solidified Charlotte's original gut reaction to Val. "What's the plan for it?"

"Well, first I've got to get that tree off the roof, so we can install a new metal roof," Wayne began. "Repair or replace any logs that are rotten and then insulate. Add larger picture windows, repair—"

Val was taking notes. "Bathroom? Kitchenette?"

"Both," Charlotte said.

"You'll need septic if you want running water. I'll need to pull a permit."

"I need running water," Charlotte confirmed. "Power will be solar."

"Okay," Val said. "I'll get a permit for that as well."

After the tour, Danica and Charlotte stopped by the

chow tent and grabbed a plate of food for lunch from Aspen. Wyatt seemed to always find his way back to Aspen, and this day was no different. The handsome cowboy could always be found loitering by her station during his breaks, but when he saw Charlotte come into the tent, he said to Aspen, "I'll see you tonight."

"Okay," Aspen said with a pretty pink flush on her cheeks.

After Wyatt left, Charlotte said to her friend, "That cowboy is smitten with you."

Aspen smiled while she loaded up their plates with chicken and potato salad.

"But if he's bothering you—"

"He's not." Aspen made the denial in record time.

"Okay," Charlotte said, "but if that changes..."

Aspen nodded. "He's harmless."

Danica and Charlotte carried their plates over to the main house. Mick had followed them to the chow tent and then tagged along back to the main house. Charlotte helped the dog up the steps and then let him go first into the house. Together, they sat down at the kitchen table to discuss the events of the day, and Danica gave her an overview of the plans for the house renovation.

After lunch, Danica and Charlotte went out onto the porch to wait for her sister's ride to take her back to the resort. Together, they sat on the front porch swing, gently rocking back and forth and enjoying the shade.

"I'm going to miss this," Danica said.

Charlotte reached over to squeeze her sister's hand. "I'm going to miss you."

They sat in silence for quite a while. and then Danica said, "I get the *why*."

"What do you mean?"

"I get *why* you're in love with him."

Caught completely off guard, Charlotte snapped her neck around to stare at her sister. It was as if Danica had taken an X-ray of her heart and found her feelings for Wayne hidden in there.

"Is it that obvious?" she asked Danica. They were, after all, triplets and even though decades of separation had nearly shattered their innate bond, this intangible telepathy between them made it futile to attempt to deny the truth.

"Yes," Danica said, "I think to everyone."

That was news to Charlotte: she believed that they had kept their relationship private. They stole kisses and held hands on walks in the woods, and she supposed wherever Wayne was, that's where folks would find her and vice versa...

"And I understand the *why*," Danica repeated. "He's handsome, gentlemanly."

"He's a great animal person."

"And I love the silver in his goatee," her sister said. "Grant started to dye his hair, and I'm not a fan. But if I do it, then I guess all's fair."

Charlotte nodded. "The first time he kissed me, he had his shirt off, and the gray in his chest hair was *glistening*. Honestly, I'd never seen anything more sexy."

"He's a real man."

"A real cowboy."

Sharing her feelings for Wayne with Danica had felt like a valve had been turned and pressure relieved. She supposed that she had known for a while now that she loved him; today was the first time she had said out loud that she was *in love* with him. The sum total of Wayne's life experiences had manifested as lines on his face, gray in his hair, scars on his arms and hands, and the fading of his tattoos. All of these signs of aging—unique only to Wayne's face—added to his appeal for her. He was rugged and strong, and she had never felt for any other man they way she felt about Wayne. And even though red flags and warning signs were buzzing around in her brain, she had decided to accept the pain of losing him down the line in order to enjoy every moment she had with him *now*.

The Mercedes limousine pulled through the gate, and Danica sighed. Together, they walked with linked arms to the car. They hugged each other tightly, neither ready to let the other one go.

"Thank you, Danny," Charlotte said. "None of this would be happening without you."

Danica stepped back, took her hands in hers and said, "Actually, none of this would be happening if it weren't for *you*, Charlie. For years, I would get so annoyed by your singular focus on keeping this ranch intact and in the family for generations to come. But now I get it. I'm only sorry that it took me so long to see in this place what you've always seen. Our history, our legacy, our future."

Wayne was always in the habit of searching for Charlotte when he was making the rounds to check on the multiple projects that were ongoing. Most of the time she found her way over to him and joined the crew. But there were some days when she was waylaid somewhere else on the ranch, and he would miss her in a way that he didn't even know was possible for him. The more time he spent with her, the more time he craved. Charlotte found him in the Everything Building.

"Hey." Bowie ran over to her when he saw her, wagging

his tail, and sat down beside her so she could hug him and give him a scratch on his chest and belly.

"Where have you been?" he asked. His tone was disgruntled, and he didn't try to soften it.

Charlotte frowned at him. "I was meeting with Danny and Ray."

Wayne felt irritated and frustrated, but he wasn't entirely sure why.

"I sent you a text," she said to him, the look in her beautiful, deep-blue eyes a mixture of concern and confusion. "Didn't you get it?"

Wayne felt around for his phone in his pockets; he didn't find it. "I must have left it somewhere. Damn it."

He turned his back to her, vaguely aware that he was being a bit of a jackass yet didn't know how to change course.

"Hey." Charlotte walked around so he was facing her again. "Are you mad at me?"

He looked up at her. "Yes."

Her eyebrows drew together. "Well, knock it off! I haven't done anything to you."

Wayne felt like his insides were being ripped apart at the seams and then stitched again into something else entirely. And as far as he was concerned, it *was* Charlotte's fault. She, with her pretty face, her warm smile, her sexy body, her strength, gumption and soulful, kind eyes had changed him, made him question his vision for his life. He resented it and resented *her*. She had made him *feel* in a way that he had believed himself incapable of.

Wayne tossed the wrench he had in his hand back into the toolbox, walked around the workbench to where Charlotte was standing and took her hand in his, leading her into the small air-conditioned office that had once been her father's hub of all things Hideaway Ranch.

He closed the door behind them and then drew her into his arms and kissed her: every emotion he had was poured into that kiss. He felt the curves of her body pressed against his; he breathed in the scent of her warm skin. He lifted his head up, sought out her eyes and felt encouraged that Charlotte had melted into his arms and had kissed him back with an intensity that matched his own.

He took off her hat, released her hair from the ponytail and fanned it out across her back. She put her hands lovingly on his face. Then she leaned in and brought her lips back to his, giving him every signal that he needed to say what had been on his mind for far too long.

In between kisses Wayne said, "I love you, Charlotte. I love you."

Charlotte molded her body to his, wrapped her arms around him and rested her head on his shoulder. He felt the vibration of her words over his heart as much as he heard them with his ears.

"And I love you, Wayne. So very much."

Chapter Eleven

Wayne had begun to figure out how to balance his workaholic personality with his fledgling relationship with Charlotte. She never brought up the future or pressed him on permanency, focused on the now of their connection, and this was a relief to him. Yes, he loved her with every fiber of his being, but he wasn't so sure what that meant long-term.

"Ready to ride?" he asked after he picked out Cash's hooves.

"I've never been so ready," Charlotte said, brushing the dust and dirt off the horse's body.

Charlotte groomed Atlas while he tacked up Cash. The saddle was a good fit, but the matching bridle didn't have enough holes to set the bit in the right position.

"Do me a favor," he said to his cowgirl. "Look in the cutlery drawer in my trailer and see you if find a leather hole punch."

"In the cutlery drawer?" She sent him a teasing smile.

"Don't forget, I've been a bachelor for a while."

Wayne took advantage of the view of Charlotte walking away from him in snug-fit jeans that showed off her curvy muscular body to its fullest. When she turned her head and caught him looking, she smiled at him, letting her hips swing just a little bit more to give him a nice show. Charlotte's sassy, teasing nature was one of the many things he loved about her; she was, he believed, a perfect fit for him at this stage of his life. That was something he had never thought to find again in this lifetime. He had believed a person only had one true love in a lifetime.

Wayne had just finished saddling and bridling Atlas when Charlotte returned with the hole punch.

"Thank you," he said when she handed it to him. "Was it there?"

"No, actually." She shook her head with a faint smile. "Junk drawer."

Wayne focused on fixing the piece of the bridle that held the bit in place. He checked both sides of the bridle and felt satisfied with the fit.

Atlas was standing quietly, waiting patiently, his eyes drooping down in relaxation with the reins of his bridle looped over a stripped-down log that had been turned into a hitching post by her father.

Charlotte pulled the reins over the gelding's head, grabbed the horn with her left hand and, putting her left foot in the stirrup, got a boost from Wayne so she could swing her right leg over Cash's back. She slipped her right foot into the stirrup and then settled into the saddle. On the way up, Wayne had given her backside a quick pat.

"We're right out in the open," she said to him. "Aren't you afraid someone might see you copping a feel?"

Wayne smiled while he tightened Atlas's girth. "Not really."

"Not really?" Charlotte asked him. "Who are you, and what did you do with Wayne?"

Wayne swung into the saddle, turned Atlas so he was side-by-side with Cash and winked at her. "Do you want to talk or do you want to ride?"

Charlotte had taken them on a path that would allow him to see, for the first time, some of the natural beauty of the pristine, untouched land that was a part of the Hide-away Ranch holdings. They warmed up the horses, walking them at first and then trotting them along a roughed-in road. As far as the eye could see, vast pastures and rolling hills greeted them.

"Over that hill, there is a spring-fed lake." Charlotte pointed, her golden skin flushed with joy and the exertion of riding.

"Lead the way."

Charlotte guided Cash off the old, forgotten road, and then she turned her head to look at him over her shoulder with a mischievous grin. "Try to keep up!"

Before he could process those four words, Charlotte let Cash have his head and yelled, "Yah!"

The blue roan lunged forward, breaking into a full gallop. Cash was quick off the leg, while Atlas was a big, muscular guy that took a lot more convincing to break into a gallop. By the time he got his act together, Charlotte was way ahead of him. She was standing up in her stirrups, taking her weight off Cash's back; she leaned forward, one hand holding on to her cowgirl hat while the other held the reins.

"Come on!" she yelled loud enough for Wayne to hear. "Cowboy up!"

Atlas had height and muscle mass on Cash, but he wasn't fleet-footed enough to overtake Charlotte's lead. But they did catch up. Together, they raced side by side through a meadow, laughing with joy as they slowed their speed up a small hill and then went full-force down the other side. Wayne had seen Charlotte ride in an arena when they were trailing the horses, but this was the first time he had seen her in her element, free from the confines of a small space. To watch her ride was a thing of beauty: she was fearless, charging ahead, completely grounded in the moment, confident in Cash and her own ability to handle any challenges in the terrain. Seeing her like this, wild, free, more talented in the saddle than he'd ever seen anyone else, made him fall more deeply in love with her than he had been before.

At the bottom of the hill, Charlotte asked Cash to slow to a canter, settling back into the saddle and then bringing him to a trot.

"That was amazing!" she said, now walking Cash toward the lake so he could catch his breath.

He wasn't imagining it. Charlotte was looking at him with a new respect. "You kept up with me."

Wayne laughed—a real laugh. "Just barely."

At the lake, they dismounted and allowed the horses to drink their fill before ground-tying them and letting them graze on the grass nearby. They cupped their hands to drink from the lake and then splashed water on their faces. Teasingly, Charlotte flicked water at him, and after that ride, his mood boosted, he grabbed her, held her up against him and swung her around while she laughed, her hat falling off her head onto the ground at his feet.

He let her down gently, stealing a kiss before they sat down on the soft grass near the lake's edge.

"That's the best time I've had in a long time," Wayne said, enjoying the feel of Charlotte's body leaning back against his.

"Me too." She sighed happily.

She leaned back her head and offered him her lips, and that one kiss led to another and another. Soon he was lying on his back with Charlotte in his arms. In one movement, Wayne rolled her onto her back so he could admire her lovely face.

He gently brushed her hair off her face, his eyes locked with hers. "You are so beautiful, Charlotte."

She reached up to touch his face sweetly. "You are so handsome, Wayne."

The next kisses led to buttons and zippers being undone and hands exploring. He was lost in the moment, focusing his entire being on the incredible woman in his arms; he was leading them to a place they had never gone before, and Charlotte was urging him on, kissing him on his neck and making sweet sounds of pleasure.

And then Bowie, who was supposed to still be back at the ranch, bounded out of the tall grass, leaping like a gazelle, barking happily while he landed on top of Wayne's back.

"Damn it, Bowie!" Wayne rolled to the side, trying to stop the dog from licking his entire face with his tongue.

Charlotte sat upright, her face glowing, her lips still parted slightly from his kisses. She reached over and hugged Bowie, ruffling his floppy ears.

"What are you doing here, you naughty puppy?" she

said, ducking her head to stop Bowie from licking her entire face.

"I think he's jealous," Wayne said after he accepted a rambunctious dog had destroyed the romantic mood.

"Yeah!" Charlotte wiped the dog spit off her cheek. "Of *me*, not *you*! He's been in a bromance with you since he met you."

"Well," Wayne said and got up onto one knee and put his hand on his kneecap to support his weight as he pushed himself to a stand. He held out his hand to her. "At least you know he has good taste."

The day after their ride, all of the permits came in for the main house renovation and expansion, as well as the plumbing, electrical and septic ones for the historical cabin. Charlotte was so excited to get started on the cabin that she barely slept the night before, mentally drawing out designs in her head and imagining how it would look when it was finished.

At first light, she went to Wayne's trailer and knocked on the door.

"Good morning, darlin'." Her cowboy greeted her with a kiss and a smile.

"Good morning." She quickly closed the door before Bowie could slip through. The relationship between Hitch and Bowie was slow going.

"Coffee?"

She nodded before loving on Mick and carrying Hitch over to the table with her. Wayne put a mug of coffee on the table in front of her while she had a special moment with Hitch, kissing the cat on his head, scratching him under his chin, as the cat walked back and forth in front of her, rubbing up against her and bumping her with the top of his head.

"All of the Westbrook men love you," Wayne said after taking a sip of coffee. "Mick, Hitch and even my kid brothers."

"I even have the stamp of approval from the three Ws?"

"Come again?" Wayne asked. "The three what?"

"The three Ws. That's what I call your brothers in my head."

"That's a good nickname for them." He chuckled. "It's hard to get the three Ws to agree on much, but they are unanimous when it comes to you."

Charlotte felt a blush warm her cheeks. "That's nice."

His eyes locked with hers, and she liked the love she saw in his deep-set eyes. "It is that."

"So today's the day," she said.

"A long time comin'."

"Too long."

He nodded. "First things first, the boys and I have to climb up on that roof and cut that tree down to size so I can lift it off. Then we've got to peel back that rusty metal roof so we'll have a better idea what we're looking at. I've pulled Wyatt, Waylon and Wade off their other jobs. I trust them. I know what they can do, and I know they'll be safe."

She nodded. "I'm going to be filming it. Aspen thinks it's a good idea to document the transformation of the cabin. She's been getting a lot of traffic on her social media since she's been posting from the chow tent and the greenhouse."

"Just as long as you're safe." Wayne's brow lowered with concern, and he tapped his finger on the table to emphasize his words. "That's top priority."

"I know how to handle myself on a job site," she said, her ego bruised ever so slightly.

"I know you do," he acknowledged, "but you're important to me. Very much so."

As the sun rose up over the horizon, the forecast called for a hot, dry day, perfect for starting the cabin project. They left the trailer to be greeted by a bustling ranch that now included additional workers and trucks as the renovation started at the main house. Wayne held a quick tailgate, doling out assignments, answering questions and troubleshooting. Once the workers were sent on their way, Wayne said to his brothers, "Where's Wade?"

"He left," Waylon said.

Wayne leaned, titled his head as if he hadn't heard right. "Excuse me?"

"He left," Wyatt said. "Left late last night."

Wayne put his hands on his hips in an annoyed stance. "To where? Or do I even need to ask?"

"Dallas," Waylon confirmed.

"Back to his ex," Wyatt added.

"Well damn me all to hell," Wayne snapped. "Did anyone think it *might* just be important to tell me?"

"Wade said he would. If he didn't, that's on him," Waylon said.

Wayne looked down at the ground for a couple of minutes, shook his head and used some choice curse words, then he breathed in and out slowly.

"Well, we aren't going to get any work done worrying about things we can't fix," Wayne said as he lifted his head. He set off toward the excavator, made that distinctive *pay attention* whistle and waved his hand for his brothers to follow behind.

Charlotte had enough experience with downing trees

with her father that she knew that this job was precarious and dangerous. Wayne was lifted by a crane operated by Waylon to start the first part of the task. Wayne tied strong cables around one section of the tree, cut it off with a chain saw, and then whistled to Waylon to slowly lift the cut section up and then over to set it down on the ground. There was a lot of shouting between Wayne and his brothers, not in anger but in urgency to get the job done without anybody getting injured. It was important for the communication to stay open and for all three brothers to know where the others were.

Wayne yelled to Waylon, "Bring it back!"

While Wayne tied up a new section of tree, Wyatt went to work on cutting limbs off the section on the ground; after removing the branches, he would cut the trunk into smaller pieces. Then, all of the branches and smaller sections of trunk would be fed into the industrial wood chipper they had rented for this job in particular. Any sections of the tree that could be salvaged and repurposed were set off to the side.

Charlotte had been filming, but staying on the sidelines just wasn't for her. She slipped her phone into the back pocket of her jeans and grabbed the pair of work gloves she always had in her back left pocket. She put on the protective goggles she had hooked onto the collar of her T-shirt and then she started hauling branches over to the nearby wood chipper.

Wyatt saw what she was doing and gave her a wave of acknowledgment. Working together, they made short work of the first section of the tree and then began on the second that Waylon had lowered to the ground. There were four in total; when the last one was laid on the ground, Charlotte heard the whistle, so she looked up and over to find Wayne.

"Bring me down!" Wayne yelled at Waylon.

Waylon carefully lifted Wayne off the roof and set him down on the ground far enough away from the remaining massive trunk that was leaning on the cabin to be safe. Wayne traded places with Waylon, who climbed up on a ladder to put a thick chain around the tree so Wayne could then move it off the side of the cabin.

"All set?" Wayne yelled over the sound of the crane.

Waylon had moved the ladder out of the way and then gave his brother a sign of approval. Charlotte stopped what she was doing to watch that trunk being removed from the cabin; she had been waiting for this moment for a decade, and all sorts of emotions—relief, happiness, gratitude—welled up unexpectedly. In order to keep herself in check, Charlotte got out her phone and began to document this transformative moment.

Wayne started to move the huge trunk off the side of the house, and Charlotte held her breath anxiously until she heard the loud, distinctive sound of a giant tree trunk landing on its side, crushing everything beneath it.

They all cheered when the tree was completely off of the structure and gave each other high fives. She ran over to the crane, climbed aboard, and in front of Wayne's brothers, she hugged and kissed him.

"You are the best, Wayne!" She hugged him again. "The very best!"

"Thank you." Wayne put his arm around her and kissed her back. "If you're happy, then so am I."

"I'm happy." She smiled brightly at him. "Very."

Charlotte jumped down from the crane followed by

Wayne. They walked over to the chipper to discuss next steps for the cabin.

"The tree did some serious damage to the roof. How much I don't know," Wayne reported.

"I remember my dad telling me that his father replaced the wood shingles with the metal."

"Waylon has the most roofing experience," Wayne said. "Are you willing to get up there and get that metal loose so I can pull it open like a sardine can?"

"I can do that," Waylon said.

"We'll continue to get this wood into the chipper," Wyatt said.

Wayne nodded before he headed back to the crane. He turned back and pointed at Charlotte, saying, "Be careful."

"I will," she said, resisting the urge to be annoyed by his concern. He loved her, she was important to him, and she needed to expect that he was going to worry about her safety.

She worked with Wyatt steadily until there was only one stripped-down part of the log that was hollow on the inside from rot left to cut down into smaller pieces.

"I've got to take a break," he said, grabbing a canteen that he had put on the ground nearby.

He offered her a drink, and she accepted.

"So, you and Wayne," Wyatt said after a minute or two.

She nodded, not sure how much, if anything, Wayne had shared with the three Ws.

"I like how close the four of you are. I mean, I was shocked when Wayne said if he called you guys to come help him that you would drop what you were doing and come."

"Wayne's been more than a brother to us. He helped Mom raise us. Dad was just...Dad," Wyatt said.

"Wayne told me about how your mom taught him how to ride."

Wyatt spun his head around to look at her. "Wayne told you about that?"

She stared at him. "He did. Why?"

"Because Wayne doesn't talk to *anyone* about our childhood, not even us, and we lived it with him."

"He still keeps me at arm's length," she said, her eyes finding Wayne while her mind digested this new information. She supposed that it was special that he had revealed anything from his formative years. She didn't know if there would ever be a time when Wayne truly let her in.

Wyatt said, "He's like that with everyone—even us. Those waters run deep. But don't give up on him. The way he looks at you, the way he talks about you, I have this gut feeling that you might just be the one who breaks down those walls."

"I suppose time will tell."

"Yes, ma'am."

Wanting to shift the focus of the conversation away from her relationship with Wayne, Charlotte asked, "So, you and Aspen."

The moment he heard Aspen's name, Wyatt's eyes lit up like a kid at Christmas. "Yeah. I love her."

"You love her?" she said. "Are you serious?"

"I am serious. I love her. And I think she loves me too," Wyatt said, completely devoid of any discomfort about discussing his feelings about her pretty blonde friend.

"She's an incredibly special person," Charlotte told him.

"Two hundred percent, she is."

"She's one of my dearest friends. If you're just looking for a summer romp, you need to back off."

"I'm serious," Wyatt said. "Aspen's the kind of woman that you marry and settle down and have a family with."

"Marry?"

He nodded his head, then he looked at her directly with eyes so similar to Wayne's but without the pain and hurt from decades of hard knocks.

"I'm going to marry Aspen one day, if she'll have me. The moment I saw her, I thought, *That's my wife*. I'm going to marry her."

The conversation was cut short by the grating sound of rusty metal being bent and pulled. Wyatt and Charlotte stood up to watch the last part of the roof popping free and curling over until it was completely removed from the cabin gables and set down a few feet from the tree trunk.

Charlotte clapped her hands and gave Wayne and Waylon a big whoop of appreciation. "I've got to go look inside the cabin now that the roof and tree are gone."

"You go," he said. "I've got the rest of this."

"Are you sure?"

"Yes, ma'am."

"Oh my Lord, would you *please* stop with *ma'am* stuff?"

He nodded. "Yes. I sure will."

Charlotte was already on the move and threw a "Thanks" over her shoulder as she jogged over to the cabin. She was convinced that in a short amount of time, her dream of turning this cabin into a home would become reality.

When Wayne pronounced the cabin safe-enough to enter, Charlotte walked onto the front porch, her heart racing at the door. With her fingers trembling from excitement, she pushed on the thick oak door with enough force to push it open. But it wouldn't budge.

"There might be some debris in the way." Wayne stepped up beside her. "Let's push it together."

Together, they forced the door open, allowing them access to the narrow entryway that led to the two first-floor rooms on either side of it. There was a sleeping loft that was originally accessed by a wooden ladder, but that had crumbled long ago. Charlotte hoped to build actual stairs so she could use the loft as her bedroom, while one of the downstairs rooms would be a small kitchen and dining area, and the second room would be a cozy living room. They would still need to find a place to install a small washroom with a sink, toilet and shower.

Charlotte reached behind her and grabbed Wayne's hand as they walked across the threshold into the cabin. Once inside, Charlotte overlooked the musty smell, the limited light and the evidence of animal droppings. The white oak planks used to build the floor could be repaired and finished beautifully, and the oak logs themselves were still in remarkably good shape. And the fireplaces! The home had two hearths made of stone; they added to the character of the cabin.

Charlotte wished that she hadn't been feeling so emotional of late. Perhaps it was the relief that after years of worrying, years of trying to keep everything running alone, she finally had support from her sisters, Wayne and his brothers, and her distant relatives at Sugar Creek Ranch.

Tears were running unchecked down her cheeks as she walked into the kitchen area. The ceiling was very low, and that would take some getting used to, but she could see herself making this little cabin into her forever home.

Wayne saw her tears, and he immediately wrapped her up in his arms.

"Thank you, Wayne." Charlotte held on to him, comforted by his warm embrace. "You don't know how much this means to me."

"Actually," her cowboy said, "I do know how much this means to you. I really do. What I don't exactly have sorted out in my mind is why the heck it means so much to *me*."

Chapter Twelve

"Are you supposed to be loitering by the greenhouse?" Aspen tossed her long blond braid over her shoulder as she placed a perfect little tomato plant into rich soil in a terra-cotta pot.

Wyatt was leaning against the doorjamb to the greenhouse. "I may or may not be playing hooky right now."

Aspen looked up from her chore. It hadn't taken much for Wyatt to grow on her: he was ruggedly handsome, with piercing blue eyes, a killer smile and a body that was naturally lean from his work as a roaming cowboy.

"Your brother isn't going to like that." She stood upright, satisfied with the new plant; she brushed her hands together to clean off some of the soil. "Have you come to admire my work?"

Wyatt took a step into the greenhouse. He had a spark in his eyes, and she was charmed by his crooked smile that always drew her attention to the sexy dimple in his chin.

"Actually, I came to admire you."

"You don't give up easily, do you, Wyatt?"

"No, ma'am, I don't. Not when I know what I want. And what I want right now is to give this to you." Wyatt brought his hand from behind his back, and he offered her a single yellow wildflower with an orange spiny center.

Aspen smiled when she saw the flower and then she began to chuckle, which then turned into a laugh.

She accepted the flower and at the same time reached over to put her hand on his forearm. She could tell that she had ruined the sweet gesture for him, and it made her feel terrible.

"I am so sorry, Wyatt, truly I am. It was so sweet of you to think of me."

When he didn't look convinced and a hurt look lingered in his eyes, even though he was doing his best to cover that up, it made her feel like the worst person. "Do you know the name of this flower?"

Wyatt was frowning, an expression she hadn't seen from him before. He was usually positive, happy and kind.

"This is called a sneezeweed."

She smiled at him, and pretty quickly Wyatt smiled sheepishly back at her. "Sneezeweed?"

"Yep," she said. "People used to dry these out, crush them and then turn them into snuff."

"So, not a type of sunflower?"

"No," she said, doing her best to make him feel better. "They used it to ward off evil spirits."

It took some explaining, but she did manage to turn the moment between them around. She apologized again, hoping that they could move past it. She did give him a hard time, but she genuinely liked Wyatt, and she had come to look forward to his visits.

"Well," Wyatt said and tilted his head to examine her, his eyes narrowed slightly like he was hatching a plan, "if you want to make it up to me…"

"Oh boy, here it comes."

"You can go out to dinner with me."

She cocked one eyebrow at him. "I'm not sure the punishment fits the crime."

"That's the deal," he said. "Take it or leave it."

She looked up at the ceiling, pretending to contemplate the dinner invitation, and after some phony deliberation, she smiled at him and said, "You drive a hard bargain. But I'll accept my punishment."

Wyatt's eyes lit up, and it was endearing to her that he got so excited over sharing a meal with her.

She put her hands on his shoulders, guided him around and gave him a push. "Now get back to work before your taskmaster of a brother catches you with me!"

Wyatt tipped the brim of his hat to her, winked and headed off toward the cabin. But then she called him back. "Hey! When, what time and where?"

"Anywhere, any day, anytime," Wyatt said. "Tomorrow for dinner?"

"I can't do Saturday."

"Then, what about Sunday?" he asked. "What are you doing Sunday?"

"I'm going to church."

"I'll go with you."

"To church?" she said, incredulous.

"If it's important to you, it's important to me."

"Okay," she said after some thought. "And, then I'm having lunch with my grandma Edna."

"Church and lunch with Grandma Edna."

Aspen had a mix of emotions as she watched Wyatt

walk away with his cowboy swagger. She had just, to all intents and purposes, invited Wyatt to meet her family, her church family and her most important person, Grandma Edna.

"What was I thinking?" she said to herself, her feet seemingly fused to the ground.

When Wyatt passed by some of his fellow cowboys working on repairing the round pen near the paddock, Wyatt raised his arms like a prizefighter that had just won a match and shouted, "She said *yes*!"

A couple of weeks into the main-house renovation, Charlotte felt exhausted. Between the dust, the noise, the demolition, increased communication with Danica, who was trying to micromanage the project from California, and Aurora's anxiety over making Danica happy—all this was making it nearly impossible for her to keep up.

"You look like you haven't slept." Wayne put a cup of coffee in front of her.

She held her head in her hands, groggy and fighting a migraine. "I haven't."

Hitch was trying his best to make her feel better, rubbing up against the crown of her head, purring for her and licking the back of her hand. She lifted her head up, wrapped her arms around the fluffy cat and hugged him to her body. She kissed him and then rested her cheek on his head.

"I can't have you on the project if you're exhausted." Wayne joined her at the table. Mick was staring at her with his head resting on the table across from her. He was whining a bit because he could tell that she was not feeling well.

"I know," she agreed. "This is just all too much. People everywhere, noise everywhere, Danny and Ray blowing up my phone all hours—I mean, I'm glad they're invested, I really am, but I also want my life back."

Bowie was scratching on the trailer door and barking incessantly to be let in.

"Bowie! Stop!" she yelled at the dog, which only hurt her head more.

Her eyes closed, she said, "I'm sorry. That was awful."

"You're exhausted," Wayne said, getting up and opening the door for Bowie.

"You're going to let him in?" Charlotte lifted up her head, her eyes squinted because the impending migraine was making her sensitive to the light.

"Yes," he said. "It's past time. If he bugs Hitch, Hitch will school him."

Charlotte breathed in deeply and let it out. "Okay. I'll let you handle it."

Bowie bounded in and nuzzled her arm, and she leaned her head down, looked in his eyes and apologized for yelling at him. Bowie then lifted his nose to sniff Hitch, and the feline hissed at him, growled and boxed the dog on his nose. Bowie decided to leave the cat alone and go on a sniffing mission in the new space. When he was done, he returned to Wayne and squeezed his large body onto the sliver of bench left by Wayne's side.

"What can I do for you now?" Wayne asked.

She shook her head. "I don't know."

He reached out to take one of her hands in his. "Why don't you stay here and rest?"

She looked up at him. "I hate to miss a day at the cabin."

"I know you do, but we're still cleaning out the space and installing a tarp because of the rain that's heading our way." He squeezed her hand. "Rest today and you'll feel better tomorrow."

"I might just take you up on that."

"I wish you would."

Hitch moved down from the table onto her lap when Bowie insisted on sniffing his fluffy tail.

"Okay," she said, petting Hitch's head. "I will. But then I need to find a long-term solution. It's just too messy and noisy in the house. I'm basically living out of boxes now."

After a minute of thinking Wayne suggested, "Why don't you stay here?"

"Here? In the trailer?"

"Sure." Wayne put his arm around Bowie, who thanked him by licking his face. "Why not? I can bunk in Wade's tent—he's not coming back anytime soon."

"He's not?"

"No," Wayne said, the disapproval and disappointment thick. She didn't ask him to elaborate, and he didn't offer as he continued. "So get some rest and think about it. We don't have to decide right now."

Charlotte went to the back of the trailer to the bed, pulled off her boots and climbed under the covers. Wayne gave her some ibuprofen for her headache and then pulled the covers up over her shoulders and gave her a quick kiss. Mick and Hitch joined her as she burrowed her head into the soft pillow.

"Get some rest, feel better," he said. "I'll take Bowie with me."

"Thank you," she mumbled, feeling more comfortable in Wayne's bed than she had all week in her own. "I love you."

The minute she was completely snuggled into the bed, she began to drift off quickly, but she did hear him say, "I'm a lucky man."

* * *

Charlotte awakened later that morning with Hitch sleeping on the pillow above her head and Mick sleeping with his back pressed up against hers. She fumbled for her phone on the small nightstand to see the time.

"Eleven fifteen," she said in a raspy, barely awake voice. "Geez, I've lost half a day."

She sat up, careful not to disturb her canine and feline sleeping buddies. She scooted to the end of the bed, pulled on her boots but didn't zip them up, and then asked Mick if he needed to go out.

Mick got up, walked to the edge of the bed and slowly got down. On the way out, Charlotte rinsed out her mouth with some mouthwash she found in the bathroom and opened the blinds near the dining table so Hitch could soak up the afternoon sun once he awakened from his nap.

Charlotte stepped outside, realized that she needed her sunglasses from inside the main house, and was grateful for the fact that her headache was gone and the rest had done her some good. She felt more herself now.

After she grabbed her sunglasses from inside the construction zone, she saw Aspen working in the greenhouse. She had to walk past the enormous dumpster in the front of the house and even though she *knew* it had to go, it was still upsetting to see her mother's threadbare, horribly uncomfortable couch tossed away. She averted her gaze from the dumpster and continued on to the new greenhouse.

"Hey!" she greeted her friend warmly.

"Hi!" Aspen put down her watering hose and met Charlotte halfway to give her a hug.

"So? What do you think of your greenhouse now?"

Aspen asked, a smudge of dirt on her cheek and her T-shirt wet in spots from a combination of water and sweat. Even dirty and sweaty, Aspen made a pretty sight.

"It's incredible." Charlotte really took a moment to look at everything Aspen had accomplished with the help of the loaner cowboys from Sugar Creek. She ran her hand over the repurposed windows from her father's collection. "These windows make it so special."

"I know," Aspen said with a nod. "I was so honored to have them in my design."

Aspen talked her through all of the plants in the greenhouse, and then they discussed the menu that she had been working on with Rayna.

"I think we're actually done." Aspen leaned her hip against the wooden table that ran the length of the greenhouse. "Once you have a kitchen again, I can walk you through any of the recipes you feel uncomfortable with."

"Sounds good," she said.

"Let me show you the build on the chicken coop before you go," Aspen said, following her out of the greenhouse.

They walked the short distance to the coop. It had been important for safety and easy access that it be in proximity to the greenhouse. Aspen ran through the safety features that would stop predators from making easy prey out of the chickens that would soon be arriving. Over time, Aspen's role had expanded, and Charlotte was grateful that she had been willing to offer her expertise to the project.

"I can shoot my content from anywhere," her friend had said.

Charlotte was also pleased that Aspen had been able to capitalize on the homesteading angle and had actually increased her following since she'd begun posting about the greenhouse, chicken coop and her new miniseries called Chow Tent Cuisine.

"How do you feel about goats?"

Charlotte looked at her sideways. "Do you mean in general?"

"No," Aspen laughed. "Ray and I think it would be amazing to have goat milk on the farm. We can make goat-milk cheese, ice cream, fudge——"

"Goat-milk milk," Charlotte interjected.

After a second, Aspen laughed along with her and rolled her eyes at herself. "Okay, I get it. Ray and I seriously geek out together about cooking. But seriously, are you pro goat?"

Charlotte said, "I'd like to think I am. Just as long as we can keep them safe, and you'd have to run it by Danica about the budget."

The expression on Aspen's face at the thought of getting one step closer to having goats on the ranch could only be described as elated. Excitedly she said, "We can use discarded materials. It won't blow the budget, I promise."

"Well," Charlotte said and shrugged, "I'm not the one you have to promise. The budget is Danny's baby."

"Okay," Aspen said. "I'll talk to her today. But I can tell her that you're a *yes*?"

"Yes. I say *yes* to the goats."

Aspen hugged her tightly. "Thank you, thank you! You won't regret it, I promise you."

"Good luck with Danny."

She moved to attend to other tasks, when Aspen jogged back to her. "Wait! I forgot to tell you something fun!"

Charlotte turned around.

"I'm going out with Wyatt."

Charlotte said, "Finally putting him out of his misery?"

Aspen's face was alight with excitement and that incredible love high a person experienced when they found a new love connection. "Yes. He's going with me to church, and then we are going to have lunch at the assisted-living facility with my grandma Edna."

"Well that's—"

"A perfect date for me?" Aspen clasped her hands in front of her body.

"Yes. A perfect date for you." Charlotte was happy for Aspen and Wyatt. "I think he's a good one, Aspen. I really do."

Aspen nodded, her creamy cheeks flushed a pretty shade of pink. "So do I."

After she dropped Mick off at the trailer so he could keep cool, she walked along the new road that had been carved out by Wayne and his excavator. She waved when he saw her. Wayne whistled at Wyatt and Waylon and made a circle with his pointer finger in the air to let them know that he was shutting the project down for a minute. The brothers were installing a tarp on the roof in preparation for the storm that would be hitting them sometime overnight.

Wayne jumped down and winced on landing and put his hand on his knee. Charlotte saw it but didn't intend to ask him about it. She was forty now, and her body loved ranch work—it was a way to keep fit—but all of her joints were rebelling with stiffness and achiness that got progressively worse as the years went by. Wayne was fifty, and it didn't matter to her one bit that he got stiff:

that man would die working the land, and that dedication and work ethic was what her father had had, and it was what she respected in a man.

"I was coming to check on you." Wayne smiled at her behind his bushy goatee.

"Did you miss me?" She smiled up at him flirtatiously.

Instead of answering her, he put his hands on the upper part of her arms and pulled her in for a kiss. Lately, they had both been freer with the connection they shared, and it felt right for her. She was a grown woman falling in love with a grown man: their relationship belonged to them and no one else.

His concerned eyes roaming her face, Wayne said, "You look better."

"I feel better," she said. "Thank you for looking after me so well."

He winked at her, and then his eyes traveled down to her shirt and he started to fasten a couple of the buttons. "That's a little low, don't you think?"

At the same time, she started to button him up. Wayne always seemed to have his shirt undone almost all the way. "Don't you think *this* is a little low?"

After they had made each other decent and laughed about it, Wayne put his arm around her shoulders. "Are you ready to see what we've been doing while you've been playing hooky?"

"I can't wait."

Together they walked over to the cabin. When they reached the porch, Charlotte's eyes widened in surprise. "Wayne!"

"Check it out," he said, a ring of pride in his voice.

Charlotte walked ahead of him through the door. Wayne and his brothers had cleared out all of the debris, broken furniture, and odds and ends out of the two rooms on the first floor.

"How did you get this done?" she asked. He had understandably prioritized shoring up the roof, repairing the two stone chimneys in advance of the storm. She hadn't expected anything to be done inside until those jobs were complete.

Wayne joined her in the kitchen area, his thumbs hooked on the front pocket of his jeans. "We ran ahead of schedule."

She walked around the room in awe until she reached one of the two stone hearths. Both hearths had a decorative arch in the design. She imagined that this was her ancestor's gift to his wife—this one seemingly feminine touch that would have no doubt been considered frivolous to the husband when they were first carving out a life in this often inhospitable yet glorious part of the country.

She turned to smile at him, to offer him her genuine thanks. "I suppose I should play hooky more often."

Wayne gave her a real tour of the cabin now that the debris had been cleaned: he pointed out logs and floor planks that would need to be replaced, the plan for the bathroom.

"I've got one more surprise for you," Wayne said, "but you've got to climb up to see it."

Charlotte climbed the temporary ladder that gave her access through a square cut in the floor of the loft; when she reached the top of it, she stopped when she saw a stockpile of wooden roof shingles.

She moved off the ladder, and even though the ceiling was low, she could still stand up right in the center where the pitch of the original roof was the highest. She went to the stacks, knelt down and picked up one shingle, running her hand over it reverently, realizing that the hands of her ancestors had made it.

Wayne joined her. She stood up, still holding the wood shingle in her hand. "I've been up here a million times. I've never seen these before. Where did you find these?"

"In your father's shop."

Charlotte took a deep breath in and closed her eyes. "Of course they were. Of course he would save these."

"We can use these any way you want," Wayne said, his legs spread slightly in a stance he often used, his arms crossed in front of him.

"When I thought about the roof, I didn't know we had these. I know I have an old photograph of this cabin somewhere with these exact shingles on the roof," Charlotte said, very tempted to revise the forest green metal roof she had selected.

"Or we could use them as an accent wall up here," Wayne said, smoothing his hand over his facial hair. "Or in the living room."

Her mind racing with new ideas, Charlotte knew it would take some time for her to make a final decision.

"Do we have enough for the roof?" she asked after they climbed down the ladder into the area that would be the living room.

"Not quite," Wayne said, "but Waylon had an idea to use more modern wood shingles placed sporadically to fill in for the shortfall of the original ones."

"Wow," Charlotte said, still processing this incredible find. "It's so tempting."

"Well, the sky is about to open up on us, so you've got some thinking time. We are going to be waterlogged like crazy when that storm blows through."

Before they headed outside, Wayne stopped her. "Have you given any thought to moving into my camper?"

"Yes." She nodded.

"And?"

"I can't kick you out of your own house, Wayne. I wouldn't feel good about it."

"I wouldn't have offered if it bothered me."

"But it bothers *me*!"

"Well, something's got to change. I need you on this build, and you need to be able to sleep." He caught her eye, and she could see how sincere he was. "How'd you sleep in my bed today?"

She smiled a faint smile. "Like a baby."

He looked pleased. "Then, it's settled."

"How about we both stay in the camper?" she asked.

"That's a thought."

"Do you think we would get fed up with each other?"

"Of course we will. When we do, we've got nothing but space out here."

"If I stay with you, we'd be announcing our relationship to the ranch."

"Do you care?"

"Not really," she said. "Do you?"

"I don't give a rat's behind," he said. "But if we're sharing a bed…"

She waited, having a pretty good idea where he was going.

"I'm just a man."

She reached out to grab one of his hands while holding his gaze. "And I'm just a woman who's tired of taking things slow."

Chapter Thirteen

It seemed that the universe had given them a break—time to cover the roof area of the cabin with a tarp before the sky above turned a charcoal gray with fast-moving clouds, high-pitched gusts of wind that sounded like wolves howling and driving rain that dumped buckets upon buckets of water. Everyone on the ranch hunkered down or took their leave elsewhere since all outside projects had been halted for nearly a week while the weather cleared.

"Where'd you go?" Wayne asked, propped up in the bed he had shared with Charlotte, two dogs and a touchy cat. If anyone had told him that he would even contemplate such an arrangement, much less *do* it, he would have called them crazy. But here he was, trapped in a small camper while a storm system stalled right over their part of the state, forcing them all inside. Yes, it was super-tight quarters, but the cramped space had forced the five of them to bond. Hitch had called a tentative truce with Bowie, but he still hissed, growled and boxed him on the nose several times if he tried to sniff him for an unacceptable length of time.

"I'm coming." Charlotte turned off the light in the bathroom and came into his view.

She was wearing a white ribbed tank top she had borrowed from his drawer; she had tied the excess material into a knot that fell just above her belly button. On the bottom, she wore a pair of form-fitting women's briefs covered in pastel-pink and blue flowers. The thin material of the tank top clung to her small, pert breasts, and the cotton underwear hugged the lovely curves of her bottom, hips and thickly muscled thighs. The matching black-and-gray tattoo armbands that looked like rope holding two long feathers reached her elbows and accentuated the strong biceps of a homesteading woman. The same freckles that were on her cheeks and across the bridge of her nose were also on her shoulders, and he loved to kiss each and every one of them.

"God bless." Wayne couldn't stop staring at her. "You are one beautiful, sexy woman."

Charlotte touched her hair self-consciously. "Do you think I should cover my gray?"

Wayne shook his head: her hair was flowing over her shoulders, wild and wavy and brown with silver threads. "Don't change a thing. It's sexy. You're sexy."

"I don't know," she said, looking at her reflection in the bathroom mirror from her spot in the narrow aisle. "I look so much older than Danny and Ray now."

"Quit finding flaws in yourself." He held out his hand to her. "Come over here and pay attention to me."

That made Charlotte laugh, and when she did, a light

shined in her pretty blue eyes. When he looked at her, he never saw flaws, he only saw her beauty. He supposed that was his way of being in love.

Charlotte sat down on the bed beside him, one foot tucked under her leg, taking his outstretched hand in hers.

They had consummated their relationship: their love and desire had manifested in many ways. Sometimes it was hot, heavy, urgent, and the next time it was slow, gentle, tender. For the first time in recent memory, Wayne had been grateful for the rain. It had given him concentrated time to explore every lovely inch of her body. Making love with Charlotte had been transformative for him in a way that felt foreign—he felt more connected, more attached and vulnerable. All emotions that he had managed to avoid for over two decades.

"Why do you look so serious?" she asked.

He looked down at their fingers threaded together before he met her gaze. "Are you the marrying kind, Charlotte?"

She looked shocked at the question, and he was shocked that he had even broached the topic.

She shrugged one shoulder with a little frown and her brows drawn together. "I haven't given it much thought, really."

"Oh no?"

"No," she said. "I mean, I want to find someone to share my life with, but I don't think that I care one way or another if the state gets involved."

His mind was screaming for him to turn back from the ledge that was this topic of conversation, but instead of listening to his brain, he followed his heart and leaped off that cliff without a parachute or a plan.

"Can you see sharing a life with me?"

This time, Charlotte pulled her hand out of his, picked up Hitch, who was curled up next to her leg, and held him in her arms like a shield.

"I've upset you."

"I just don't know what the point is, Wayne," Charlotte said. "I knew when we got involved that we weren't going to ride off into the sunset together. That's the pact with the devil I made. You've been on the road for half of your life, and I don't have any illusions or daydreams about puppy dogs and rainbows that you are going to change a twenty-five-year lifestyle and settle down with me. I promise you that isn't a thought I've even had."

He had completely derailed his hope for a morning of lovemaking, and he was kicking himself in the rear for it.

When he didn't respond for fear of digging a deeper hole, she spoke.

"If you're asking if I think we could make something work, the answer is yeah, sure. I know that you love me, and I love you. But you're nowhere near ready. And maybe I'm not either."

Wayne realized that it was still best to let Charlotte continue; he seemed to have pushed a button that he hadn't meant to.

"You never laugh, Wayne. You hold yourself away from everyone, even your brothers, and if they can't break through, how can I? There is something or *someone* between us, and as long as that's the case, all we have is the here and now. So if you're feeling guilty because we had sex and you're afraid that you're going to leave me brokenhearted when you hook up the camper to your truck and drive away, don't. I don't bruise easy, and I can take care of myself."

After Charlotte said her piece, she got up and started to jerk on her jeans.

"Charlotte." He sat upright. "Come on, where are you going?"

She tugged on her T-shirt and boots and shrugged on a yellow rain slicker. "I need some space."

Charlotte slammed the trailer door behind her, and Wayne felt all of the eyes of the animals on him.

"Okay," he said to them, "I get it. I screwed that up royally."

The storms had waterlogged the ranch, making the ground muddy and slippery. Debris was scattered everywhere, with fallen tree branches and soggy leaves. The only upside was that all of the newly constructed structures had held up and were watertight. Everyone was on cleanup duty, and that meant Wyatt had to postpone his date with Aspen. It made him worried that given extra time, Aspen might back out. He believed that she just needed time to get to know him, to see that he was sincere.

But the next Sunday came, and she hadn't backed out. Wyatt had gone into Bozeman to buy some new Wranglers, a button-up shirt and a tan leather Western-cut blazer to wear with a bolo tie that had belonged to his maternal grandfather. He cleaned up his boots and hat and was extra careful shaving his face. While he was in Bozeman, he had cleaned out his truck and had it detailed just in case Aspen chose to ride over to the assisted-living facility where Grandma Edna lived.

Aspen had decided to let him escort her to church, and it was not lost on him that he would be meeting her family on the first date. In his way of thinking, this was a

serious move on her part. And it was going to be a make-
it-or-break-it moment for him: if her family didn't like
him, he was certain that he would be a one-hit wonder
relegated to eternal platonic friendship with the woman
of his dreams.

"Just be yourself." Charlotte had seen him getting into
his truck and walked over to give him some words of en-
couragement. "And they'll see who you are."

"Thank you, Charlie," Wyatt said, reaching out of his
lowered truck window to squeeze her hand in gratitude.

She smiled at him and waved as he cranked the engine. Charlie Brand was a one-of-a-kind woman, and his
brother would be a fool if he didn't put a ring on it and
take her off the market. He didn't intend to make that
same mistake with Aspen.

All the way to Bozeman, Wyatt worked on calming
his nerves; he wasn't used to being this anxious about
anything. That wasn't usually his personality. But this
nearly uncontrollable anxiety he was feeling only confirmed for him just how serious he was about Aspen.

"Here we are." Wyatt pulled into the parking lot of
Bozeman United Methodist Church. His family on his
mother's side was Baptist and didn't miss Sunday service
unless they were gravely ill or dead; his father was an
atheist. He had managed to land somewhere in between,
but he couldn't remember the exact last time he'd been
in church on a Sunday. He just knew that it had been a
mighty long time, and if he hadn't met Aspen, it would
have continued to be a mighty long time.

Wyatt locked the door to his truck, buttoned up his
blazer and took one last look at his face in the side mirror before he rolled back his shoulders and did his best

to feel confident as he joined other parishioners walking from the parking lot to the church.

"Welcome." A short, stout elderly woman wearing a flowered dress and a pillbox hat smiled at him with her pink-tinted lips as she handed him a program. He thanked him and filed into the line that was moving slowly into the church.

Wyatt quickly wiped sweat off his brow. His damp palms marked the paper of the bulletin. He scanned the church for Aspen; he had texted her that he had arrived, but she hadn't texted back. Wouldn't he look like a grade A fool if he got stood up at church?

Finally, he saw Aspen stand up and wave at him from the other side of the church. Relief mixed with apprehension kept him company as he wound his way over to the pews where Aspen and her family were sitting.

Aspen met him in the aisle, and the welcoming look on her heart-shaped face worked to calm his nerves to some degree.

"Wyatt," she said, "I'd like to introduce you to my dad, Santiago."

Santiago Hernandez was stocky and, with thick muscles and a strong handshake, built like a Mack truck. Aspen's father didn't smile at him; he gave him a quick nod, the look in his dark brown eyes inscrutable.

"Hello, sir," Wyatt said as he shook his hand.

"That's my mom, Georgina."

"Ma'am." He tipped his hat to Aspen's mother politely. Georgina Hernandez was a slender woman who was dressed in a navy blue dress with a simple strand of pearls around her neck and matching teardrop pearls on her ears. Aspen was definitely her mother's daughter.

"And you know my sister, Aurora," Aspen continued the introductions, "and her husband, Dale."

Dale gave him a nod. Aurora's husband seemed bored, but he didn't know the guy well enough to be certain. On Aurora's lap were two adorable toddlers, fraternal twins Arabella and Axel.

"Why don't you sit right next to me so we can get acquainted?" Georgina said to him. She tapped on her husband's arm. "Scoot over a smidge, dear. I'd like to get to know this young man."

Being sandwiched in between Aspen's parents in a church had to be one of the most uncomfortable experiences of recent memory. He had wrongly believed that he would at least be able to sit next to Aspen during the service.

"So tell me a little about yourself," Georgina said to him. "Tell me about your people."

"I'm from Texas," he said, starting to feel hemmed-in, sweating profusely beneath his blazer. The leather had definitely been the wrong move.

"Family values," she said with an approving nod.

"Yes, ma'am."

"Are your people Methodist?"

"No," he said, not sure where the land mines were in this conversation with Mrs. Hernandez. "Baptist."

"Oh," Georgina said, her lips pursed ever so slightly, but he was certainly close enough to detect minute facial expressions.

"But," he added quickly, "they attend services every Sunday."

Georgina's lips stopped pursing and turned in a small smile, and she patted his arm and said, "Devotional."

"Yes, ma'am." He nodded. "Devout."

As long as he was talking about his mother's family, it wasn't officially a lie. Wyatt didn't see any point in confessing his father's atheism until after the ink was dry on their marriage certificate.

The service seemed to last a lifetime, and Wyatt was experiencing something akin to a heat rash under his clothing. All he wanted to do was run out of the church, strip out of his jacket and shirt, and scratch every single itch he was having until he found some relief. But instead of following that instinct, he sat stiffly between Santiago and Georgina, doing his best to sing along with the hymns and following along the sermon in a pew bible. He did sincerely thank God when the sermon seemed to finally be over and the collection plate was beginning to be passed around.

And that's when it hit him: he didn't carry cash. Trying not to jostle his potential future in-laws, he leaned forward and tried to fish his wallet out of his back pocket. He finally wiggled the wallet free and he looked in every single compartment in hopes of finding even a single dollar. He closed his wallet feeling Santiago's eyes on him. They were sitting in the back section of the pews, and Wyatt had a long, long wait before the plate reached his row. Santiago placed a crisp one-hundred-dollar bill in the plate and then passed it to him.

"I'm sorry," Wyatt said to Georgina, "I forgot to bring cash."

Georgina took the plate and passed it on to Aurora. "Don't you worry. God doesn't hold our fallibility against us. You'll remember next time."

"It's only the way we fund good works in the world in the name of our Lord and Savior Jesus Christ," Santiago said, his eyes facing forward.

"Santiago," Georgina said, "stop teasing. Wyatt doesn't know you're teasing."

When the service was finally over and Wyatt was put out of his misery, Aspen sent him an understanding look. He only hoped his willingness to go to church with her family had earned him some sort of attaboy points with her.

In the parking lot, Aspen said to her family, "I'm going to ride with Wyatt. Make sure he gets to Grandma's place okay."

Santiago had his hands in the pockets of his black-and-silver-stitched Western blazer. "The boy doesn't carry cash, but I'm sure he has a cell phone."

Aspen kissed her dad on the cheek. "We'll see you there."

Once inside the safety of his truck, the sweltering blazer tossed into the back seat, Wyatt said, "Well, your dad hates me."

"No," Aspen said, "he doesn't. He's just hard to get to know."

Wyatt started the truck and let Aspen give him directions to the Springs, the facility were Edna Hernandez lived.

"Turn onto Main Street," Aspen said. "Then we'll take a right onto Seventh Avenue and that will turn into Baxter."

Wyatt followed her directions, still feeling out of sorts from his time in church. He didn't think it had gone so well for him, and that had put him in an unusually down mood.

Aspen turned her body toward him. "How did you like church?"

He shrugged. "It was fine."

"Fine," she repeated and turned her body away from him.

"Look," Wyatt said, "I didn't have money for the plate, and from my viewpoint, that didn't go so great, and I had a lot riding on this."

"And what's that?" Aspen said.

"My life." Wyatt gripped the steering wheel harder. "My future. My marriage. *You!*"

Aspen took her time responding to him; when she did reply, she said, "Let me ask you some questions."

"Shoot."

"Would you want kids?"

"Yes," he said. "Eventually."

"I'm thirty, so *eventually* could lead to *never* for me."

"Do you want to be a mom?"

"Yes." He heard the emotional catch in her one-word response.

"Then, we can get started right away."

He turned his head to look into her eyes so she knew he was dead serious. Her cheeks flushed, and she broke the contact.

"Would you raise our children Baptist or Methodist?"

"Methodist."

"Would you attend church with me every Sunday?"

"I suppose I would."

"Even if there's a big game on?"

"I don't watch sports."

"Oh! Turn right onto Nineteenth Street!"

He turned onto Nineteenth, took a left at Cattail Street not too long after and then made a right on Catron Street. One quick right took him into the parking lot of the complex. He parked his truck, turned the engine off and rested his hands on the steering wheel with a sigh.

After a bit, he leaned back and looked at Aspen and she looked back at him.

"I didn't expect you to show up today," she said, quietly, honesty there for him to read in her eyes.

"Why not?"

"Because, once I tell men that I'm...a virgin—" Aspen crossed her arms over her chest "—they disappear."

"That's because they don't love you," he said simply. "And I do."

"How do you know?" she asked. "How are you so certain?"

He reached out to hold her hand, and she let him. "I don't know. I just do. I can't even begin to explain it to myself, much less explain it to you. All I know is that the instant I saw you, I thought, *I'm going to marry that woman*. That's it."

Aspen gave him a broad smile that brought out her dimples. "Well, if you really do want to marry me, you're going to have to pass the Grandma Edna test."

"Grandma Edna is going to love me," he said, feeling his mood lifted and his usual self-confidence replacing his uncertainty. "You'll see."

Charlotte had never tried to work with a man with whom she was at odds romantically. She'd never made the mistake of getting involved with the men her father had employed on the ranch. It hadn't always been easy and there had always been innocent flirtations, but that was the extent of it. And now she could appreciate why her father always ran interference between her and the seasonal cowboys who came rolling through. Both of them had swept their disagreement during the storm under the rug, but it was still lingering like a foul odor of unknown origin. What really ticked her off about it the most was that it was negatively impacting their working relationship; the first snow was on the horizon and time was too precious to waste.

The work on the cabin, once the rainwater receded and the ground dried, had been moving forward with a crew coming to install a septic tank, while the two of them, on separate sides of the cabin, focused their efforts on painstakingly finding rot in the logs so they could be replaced prior to putting on the metal roof. Everything about the restoration of the cabin would rest on their success at repairing any rot in the structure.

"How's it going?" she asked Wayne, offering him a cold bottle of water as a peace offering.

"Not bad." Wayne accepted the bottle and twisted the cap off. "You?"

"I think I've got it all marked," she said. "Now for the hard part."

He chugged the water quickly and then replaced the cap. "There's a lot of rot."

"I know," she agreed, the scope of the job ahead of them daunting.

They stood together in what felt like an uncomfortable silence before she said, "Listen, I really think we need to clear the air between us."

"I'd say so," he said with a frown. "You moved out."

"We needed some space."

"I didn't say I needed space." He shook his head, running his hand over his facial hair.

"No. I guess I needed the space."

"I'm glad we worked that out."

Charlotte was already feeling frustrated by the conversation. Yes, she loved Wayne. Yes, she loved being with Wayne. But no, their relationship, at this moment, was not more important to her than the work they needed to get done on the cabin.

"Look…" she started again, "can we just…?"

He met her gaze. "Yes."

She gestured to all of the marks on the side of the cabin indicating rot. "I mean…we have so much…"

"I know." He nodded. "You're right."

"So, moving on." She slapped at a bug that landed on her arm.

He nodded, squinted his eyes a bit and then asked, "Are you moving back in?"

She had been on the fence with that. Ultimately, the camper was a heck of a lot more comfortable than the cot she had set up in her father's office. And she had missed Wayne; she had missed their family time. She believed in her heart that one day Wayne would leave… But she could miss him later. She didn't have to miss him right now.

She nodded, and that brought a pleased smile to his face, the first smile she had seen since their falling-out.

"I do want to apologize," Wayne said. "I didn't mean to upset you."

"I just thought that we had an understanding." She shrugged. "Day by day."

"We did," he acknowledged, "we did. But we took a pretty big step, and I wanted to know how you felt is all."

She laughed. "And now you know."

"Yes, ma'am, I surely do know." He kept smiling. "Are you ready to rock and roll?"

She nodded, put on noise-dampening headphones and protective goggles, and then turned on the Sawzall tool to start cutting out the rotted wood. Right behind her,

Wayne had a large chisel in his hands, and he started to dig out all of the rot. She hadn't known how Wayne would respond to their discussion; now she knew that he was made of the same cloth as her and her father. Work came first, and anything and everything else could wait until the job was done.

Chapter Fourteen

"It's baby chick day!" Aspen waved at her from the driver's window of her cactus-green Bronco.

Aspen parked and rushed around to the other side of her SUV and opened the passenger-side door. She had been preparing for these baby chicks like a new mother nesting for her newborn to arrive. She had purchased every creature comfort for the soon-to-be-spoiled chicks and had set up a brooder that would provide a safe, warm place for the chicks to grow until they could safely go outside.

Aspen opened the top of the cardboard box with twenty-four yellow and brown fluffy chicks that were peeping sweetly.

Charlotte had raised many chickens in her day, but it had been fun to watch Aspen prepare for her first chickens ever.

"Just look at them, Charlie." Aspen looked down at her baby chicks. "Aren't they the most beautiful chicks you have ever seen in your life?"

"Absolutely, yes."

"Would you make a video for me?" Her friend handed her the cell phone. "My followers have been waiting for this day!"

Charlotte followed Aspen as she carefully carried the box of chicks to the enclosure and coop that had been designed to keep the chickens safe. This building could be closed at night for extra protection from predators and harsh winters.

Aspen knelt down beside a metal watering tub that had been turned into the brooder. Inside there was a red lamp for warmth, a long feeder filled with chick grain, a safe waterer and shavings for bedding.

"It's finally time to put these precious baby chicks in their new home. This brooder will keep them warm and safe until they are old enough to explore their coop and enclosure," she narrated for her post.

While Charlotte filmed, Aspen gently transferred the chicks to the brooder, her face alight with joy at her flock. "Watch how I show the chicks their water. I just carefully take one and dip its beak into the water and now they will take a drink. See? And then this chick will show the rest how to get water. Isn't Mother Nature amazing? Okay! Thank you for watching, and I'll see you again real soon with another update on my flock."

Charlotte stopped videoing and handed the phone back to Aspen. She sat down next to the brooder and petted the soft fuzzy feathers of the chicks.

"I always want them to be safe," Aspen said, her eyes

tearing. "It's so hard to be safe when *everything* and *everyone* wants to eat you."

Charlotte reached out to put her hand reassuringly on Aspen's arm. "I promise you that we won't eat these chickens."

"Even after they can't lay eggs anymore?"

"Even then." Charlotte smiled affectionately at her friend. "I promise. These chickens will die of old age."

"That makes me so happy," Aspen said.

They left the baby chicks to get some rest after such a big day.

Charlotte promised to check up on them while Aspen was not on the property. Before they parted ways, Charlotte asked her, "So how did things go with Wyatt? I've been so busy trying to fix the cabin that I feel like I haven't had a chance to catch up with anyone."

"I have to give him a lot of credit," Aspen said. "He weathered church with my family. My dad can be a tough nut to crack, but once his mother took an immediate liking to Wyatt, Dad changed his tune. Dad doesn't toe the line with anyone, but when it comes to his mother, Grandma Edna has the final word on all matters."

"So…will there be a second date?"

Aspen stepped closer to her and lowered her voice, even though there wasn't anyone nearby to hear them. "Can I tell you something that I haven't even told Aurora?"

"Of course."

"I hardly ever keep anything from her, but sometimes she can be…"

"I understand. I really do."

"I know you do. Of course you do." Aspen nodded.

Sometimes, multiples could be too quick to put a negative on things, especially when it came to love. Outside relationships could sometimes seem like a threat to the special bond they shared.

"I think I love him, Charlie."

"Wyatt?" Charlotte was not expecting that. "Are you serious?"

Aspen nodded. "I really think that I do."

"And it's not just his certainty influencing you?"

"No." Aspen shook her head and put her hand over her heart. "This is coming from inside of me."

Charlotte hugged her friend tightly. "Then, I'm happy for you, Aspen. The two of you are going to make some beautiful babies."

Charlotte spent some extra time in the shower; her entire body ached right down to her fingers from removing rotten wood and sometimes entire logs from the walls of the cabin hour after hour, day after day. It had been painstaking, grueling, exhausting work that had taken a full week.

"Come here." Wayne opened his arms to her.

Charlotte crawled into the bed, careful not to disturb the animals on their staked-out parts of the bed. Wayne helped her slip under the covers, and she fit her body next to his, her arm around his waist, her head on his chest. He covered her body with the blanket and rested his arm on her shoulder.

"Mmm," she murmured contentedly, her eyes already closed.

"That was a tough one," he said.

"I thought it was never going to end," she said, her voice raspy from fatigue.

"But we got it done. You and me."

She whispered something under her breath, too tired

to talk anymore. Wayne kissed the top of her head, shut off the light and held her in his arms as she drifted off to sleep. Several hours later, Charlotte awakened, slid out from underneath Wayne's heavy arm, scooted to the end of the bed and then felt her way in the dark to the bathroom. On the way, she stumbled over Mick.

"I'm sorry, sweet boy." Charlotte knelt down to pet him. "What are you doing down here?"

The minute she touched him, she knew something was wrong. She stood up, switched on the light and knelt back down.

"Wayne!" She reached behind her and jostled his foot. "Wake up!"

"Mick." She ran her hand over his body; he wasn't moving, but he was breathing. His legs were stretched out stiffly from his body. "Mick. Please, Mick."

Wayne sat up, pushing his long hair away from his face. "What's wrong?"

"It's Mick! I think he's having a seizure."

That snapped Wayne awake. He threw off the covers and stepped over her and his dog so he could kneel down by his head. He gently cradled his head and talked to him, doing his best to comfort him, while Charlotte grabbed her phone. She called the only vet who might answer the phone this time of the night. The ringing was grating, as was Bowie whining at the end of the bed. She just needed the vet to answer the phone.

"Pick up. Pick up. Pick up," she repeated under her breath. "Please pick up."

"Hello?" Dr. V answered the phone with a sleepy voice.

"Dr. V! It's Charlotte Brand."

"Charlotte Brand?" the vet repeated.

"Yes. Please help us. Please. Our dog Mick—he's having a seizure. I think it's a seizure."

Dr. V woke up quickly and asked her targeted questions. "Do you know how long he's been in that state?"

"No," Charlotte said. "When we went to bed, he was fine. I got up to go to the bathroom, and I found him."

"It does sound like he's having a seizure," Dr. V said. "Bring him to my Four Corners office. Address is online. I'll meet you there. I'll do what I can."

"Thank you, Dr. V," Charlotte said, holding back tears. "Thank you!"

As she was ending the call, she heard the vet say, "Rob, honey. I have to go to the office. It's an emergency."

She got dressed while Wayne kept Mick company, and then they traded so he could throw on his clothes. Wayne pulled an old quilt out of the cabinet and they wrapped Mick up in it. Charlotte grabbed her wallet, her phone and the keys to Wayne's truck. He got into the passenger side, holding Mick in his arms, and she got behind the wheel.

"It's going to be okay," Charlotte said as she cranked the engine, turned on the lights and shifted into gear. "Dr. V is going to help you."

Wayne spoke to Mick in hushed tones, his voice wavering with emotion, and petted the dog on his head.

"I love you, old man," Wayne told Mick. "You've been the best friend any man could have. You're so good, Mick. You're so good. I love you so much."

It was a forty-five minute drive on dark roads to Four Corners. Mick seemed to improve halfway, and he actually wagged his tail twice and licked Wayne on the nose. But then he had several back-to-back seizures. All Charlotte could do was drive and pray. Drive and pray.

They pulled into Dr. V's clinic; the lights were on and she met them at the door.

None of them bothered with pleasantries. Dr. V. asked them to take Mick to a room with an examining table. The vet began to examine him, confirmed that he was having a seizure and then gave him some medication to stop it.

Charlotte stood right next to Wayne, hoping that her presence would help him cope with this emergency as being next to him was helping her. She loved Mick as much as she loved Bowie. He was a part of her heart, part of her family now.

"Hey, boy," Wayne said when Mick's eyes seemed to focus in on his face. "There you are. I love you, Mick. I love you."

Mick's eyes shifted from Wayne to her; she leaned down and kissed the top of his head and told him that she loved him. Then, Mick took one last breath in and then exhaled a long sigh. Charlotte's brain knew before her heart would accept it that that had been Mick's last breath.

Dr. V checked for a pulse; she checked for a heartbeat. After a minute, she shook her head. "I'm so sorry. He's gone."

Wayne's face drained of color; he stood motionless, his hand resting on Mick's head. The tears Charlotte had been holding back broke through the dam as she laid her body over Mick, hugging him and petting his fur. Wayne pulled the blanket still beneath his dog's body and covered him, tucked the edges tightly around him and then picked him up in his arms. Wayne sat down on his haunches, holding Mick, his face buried in the dog's neck. Wayne began to sob; Charlotte sat down on the ground beside him, put her arms around him while he held the lifeless body of their beloved Mick. Charlotte kissed the top of Mick's head, with tears of sadness and sorrow pouring out of her eyes and onto her cheeks.

Dr. V had left the room to give them privacy. Charlotte didn't want to leave Wayne's side, but she had to be strong for him. She needed to handle things so he could focus all of his energy and emotion on coming to terms with his loss. She found the kind veterinarian hugging her husband in a small office adjacent to the exam room.

Dr. V turned toward her, her blue eyes red from her own tears.

"I'm so sorry." Dr. V said.

Charlotte felt so grateful for the dedicated veterinarian that she hugged her tightly for a moment or two.

"I know you are," she said. "We are so grateful for you."

Dr. V nodded while she wiped the tears from her eyes and cheeks with her fingers. "Thank you for saying that."

"Thank *you*, Dr. V."

After a solemn silence, Dr. V asked, "How do you think Wayne would like to handle his remains?"

"I really don't know," Charlotte said. "I'll have to go ask him. Will you be able to send us a bill?"

"I'm not going to charge you for this." Dr. V suddenly looked as weary as she felt. As much as she didn't want to disturb Wayne, they needed to allow the vet to return home and get some sleep.

Charlotte thanked Dr. V once more before she returned to Wayne, who hadn't moved. She rubbed her hand on his back. "Wayne, the vet needs to know how you would like to handle Mick's body."

Wayne stood up and carried Mick back to the exam

table and set him down. Wayne petted Mick's face and his ears and kissed his head several times.

"Would you like to bury him at Hideaway Ranch?" she asked quietly.

Wayne stared down at Mick; he shook his head. "I don't know what to do."

Charlotte put her arm around Wayne's back, and he adjusted so his arm was resting across her shoulders. In that moment, she had never felt closer to Wayne. He was accepting her comfort instead of pushing her away.

"We have a special place on the ranch. We call it the bluff. It's where my father proposed to my mother. We sprinkled our parents' ashes there earlier this year. Would you like to do that with Mick too?"

She waited for a while for an answer and was starting to believe that Wayne hadn't heard her.

"Yes," Wayne said in a gravelly voice. "That's what I want. I want him to be free, not stuck in a dark hole."

"Okay." She held on to him. "That's what we'll do."

After they said one last goodbye to Mick, and after Wayne had removed the wide collar that held his dog tags from Mick's neck, Charlotte hugged the vet and thanked her profusely. "We will never forget this kindness, Dr. V."

"Thank you," Dr. V said, turning the lights off in the clinic and following them out the door. "I only wish I could have done more."

The drive back to Hideaway Ranch was quiet, each of them lost in their own thoughts. She drove them all the way back to Big Sky without a word being spoken between them. Wayne was a man of few words at the best of times. It made sense that he should be rendered mute during a tragedy.

"We're home," Charlotte said, parking the truck by the camper.

They both got out of the truck and met by the hood. Wayne pulled her into his arms and held her tightly. "Thank you, Charlotte."

She reached up, put his face between her hands. "We're here to help each other through the tough times, Wayne. What else are we here for, if not that?"

They walked together the short distance to the camper, opened the door and went inside. The fact that Mick wasn't there to greet them with his wagging tail, his kisses and his soulful brown eyes hit her the minute they walked through the door. His presence would be missed, and his death had ripped at their hearts.

Bowie rushed over to them, and they both seemed to hug him more tightly and kissed him a few more times. Exhausted and emotionally drained, they stripped down and climbed into bed. Wayne put Mick's collar on his nightstand and then turned off the light. Charlotte reached up above her head and petted Hitch. The cat meowed, rolled over on his side so she could rub his belly and began to purr. And that was how she managed to fall asleep—Hitch serenading her with his loud, rhythmic, wonderful purr.

The next morning, Wayne didn't awaken before dawn. He slept in, which had never happened before. And even though he didn't drink, when he opened his eyes, they were bloodshot, and he looked as wrecked as if he had been on a weeklong bender.

Charlotte sat on the bed next to Wayne. She ran her fingers through his hair and rubbed his back. "Why don't you get some rest, Wayne? You've been working nonstop since you got here. And now, losing—" she stopped short of saying his name "—you're exhausted. Stay in bed and I'll check on you later."

She kissed him on the forehead, and then she said to Hitch, "Keep him company."

Hitch looked at her with his large golden eyes, stood up, stretched and walked over Wayne like he was a bridge to flop down next to him. "Smart boy."

To Bowie, who was resting his head on Wayne's hip, she said, "You keep Wayne company too, sweet boy."

She stood up and was about to turn away when Wayne reached out and caught her fingers.

He looked up at her. "You're a good woman, Charlotte. A kind woman."

"Thank you, Wayne," she said. "I try to be."

She kissed him lightly on the lips, told him that she loved him and then turned off all the lights so he could rest. She went to the barn to feed the horses; they were stirring in their stalls, whickering for their breakfast. She filled a large red scoop with each horse's specific ration of grain and poured it into round black rubber feed bowls.

"Good morning, Charlie."

Charlotte had been deep in thought, unable to stop thinking of the horrible events of the night before and was completely startled. She straightened and spun around toward the sound of the voice.

"Flint! You just took years off my life."

The lanky cowboy looked properly chagrined. "I'm sorry. That wasn't my intention."

She finished her job, and then Flint pitched in. The horses scarfed down their feed, and then they haltered the horses and walked them to the pasture.

"Next stop, chicken coop."

"Mind if I tag along?" Flint asked.

"Not a bit."

They walked together toward the coop, not having much to say until Charlotte asked, "Where have you been, by the way? I haven't seen you around for a while now."

Flint chuckled. "Boss man had me rotated back to Sugar Creek."

Charlotte stopped walking. "He didn't."

"Yes, ma'am, he surely did," Flint said. "But I don't blame him. I'd probably have done the same."

They reached the coop and made sure that the chicks, still too young to be out on their own, had water, fresh bedding and food, and that the heat lamp was the right temperature.

"They're comin' along," Flint said.

"Yes, they are," she agreed. "So how'd you manage to rotate back in?"

"A couple of the hands left town during the storms and never came back," Flint explained.

"Well," she said, ready to head into the main house and dig through the construction zone to find a place to plug in a coffeepot—*if* she could even manage to find the pot or the coffee, "welcome back."

She walked a couple of steps away from the young man when he said, "So, you and the boss man."

Charlotte turned back to him. "That's right."

"He's a lucky man."

"Thank you, Flint," she said. "I'm a lucky woman."

Later that morning, it was overcast and dreary, but the forecast didn't call for rain. Charlotte couldn't find the coffeepot or the coffee, which was a worst-case scenario for her. She needed that jolt of caffeine to get her jump start, and she would not risk awakening Wayne by making the coffee in the trailer. She was tired from the night before, still battling an odd combination of disbelief and grief, and a headache was creeping up on her.

She was about to head to the cabin to check on the progress of the plumbers installing the bathroom components, hooking up the septic and bringing water to the roughed-in kitchen when a heavy-duty truck hauling a trailer came into view. The driver waved to her as he drove into the central area of the ranch.

"Goat day!" She shook her head at her forgetfulness.

The driver parked and got out. He was a heavyset man with a round belly beneath a faded pair of overalls.

"How do?" he greeted her in a booming voice.

"I'm well." Charlotte offered her hand.

They shook hands, and he pulled a rumpled invoice out of the bib of his overalls, shook the paper out to unfold it and squinted his eyes to read the writing on the print before he chuckled to himself and felt on the top of his head for a pair of reading glasses.

"Looks like we have a delivery for six Oberhasli goats and two miniature donkeys."

Charlotte frowned. "No donkeys."

The gentleman took a closer look at the invoice. He stabbed the paper with his finger. "Right here. Two donkeys."

Charlotte accepted the invoice and read it silently, and sure enough, two donkeys were paid for in full along with six goats. The purchaser was Rayna Johnson, care of Charlotte Brand.

"Okay," she said, folding the invoice and putting it in her back pocket. "I guess we are the proud owners of two miniature donkeys."

Charlotte called Flint over to help her move the goats into the enclosure. They decided to put the donkeys in the resting pasture until they could build a more suitable situation for them. Rose had loved donkeys and had raised them on the ranch; they couldn't graze all day on grass like a horse; they could handle six or seven hours of grazing, and the rest of the time should be spent on a dry lot with finely crushed gravel as footing and given limited amounts of hay and water. Donkeys that overgrazed became obese and were in danger of developing laminitis because of the high sugar content in the grass.

With the goats and the donkeys secured, Charlotte signed the delivered manifest and sent the driver on his way. The minute that chore was done, she called her sister Rayna on video chat.

"Hey, Charlie! Did the animals get delivered?"

"Yes, Ray, as a matter of fact they did."

"Oh, let me see them!"

Charlotte turned the camera around so Ray could see the goats. "They are so adorable! I can't wait to meet them and hug them."

"Yes, they are very cute," Charlotte agreed. "But I think you forgot to tell me something?"

Ray looked perplexed, and then a light bulb went on. "The donkeys!"

"Yes. The donkeys that I was given zero forewarning about."

"Let me see them!"

Charlotte obliged, walking over to the resting pasture.

Ray actually squealed with joy. "They are now officially my favorites."

"Poor goats." She made a tsk sound. "They got knocked

off the top rung in record time. Would you mind telling me *why* we have donkeys?"

"Well," Ray said very seriously, "the chickens are for eggs. The goats are for milk. And the donkeys are for fun."

Charlotte raised her eyebrows and shook her head. "Okay. You are officially cut off from any further animal-related purchases. If they eat and make manure, you are banned!"

Ray frowned at her playfully. "Spoilsport."

Chapter Fifteen

For the two weeks after Mick's death, Wayne, the man of few words, became a man of nearly *no* words. But his affection for Charlotte had deepened. Whenever she was near, he would pull her into his arms and hug and kiss her. He was deeply saddened at the loss of Mick, and she was too. She had loved Mick, and she would keep him in that space in her heart where she held all memories of beloved animals past. Even Hitch and Bowie were mourning the loss of their companion.

But it had also been a productive two weeks. They had painstakingly sealed all of the cracks in the log chinking, a synthetic sealant to seal in between the logs and the joints to protect the wood and insulate the home. Wayne had showed her a trick to seal cracks by pushing thread into the cracks with a small chisel and then running sealant over the thread. They worked steadily and focused on the task at hand. For both of them, work was what had always saved them during the tough times. And now was one of those times. She had selected large picture windows to be installed throughout the main floor to bring natural light into the dark space. Wayne removed the old windows and marked where she should start cutting with the chain saw for the new kitchen window, and she cut a large square in the kitchen wall, praying that she didn't make a mistake.

Next they built a frame for the window, nailing it into place and sealing the frame. Once the frame was ready, Wayne whistled to Waylon to bring the window up to the space in the side of the cabin. Waylon drove the tractor forward with the heavy window sitting upright in the bucket and strapped to the bucket arm. Wyatt was riding in the bucket to provide extra security to the window. There was no money in the budget for replacing it.

Wayne waved his hand for Waylon to move forward inch by inch until the window was close enough for the four of them to install. Wyatt unstrapped the window while Waylon joined him the bucket. Slowly, the brothers lifted the window just enough for Charlotte and Wayne to use the straps to pull it into place. Once set, Charlotte and Wayne moved on to the living room where they would be installing two windows. Waylon and Wyatt installed the metal fleshing and then an outside frame made of logs cut in half. This would further seal the windows from leaking or moving when the wood logs naturally shrank and shifted over time. Moreover, they added to the aesthetic of the cabin.

They were putting the second window in place when Wyatt's phone started to ring. He ignored it, focusing on the job at hand. While the four of them struggled to get the window in place, Wyatt's phone began ringing again.

"Damn it, Wyatt," Wayne growled. "Turn that damn thing off next time."

The window finally slid into place after some trimming to make the space bigger at one corner. Wyatt jumped out of the bucket of the tractor and looked at his phone.

"I've got to go," Wyatt shouted over the sound of the chain saws.

Wayne shut down the saw and lowered his headphones down to his neck. "What did you say?"

"I've got to go."

"The job isn't done, Wyatt."

"Aspen's grandmother just died," Wyatt said. "I'm going."

"Damn it, Wyatt," Wayne barked at his brother.

Charlotte put her hand on Wayne's arm to calm him. "We can do it without him, Wayne."

Wyatt waited a minute. Charlotte had known the Westbrook brothers long enough to infer how difficult it was for the younger brothers to defy Wayne. Wayne gave a slight nod to his brother, and Wyatt spun around, ran over to his truck and took off.

"What in blazes is going on?" Wayne said, disgruntled. "Wade ran off to Texas and hasn't come back yet, and now Wyatt."

Not having an answer that Wayne would accept, Charlotte put her headphones back on and picked up the chain saw and began to cut another square space for the next window. It was more difficult to install the last two windows downstairs without Wyatt's help, but they did manage to get it done. After that major job was finished, Charlotte sat on the newly built staircase steps with Wayne and Waylon drinking water and catching their breath.

"What's next?" Waylon asked.

Wayne jerked his thumb over his shoulder. "Ask the boss."

Charlotte smiled at her cowboy, happy to see him slowly pushing his way through mourning Mick. "Correction. That's *boss lady* to you."

Wyatt hadn't worn a suit since his high-school graduation. A rambling cowboy didn't have much need for fancy clothes. For Aspen, Wyatt went into Bozeman and bought a black off-the-rack suit for Grandma Edna's funeral. The service was held the following Saturday, and Wyatt sat next to Aspen in the front pew reserved for family members. Santiago, Edna's only living child, addressed the family and friends from the church lectern. Edna had attended the Methodist church for many years and had endeared herself to many. Edna had immigrated from Mexico when she was a teenager and Spanish was her first language. Santiago's eulogy was in both English and Spanish for any attendees on video chat in Mexico who didn't understand English.

Wyatt sat in his spot, holding Aspen's hand while she wept quietly beside him, dabbing at her eyes often to wipe her tears. The symbolic nature of being included as one of the family for Grandma Edna's funeral service was not lost on him. In his mind, Grandma Edna would be his guardian angel: he believed wholeheartedly that she was the reason he had been accepted into the family. He only wished that he had been able to spend more time with her.

After Santiago finished his eulogy, the minister finished the service, and then everyone was able to say a final goodbye to Edna, who was lying in an open casket at the front of the church. Aspen stood up, still holding his hand, and they followed the rest of the family up to say their farewells.

Aspen looked down at her beloved grandmother, touched her hand lovingly and then turned away with fresh tears running down her face. Aspen linked her arm with Wyatt's as he escorted her up the aisle into the doorway. While they were inside, rain had moved in; it seemed that the sky was also weeping for the loss of Edna.

"I'll ride with my family to the cemetery," Aspen said through her tears.

"Okay."

She looked up at him. "Thank you for coming."

He put his hand over her hand. "This is where I'm supposed to be. Here, with you."

Wyatt borrowed one of the umbrellas available at the main entrance of the brick church; he walked with Aspen, making sure she made it to the limousine for immediate family.

"I'll see you at the cemetery," Wyatt told her before he jogged back to the church with the umbrella.

He turned on his truck, flipped on his lights and joined the funeral procession to Edna's final place of rest. The rain had stopped, the clouds moved and the sun began to shine in the quick five-minute trip to Sunset Hills, the cemetery maintained by the city of Bozeman. He found a place to park and headed straight for the limousine; the door of the vehicle opened, and Wyatt offered Aspen his hand. He also helped Aurora out so she could turn around and take one of the twins from her husband, Dale.

"Grandma Edna loved it when the sun would come

out after a hard rain," Aspen told him as they walked toward the large tent that had been erected over the grave.

They took their seats and patiently waited for everyone to settle. The minister prayed the order of committal and offered the benediction, and then Aspen, Aurora and Georgina laid yellow roses, Edna's favorite flower, on the casket before it was lowered into the ground. At the end of the funeral and as the people were slowly trickling back to their cars, Aspen remained in her spot, staring at the place where her grandmother had been laid to rest next to her husband, Santiago Sr., who had died several years before.

Santiago walked over to where they were sitting, and Wyatt stood up out of respect for the elder.

"Thank you for coming to support our family." Aspen's father offered him his hand.

"Yes, sir."

Aspen stood up and hugged her father tightly.

"Are you coming with us?" Santiago asked his daughter.

"I think I'd like to ride with Wyatt. If that's okay."

Santiago kissed his daughter's cheek. "I want you to do what's best for you, *mija*."

Wyatt sat with Aspen as the tent and parking lot emptied, until they were the last ones left. Bottom line, he would sit in that spot for as long as Aspen needed him.

Still staring ahead, she said, "Do you remember when Grandma Edna called me over to her the day that you met her?"

Wyatt nodded. "Yes, I do."

"Do you know what she wanted to tell me?" she said. "She told me that you were my intended—my soulmate—and that I should marry you."

Stunned, Wyatt asked, "Do you think she's right?"

"Grandma Edna is *always* right."

Aspen then met his gaze. "You proposed to me on our first walk."

"I remember." He had said "Let's get married." It wasn't the proposal he would have planned, but he had meant it.

She shifted her body toward him. "Is it too late to accept?"

Wyatt forgot to breathe for several seconds. There was no way he could have anticipated this moment.

"No," he said. "The invitation to be my wife is a standing offer."

"I accept," she said simply.

"I'll have to ask for your father's blessing to marry you."

"Yes," she agreed, "when the time is right."

Wyatt held Aspen's face gently in his hands so he could look deeply into her eyes. "I love you, Aspen. Today, tomorrow, forever."

"I love you," Aspen said aloud to him for the first time. "Today, tomorrow and forever."

Wyatt sealed their promise with a short, sweet kiss. Then he put his arm around her shoulder and pulled her close, and they sat quietly, honoring Grandma Edna for paving the way for their union. Wyatt didn't share the thought he had sitting there with Aspen, but in his gut, in his mind, he knew, in the same way he had known Aspen would be his wife, that their firstborn would be a perfect baby girl and her name would be Edna Hernandez Westbrook.

Wayne and Charlotte had traveled into Gallatin Gateway to buy some materials from the hardware store. Waylon had finished framing the new windows, pressure-washed the cabin and started staining. Charlotte and Wayne had been focusing their efforts on the complex task of installing the handrail and posts on the staircase. At times, they both needed to take a break and run an errand or two so they could get their heads back into the task at hand. While they were in town, Wayne got a call. He answered the phone and then she heard him say, "Alright. Thank you. I'll be by today."

"What's wrong?" she asked.

"Mick's ashes," Wayne said robotically.

Pain—naked and raw—flashed across Wayne's face.

She reached over and put her hand on his arm. "We'll do this together, Wayne."

He put his hand over hers and gave a nod. Instead of heading back to the ranch, they went up to Four Corners to pick up Mick's remains. The trip was a quiet one; neither of them felt it necessary to end the silence with unnecessary words.

They arrived at the clinic and held hands as they walked into the small waiting room together. On the reception desk, there was a small battery-operated candle flickering and there was a sign letting patrons know that the candle was lit in honor of a family suffering the loss of a beloved pet.

"This is for Mick," Charlotte whispered to Wayne, losing her inner battle to keep her tears at bay.

Wayne put his arm around her shoulders and pulled her in tightly to his body.

"I'm so sorry for your loss," the receptionist said quietly.

"I thank you kindly." Wayne accepted Mick's remains. "He was the best kind of dog; the best kind of friend."

Together, they retreated to the truck and once inside they fell into each other's arms. It was a relief to cry. For both of them. They held on tight to each other for a while before Wayne felt ready to drive back to the ranch.

"Do you want to go to the bluff today?" she asked him softly.

He glanced over at the small box on her lap.

Wayne swallowed several times, sniffed and then coughed hard. Behind the dark lenses of his sunglasses, Charlotte knew that there were fresh tears in Wayne's eyes.

She put her hand on his arm. "Let's go today."

Wayne nodded yes. When they reached Hideaway, Wayne took a right onto the narrow ranch road that would lead them to the bluff. She had taken Wayne there the week before, letting him see the beauty of Mick's final resting place. Wayne had returned to that spot several times to hack away at the overgrowth along the path. Charlotte didn't try to stop him: it was part of his mourning. It was cathartic, and she wanted that for him, and she didn't take it personally when he told her that he wanted to do it alone.

At the trailhead, Wayne parked the truck. He took a pocketknife out of his jeans, ran the blade over the tape on the top of the box, and while he put his knife away, Charlotte opened the box and looked inside. Mick's ashes were housed in a small, plain box with a top that slid off to reveal the contents in a sealed plastic bag.

Charlotte carefully took the wooden box out of its shipping container and held it in her hands. Wayne came around to her side of the truck, opened the door for her and then offered her his hand. He did not attempt to take the remains from her. Together, they hiked up to the top of the hill to the bluff. When they reached the rocky out-crop at the apex, Charlotte slid the lid off the box and took out the plastic bag holding Mick's ashes. Wayne once again took out his pocketknife and cut a slit in the bag so they could easily spread the ashes.

"You were my best friend," Wayne said. "You were the best dog I've ever known. Rest in peace, Mick."

"Rest in peace," Charlotte echoed.

Wayne knelt down, and she squatted next to him. To-gether they held the bag, tipped it over and let the ashes catch the wind. After several moments, the ashes had scattered across the landscape below, and Wayne pushed himself up to a stand and then helped her up.

He put his arm around her, kept her close to him and said, "Thank you."

"I loved him too."

"I know you did," Wayne said, "and he loved you."

They walked back down the path, careful on the steep areas, until they reached the bottom of the hill where the path ended. Once inside the truck, Wayne sat with his arms resting on the steering wheel, looking out the wind-shield. She wanted to give him time, and if they needed to sit together right here and right now while he gathered himself, that's what they would do.

Wayne sat back but didn't put the key in the ignition. Still looking straight ahead, he said, "Charlotte, there's something I've been meaning to tell you."

Charlotte felt her stomach drop and her pulse sky-rocket. His words and the way he said them sent a wave of nausea over her. She swallowed several times, hoping beyond hope that he wasn't about to reveal that he was married with a full house of kids.

"I was married."

The breath that she had been holding escaped from her lips as he continued. He had used the *past tense*, not present.

"I was married to my high-school sweetheart. She was my first love. My only love." He was still looking off into the distance. "Until now. Until you."

She reached over and put her hand on his arm. "Before you continue, there's something I need to tell you."

He looked over at her and locked eyes. "I saw her picture, Wayne. When you sent me to go look for that leather hole punch, I saw the medal. I saw her picture. I never said anything because I—" she tried to gather her thoughts "—I wanted to give you the chance to tell me in your own time."

She had also been afraid that Wayne would think that she had been snooping through his belongings. When she couldn't find the punch in the cutlery drawer, she'd opened the drawer below, found the tool, and then when she took it out she saw, in a clear protective sleeve, a photograph of a beautiful young woman wearing an army uniform. Next to the photo was a medal. She had been holding this secret ever since: she had hoped one day Wayne would tell her about the woman and the star-shaped medal.

"Her name was Adelaide. Addy," Wayne told her. "We met when our fathers were stationed at Fort Sam Houston. The first time I saw her, we were at the commissary. I had never seen a girl that beautiful before."

He looked over at her. "Sorry."

"Don't be," she said. "I want to know about her."

"I'd like to say that it was love at first sight for both of us." His lip curled up in a half smile at the memory. "It took a lot of persistence for Addy to agree to go out on a date with me. She made me work for it. But by the time I dropped her off two minutes to curfew, she kissed me and then she was my girl."

"And she became your wife."

He smoothed his facial hair down with his hand. "Yes. She was my wife.

"We only ever disagreed about one thing. The military," Wayne explained. "She wanted to join the army and marry an army man and make some army babies."

Wayne clenched his jaw. "I didn't want to have anything to do with the forces. It'd ruined my father, wrecked my parents' marriage. No. I wanted a civilian life with a civilian wife. I didn't want any kids of mine to grow up like I did."

This was the first time Charlotte had ever heard Wayne mention that he had wanted a home, a family... It was a side to the man she loved that had been previously unknowable.

"But she did join up."

"She did."

"And you didn't."

"No," he said. "I worked on my stepmom's ranch and learned horses, and Addy became what she had always wanted to be: a helicopter pilot. Climbed the ranks, became a captain."

"She was a brave woman."

"Brave, beautiful, smart. A heck of a lot smarter than me."

He paused his story, and she was patient knowing that he was dredging up memories that he had worked very hard to suppress. She didn't understand why he was telling her in this moment, but she felt honored that he trusted her enough to share his memories of Addy.

"She was on leave. We were celebrating her twenty-fourth birthday. I had asked her to marry me a hundred times before. On one hundred and one, she said *yes*." He laughed at the memory. "I think she was more surprised by her answer than I was. Before she could change her mind, we had a quickie courthouse ceremony—me in my cowboy hat and boots, and her in her dress uniform—and we sealed the deal. We promised our families that we would have a fancy wedding and reception with all of the Texas bells and whistles after she finished her deployment."

Charlotte felt that awful roiling in her stomach knowing how this story was most likely going to end.

"But she died on that deployment," Wayne said in a choked-up voice. "She died."

As was his way, after any unwanted emotional episode, Wayne threw himself into his work. The cabin gave him the outlet he needed. And to Charlotte's credit, when he was done talking about Addy, she hadn't pressed him for more details. On the contrary, she sat quietly beside him, holding his hand until he was ready to drive them back to the central ranch. And she hadn't brought up his wife since. She simply continued to work by his side, supporting him the best way she knew how.

"Will you hand me that measuring tape right there?" he asked Charlotte.

Dressed in a tank top, jeans and boots, Charlotte gave him something nice to look at while they worked. He loved everything about her—her muscular body, her freckles, her golden skin, her badass tattoos and her natural hair often pulled up into a messy ponytail. She was the best damn work partner he'd ever had and for sure the most talented woman when it came to construction and homesteading. She had been given an excellent education by Butch.

They were putting the finishing touch on the stairs by installing a natural wood banister made from a large oak branch that had been stripped of its bark. The limb curved slightly here and there, and there were knots in the wood that gave it extra character. She had picked it out from a pile of discarded wood, and then they had worked as a team to strip it and prep it for installation.

"This is tricky," Wayne said, holding his measuring tape while she used a pencil to mark where they were going to attach it to the posts they had already installed. "No room for mistakes."

Because the railing was made out of a branch, measuring the wrought iron posts she had selected and cutting each down to a custom fit was the only way to make it work. Once they attached them, Charlotte measured and then drilled holes on the underside of the railing while Wayne cut the iron posts that she had selected. She had wanted to add some modern elements to the cabin so it wasn't just all wood, and he had to agree.

"Isn't it weird that I can't stand all of this noise in the main house, but I don't mind it here?" she said to him.

"Not really." Wayne smiled. "At this site, you're the one making the noise. At the main house, the noise is being done *to* you."

"Are you calling me a control freak?"

"Looks thatta way," he tossed back.

"Takes one to know one," she countered.

"Ma'am?" the plumber politely interrupted. "I'd like to get you to take a look at our work."

Charlotte's pretty blue eyes lit up with excitement, and she said to Wayne, "Come with me."

Together they followed the plumber to the kitchen first. Charlotte turned on the water faucet and there was water!

"Look, Wayne! We have water!"

"I'm feeling pretty parched right about now."

Charlotte grabbed a plastic cup off the counter, filled it up and handed it to him with an expectant expression on her face.

He took a sip, and she asked, "What's the verdict?"

"Honestly, it's the best damn water I've ever tasted."

Chapter Sixteen

"Whoa, whoa, whoa, whoa." Wayne was kneeling on the floor on the second story of the cabin where he was installing the original wooden shingles as a wall feature.

"What are you saying?" Wayne asked him. "You're getting married?"

"Yes," Wyatt said without any hesitation. "I asked Aspen to marry me, and she said yes."

Wayne breathed in deeply and ran his fingers through his hair, pushing it back off his face before he said, "What in the world has gotten into you, Wyatt?"

"Love."

"Love?" Wayne looked at him in disbelief. "What in tarnation are you talking about? You've known this girl for one hot minute—"

"No different than you and Addy."

Wayne's face flushed with anger. He stood up, and Wyatt could see that his knees were stiffening up on him. "Why would you *say* that? Why would you bring her name into this?"

Wyatt took his hat off, regretting broaching the subject. "I loved her too, Wayne. You forget that."

Wayne rested his hands at his waist. "I remember every damn thing. Every single damn thing."

"And maybe that's the problem. You're stuck in the past, Wayne. You've got to embrace what's in front of you now. *Who* is in front of you now."

Wyatt knew Wayne well enough to know that he had been majorly crossing the line; he'd never stood up to Wayne in this way, and it didn't matter that he was thirty-five: with Wayne, it had always been a one-sided conversation. Until now, until today. And his love for Aspen had forced him to stand up to his brother in a way he'd never felt compelled to before.

Wyatt also knew that as much as he would like to rewind and *not* bring Addy into the discussion, he couldn't, so he did his best to move on. "I've asked her father for her hand in marriage."

"Come again?"

"Her family has given me their blessing," Wyatt continued. "The wedding is going to be next month, and I want you to be my best man."

"What's the rush about?" His brother was looking at him like he was a mystery he couldn't seem to solve.

"We know what we want. There isn't any point in waiting."

"There's no point?"

"No. There isn't," he said. "Aspen is thirty, and we both want to start a family."

Wayne crossed his arms over his chest and rubbed his

bushy goatee with one hand. "I've done my best to guide you."

"You always have."

"I've done my best to look out for you. Protect you."

"I've followed you from one end of this country to the other, and I'd do it all over again, no questions asked. But I don't need you to protect me anymore, Wayne. I sure as hell don't need you to protect me from the woman I love."

"And that's it?" Wayne said.

"That's it."

Wayne crossed the short distance between them, hooked his arm around him and hugged him tight. "I love you, Wyatt. And if this is what you want, I support you. I'm happy for you. I don't know what else to say."

Wyatt hugged his brother back before he broke the hug and said, "How about 'Congratulations. I'll be honored to be your best man'?"

Wayne smiled one of his rare smiles at him, and Wyatt knew that his brother didn't say anything he didn't mean. So it was particularly meaningful when Wayne said, "Congratulations, brother. I'd be happy to be your best man."

That night, after he made love with Charlotte, Wayne rolled up onto his side and looked down at her flushed face with her hair fanned out on the pillow. He brushed a few strands away from her face and then kissed her lightly on her full lips. He had grown to love every single part of this woman's face; there wasn't a wrinkle or a scar or a freckle or a feature that he didn't one hundred percent love. He'd only felt that way one time in his life before…but he was older now, wiser, and perhaps more capable of a deeper depth of love. This time around, he was at an age that he could fathom his own mortality, and the idea of growing old with someone appealed to him in a way his younger self hadn't been able to fully embrace. The man he was now could deserve a woman like Charlotte.

Charlotte reached up and put her hand on his face, something that he loved. He leaned his face into it before he turned his head to kiss her palm and then took her hand in his.

"What is this look on your face?" his cowgirl asked him. "What in the world are you thinking about?"

Wayne couldn't quite explain it, but he had been thinking all day about Wyatt's conviction: he felt love and he had acted on that love. It was clean, honest and easy. He respected Wyatt's ability to take that leap without really looking too hard at how he might land. All of their lives, he had been Wyatt's teacher and mentor. But now, Wyatt was forging ahead, leading the way and being bold and brash, as a young man should.

"I guess I'm thinking that maybe it's possible for a young dog to show an old dog a new trick."

The closer they got to the end of the summer, the longer it seemed to be taking for everything to be finished. Now that Aspen was occupied with planning a wedding that was going to be held at the end of the month, Charlotte had to shift her focus from the cabin to the chickens, the goats, the chow tent and, of course, the miniature donkeys. There were still a few cowboys on site from Sugar Creek, but many had been called back to fill roles at the Bozeman ranch. She was grateful that Wayne was still working double time to finish the cabin prior to the first possible snow as early as September. She trusted

Wayne and his brothers, and even though she would prefer to be on site working alongside them, Charlotte had to forgo what she *wanted* to do in order to direct her energy into what she *needed* to do.

Charlotte was cleaning up the chow tent after lunch when the farrier arrived. She wiped her hands on a cloth and waved her hand in greeting.

"Dean Legend!" Charlotte was genuinely happy to see an old friend.

The Legend family ran a cattle ranch that shared a border with Hideaway Ranch; over the years, their cattle would break a fence and end up on their land and vice versa. Dean was the only son of Buck and Nettie Legend. They used to have a strong neighborly bond, and Charlotte was convinced that if she ever needed Dean's help, he would be there for her. And she, in turn, would do the same for him.

"Charlie Brand." Dean got out of his truck and gave her a big bear hug. Dean had always been a large guy, tall and muscular, and he was still handsome with an easy smile, a trimmed beard and light green eyes that had always made the girls fancy him. But back in high school, Dean had only had eyes for Rayna.

"Man." Dean rested his hands on his hips. "This looks like a totally different place."

"It's crazy. I know."

"Show me around."

Charlie took Dean on a tour of the place, walking him through the remodel of the main house that was near completion, the chicken coop, goat enclosure, the new dry lot for the donkeys, the upgrades to the pastures and ending up in the barn.

"I think you've got a real shot here," Dean said. "A real shot."

"We've had a rough patch, that's for sure. We can use a break."

As they walked out of the barn toward the pasture, Dean said, "I was real sorry to hear about your mom's passing."

"Thank you," Charlotte said. "She really loved you."

"I loved her. She was a very special woman."

They stopped by the main horse pasture and Charlotte gave him a background on her small herd.

"Are they barefoot?"

"All of them."

"Do you want them to stay barefoot?"

"I'd like to, but they are going to be taking guests on trail rides, so if you think we will need to put shoes on, now or in the future, I trust you," she said. "I was actually really happy to hear that you'd gotten back into farrier work."

Dean smiled. "It keeps me sane. You want me to trim them here?"

"I think so," she said. "I can bring them out one at a time, if that works for you."

"Fine by me," he said. "Let me back my truck up, and we'll get started."

Charlotte went into the pasture and haltered the little mare named Rose. She led her beyond the fence to the covered section of the dry lot.

Dean backed up his truck, hopped out and started to unpack his hoof-trimming tools.

"This is Rose," Charlotte said.

"Nice little mare you've got here." Dean picked up Rose's front hoof, brushed it clean and looked it over. "Feet are in great shape. Healthy."

"That's good news."

Dean took out his nippers and began to trim the hooves, and then he used a large file to shape them. Rose was a perfect lady, easy to handle and done in record time. Charlotte put Rose back in the pasture and then grabbed Cash.

"I like a stocky roan." Dean greeted the gelding, rubbing the space between his eyes and running his hand along the curve of the horse's back.

Dean repeated the routine, lifting the hooves, checking for their health, nipping the excess and shaping each hoof. Cash wasn't thrilled with having his hind hooves trimmed and pulled them out of Dean's hands a couple of times, but the farrier was patient with him and eventually Cash settled down.

"Another healthy set of hooves," Dean said, standing upright and wiping sweat off his brow. "Where'd you say you got these horses?"

"Sugar Creek Ranch, Bozeman."

"Right." Dean nodded, taking a swig from his water bottle. "I've heard good things."

"I can't even begin to tell you the amazing horses they have on that ranch. The daughter, Jessie—she lives in Australia with her husband and two children now—she was in charge of their breeding and training program for years. She was a genetics genius. All of these horses with the exception of that big dappled gray were bred, born and trained by Jessie Brand."

"What's the story with the gray?"

"He was a stowaway with a mare Jessie's father bought at auction."

"Some stowaway."

"Mind-blowing." Charlotte walked Cash back to the pasture and grabbed Atlas.

While Dean worked on Atlas, Charlotte asked, "How is your father? I heard he took ill last year?"

"He did. He had a stroke, and it seemed like a good time to move back here to help the folks with the family business. I have full custody of my girls, so I didn't really have anything keeping me in New York."

"That's right! I'm so sorry, I didn't even ask about your girls."

Dean paused to take his phone out of his pocket, scrolled to pictures and handed the phone to Charlotte. "Paisley is the oldest, and Luna is two years younger."

"They look just like you."

Dean laughed, his eyes alight with obvious pride in his girls. "I'm not so sure that's going to turn out in their favor, but I have to agree. They are definitely my girls."

"Daddy's little girls." She handed the phone back to him.

The farrier put his phone back into his pocket. "Daddy's little everything."

Dean worked on the remaining three horses, and then he asked, with a not-so-successful attempt at nonchalance, "So how's Ray?"

"She's good," Charlotte said carefully. It wasn't her business to gossip about Rayna's marital collapse.

"Well, that's good," Dean said. "Aren't her boys college-age now?"

"Yes." Charlotte's eyes widened at the thought. "Ryder and Rowdy are freshmen now, which makes me feel super old. They attend college in Oregon."

After that brief exchange, they dropped the subject of Rayna, and Charlotte was grateful for it. Dean and Rayna had dated in high school; everyone thought that they would marry, and the families approved of the match.

Joining two large cattle ranches by marriage seemed like a logical direction. But Ray had wanted to experience life outside of Montana, and she met her now-estranged husband in college.

Charlotte knew better than anyone that Ray had broken Dean's heart. He'd pined for her, hoped she would return and didn't really give up on their love until he heard that she had married and was about to have a baby. That was when he flipped his life upside down and got a degree in finance and went to work on Wall Street. Looking at Dean now, with his Wranglers, plaid button-up, scuffed-up cowboy boots and his lumberjack beard, it was hard to believe that the man would ever survive in New York City. But not only had he survived, he had thrived. The grapevine was pretty robust in lightly populated areas, and the talk of the town was that Dean had come back home with more than just a pretty pair of girls—he had come back filthy rich, even though you wouldn't know it to look at him now.

"Well, all in all they look great," Dean said as he packed up his tools. "We need to keep an eye on that crack in Atlas's front right. He's a heavy dude, and we don't want that crack to get away from us. Mix tea-tree oil and apple cider vinegar, and spray it on all of their hooves, front and back. That will clear up some minor thrush. The weather yo-yo is hard for all of us—waterlogged, then desert dry—but it plays major havoc with our horses' hooves."

Dean closed the door to his topper and brushed his hands off on his jeans. "I talked to Danny. She said to send her the bill, and she'll handle it from her end."

"It was so good to see you again, Dean," Charlotte said sincerely. Old friends brought back fond memories of when she was young and carefree and her parents were alive.

"It's been real good to see you, Charlie. I'll be in the stands rooting for you."

She gave him a hug goodbye; when he got into the truck and rolled the window down, he said, "Tell Ray I said hello."

"I will," Charlotte said, and then the next words popped right out of her mouth. "You can always tell her yourself and come to our soft opening."

The thought of seeing Ray in person registered on Dean's face as a mixture of terror and hope. That's when Charlotte knew for sure that Dean still had love in his heart for her sister.

"Well, let's see how things go," Dean said, wrapping his knuckles on the outside of the driver's door. "I appreciate the invite."

"You're always welcome."

"Thank you. I'll see you in six weeks. Call me if you have any issues with their hooves."

Charlotte watched Dean drive away, and she couldn't stop thinking about playing matchmaker with Dean and Ray. Her mother had always said that Charlotte liked to dabble in other people's lives and that it rarely turned out well.

"You should probably just stay out of it, Charlie," she said aloud. But the truth was, if she were being completely honest with herself, she probably wouldn't.

Over the next two weeks, all of the loose threads began to disappear one by one. The green metal roof she had picked out for the cabin was installed, they had finished screening in the porch, and the solar company installed panels on the roof and hooked up the system to the cabin. They now had electricity, running water and indoor plumbing. The kitchen was installed, and all of the appliances would be delivered by the end of the week. All of the major outside projects had been completed, all of the cowboys-on-loan had returned to Sugar Creek, and the baby chicks were old enough to explore their large enclosure that protected them from below and above. Aspen loved those chickens so much that Charlotte was rather surprised that they didn't make it into the wedding as ring bearers.

The renovation of the main house was in its last stages, and Charlotte was blown away by the transformation. Danica and Aurora had turned that dated, dreary and musty main house into a three-story bed-and-breakfast with an enormous modern kitchen and several well-appointed bedrooms for large groups of visitors. The walk-out basement had been built out to be a large dining room with incredible views of the mountains in the distance with glass accordion doors that could be pushed back to make the space open-air. Right outside of the dining area, a roomy deck was set up with an outdoor kitchen and a firepit. It was a perfect place to enjoy a chilly night by the fire or to host events.

That night, Charlotte and Wayne took advantage of the firepit; they invited Waylon, but he had retired to his tent, and Wyatt was having dinner with Aspen's family to nail down their wedding plans. It had been such a long time between starry nights next to an open flame. She had missed it and in her mind imagined that Wayne had missed those moments with her as well. Their love was real: it was, however, very much up in the air if it was a love that would lead to anything more permanent. For her own sanity, Charlotte had refused to dwell on it, trying her best to remain present and enjoy every day that they shared. But how would she feel if and when Wayne pulled up stakes and headed on down the road? Devastated. Absolutely devastated.

"It's so quiet here now," she said to him.

Wayne nodded his agreement. "It's been a minute since we had this place to ourselves."

"I'm glad that the Westbrooks are still here. I wouldn't even begin to know how to tend to all of these animals' needs by myself."

"We'll be stayin' until the job's done. But you're gonna have to hire some hands. Wyatt will stay on with you, and he has some contacts, so I'd check with him."

She breathed in deeply and let it out in one drawn-out sigh. "I'll do that. What about Waylon?"

She couldn't bring herself to ask the most pressing question, *What about you?* She had adopted this role of nonchalance and a carefree attitude about their relationship that she didn't feel anymore. But she was afraid to shed that persona, lower her shield and take a chance with her heart. Yet every time she tried, she couldn't do it. She supposed it was her defense, her protection, and perhaps she had been preparing herself for the loss of this love since the very start.

"Waylon is his own special bird." Wayne stretched out his legs and crossed them at the ankle. "I don't think he cares much for this life. He likes books. He likes to learn. There's not a heck of a lot of mind stimulation herding cattle. I think he'll make a decision to leave this life. Go to college and go all the way."

"And you'd be okay with that?"

Wayne nodded. "I would. Not a doubt. When he's ready, he'll go, and I'll support him. Until then, he's good company."

"He doesn't really say much."

Wayne chuckled a bit. "Like I said, good company."

That's when Wayne pulled his harmonica out of his shirt pocket and began to play. Bowie joined them by the fire, lying down between them. Charlotte closed her eyes, feeling weary and relaxed listening to Wayne play. As the fire died down, Charlotte yawned loudly several times and realized that if she didn't get up now she was going to fall asleep sitting up in that chair.

"Ready to turn in?" Wayne tucked his harmonica into his pocket.

She nodded while yawning. "I have to."

Wayne doused the fire and offered her a hand up.

"Thank you," she said sleepily, hooking her arm into his. This had become a habit, like combing her hair or brushing her teeth. When she was with Wayne, they always walked arm in arm. It felt rather weird when they didn't.

"Come on, my good boy." Wayne held the door open for her and Bowie. Once inside, the dog bounded toward the bed, jumped onto it and jostled Hitch by making the mattress bounce. Bowie, who really wanted to make friends with Hitch, kept his distance, didn't get too close with his perfunctory sniffing and curled up into the tiniest ball he could manage.

"Good boy, Bowie," Charlotte praised him and kissed him on the head. Then, she kissed the disgruntled cat on the head. "Good boy, Hitch."

Charlotte stripped out of her clothes, pushing her jeans

over her feet and dropping them by the table. "I'll pick those up tomorrow."

Wayne didn't pay attention to the puddle of clothes she was creating; instead, he lifted her shirt over her head and dropped it on top of her jeans. He gently guided her to the bathroom and patiently waited for her to finish her nightly routine before he took his habitual evening shower.

By the time he came to bed, she was half asleep. When he slid under the covers and turned off the light, Charlotte rolled over to curl her body into his, run her fingers through the damp hair on his chest and breathe in the woodsy bourbon-barrel scent of his soap.

She loved to put her hand on the left side of his chest, feeling the comforting sensation of his heart beating slow and steady. Her hand drifted down to his waist and then slipped down farther. She was tired, but lying next to Wayne so languid and relaxed, her body wanted what it wanted.

In the dark, Wayne kissed her forehead, her cheeks, her neck and then pushed the bed clothing down so he could explore the skin of her neck and shoulders, and then his hand touched every curve until it reached her thighs.

"You've got to go, Bowie," Wayne said to the dog, evicting him from the bed. "You too, Hitch."

After he got her alone on the bed, Wayne covered her body with his and pulled the covers up over both their bodies, and they began a sensual dance. In Wayne's arms Charlotte felt completely seen, desired and loved. He loved her with his entire body and gave her access to his soul. In his arms, she broke free of her inhibitions and let Wayne take her on a ride beyond the clouds, to a place where she could touch the stars, before they drifted back to earth wrapped tightly in each other's arms.

Chapter Seventeen

The next morning, Wayne didn't get up before dawn. Instead, he turned off the alarm, rolled over to be the big spoon, wrapped Charlotte in his arms and went back to sleep. Later, Hitch and Bowie ganged up on him so he would feed them. He got up, fed the animals, let Bowie out to do his business and then put on a pot of coffee, all the while doing his best not to awaken Charlotte. He got dressed, combed his goatee and hair, grabbed a cup of coffee and drank it slowly. Wayne recognized he was in an odd mood. He hadn't slept well the night before because of something Wyatt had said to him when he told him about his marriage to Aspen. Wyatt had told him he was stuck in the past. And damned if his younger brother didn't have a point. He was twenty-five years stuck, and until he fixed it, all of his brothers would find wives, settle down and have a family while he continued drifting

from town to town. That glimpse into his future rattled
him: that lonely life didn't appeal to him anymore.

"Wayne? What time is it?"

He checked his phone. "Eight forty-five."

"What?" Charlotte popped up like a jack-in-the-box,
wearing his thin white ribbed tank, and struggled to
throw on her jeans before grabbing a cup of coffee. She
put some ice cubes in the coffee to cool it off a bit.

"Why didn't you wake me?"

"You needed your rest."

"But the animals—"

"All handled," he said calmly. "Sit down, enjoy your
coffee."

She slumped onto the bench across from him, her hair
wild and sexy, put her coffee cup down on the table and
stared at him.

"Why are you being like this?"

"Like what?"

She waved her hand up and down. "Like this. Not
working."

"Sometimes I don't work."

"You never don't work." She shook her head. "You are
not a stop-and-smell-the-roses kind of guy."

"Maybe I wanted to talk to you."

Charlotte guzzled down her caffeine and got up to pour
another cup. She topped his up and then rejoined him.

"You're leaving," she said, her fingers turning white
from holding the mug so tightly.

"No."

"Then, what?" she asked, irritated now. "Please just
get to the point."

Wayne tapped on the table a couple of times. "I'm not
sure this is the right time."

"Oh no you flippin' don't, cowboy!" Charlotte's eyebrows drew together. "Spill it."

Wayne looked at her and realized that he couldn't go back: his only option was to go forward. He stood up, went over to the drawer next to the cutlery, took one of his few prized possessions out and carried it back to the table. Charlotte's eyes widened, and the color drained from her face for a split second before red splotches popped up on her chest and neck.

"I'm not ready for this."

"I don't have to continue," he said. "I can wait until you're ready."

"No." She shook her head. "No. I mean *yes*, I'm not ready, but *no*, don't stop. Continue." Charlotte started to itch her neck.

"Charlotte?"

"Yes?"

"Take a deep breath and let it out."

She did what he suggested, and it seemed to calm her. She threaded her fingers together and rested them on the table. "Okay."

And then he did it. In a calm voice, with a new inner peace and self-understanding, Wayne told his wife's story to the woman he loved so dearly now at this stage of his life.

"Addy was a medevac helicopter pilot. She served in Iraq and Afghanistan. She was flying into a hot zone to extract the wounded. She landed, loaded and then got back in the air. But she took on enemy fire. It crippled the helicopter, but she managed to get them back to base. God only knows how she landed that helicopter without losing a single soldier—especially since she'd been hit and was bleeding internally. She saved all of those soldiers, but she couldn't save herself. They tried to save her. I know they did. But they couldn't. She died on the table. That's how I lost her."

Charlotte reached across the table and put her hand over his. "I am so sorry, Wayne. I am so sorry for your loss."

"Thank you," he said. "You're the first person I've told this story to in twenty-five years. Twenty-five."

"I feel…honored. Thank you for trusting me with it."

Wayne opened the bag, studied Addy's picture, then held the Silver Star Medal in the palm of his hand. "She was awarded this medal posthumously. A Silver Star, for valor. After I lost her, I got in my truck and I drove, and I haven't stopped driving."

"All of these years," Charlotte said quietly, her eyes so full of compassion for him. "Because Addy was your home. When you lost her, you lost your home."

Wayne had never met anyone who could read, understand and support him like Charlotte. She gave him the greatest gift: listening without judgment.

"I haven't had a home for a long time, and I had relegated myself to never finding one. How could a man get struck by lightning twice?" he asked rhetorically. "But it did. It did strike me twice."

He carefully put the medal in the protective case along with the picture of his beloved Addy.

"When you talk about the cabin, you always say *we*. We have a bedroom, we have running water, we have a screened-in porch…"

Charlotte's cheeks turned a light shade of pink. "I don't mean anything by it…"

"I hope that's not true," he said, "because it means everything to me. We built more than a cabin, Charlotte. Together, we built our home."

"What are you saying, Wayne?" she asked. "Do you want to stay with me?"

"Yes," he said plainly. "If you'll have me."

Charlotte reached over the table for his hands. "I love you, Wayne. Of course I will have you, hopefully every single day for the rest of my life."

"Why are you so far away from me?"

Charlotte slid off the bench seat, went around to his side and then sat in his lap, her arms around his shoulders and her head buried in his neck.

"I love you, Charlotte," Wayne said. "I will do my best to be worthy of a woman like you. I will work every single day to make you happy."

Later that day, Wayne accompanied Wyatt to a jewelry store in Bozeman. Wyatt had been very decisive about the woman he wanted to marry, but he was the exact opposite when it came to buying her a ring.

"I don't want to screw this up," Wyatt told him one hour into the appointment.

"You can't screw it up," Wayne said. "She loves you, not a hunk of metal and a polished rock."

"How have you been walking on this planet for five decades without picking up even the slightest bit of information about women?"

Wayne left Wyatt for a while spinning his wheels over finding the exactly right ring for Aspen. He headed over to the post office, bought a padded envelope, addressed it to Addy's parents in Texas, and took one last look at the photograph and the medal before he slid them inside the envelope, sealed it and then sent it off. That one small gesture was his first step out of the past and into his future with Charlotte.

"Where did you go?" Wyatt asked him, annoyed.

"I had to mail something."

"Help me decide." Wyatt had two rings on the velvet display. "Which one do you like?"

Wayne looked closely at the rings: one had a brilliant-cut center diamond, set in platinum with delicate filigree work on the shank and the bands; the other ring was a princess-cut flanked on each side by fiery rubies.

"That one." He pointed to the princess-cut and rubies.

"That's what I was thinking." Wyatt nodded. He said to the sales associate, "I'll take that one, please."

Wyatt felt like the engagement ring was going to burn a hole in his pocket; he kept feeling for it, wanting to get it placed on Aspen's finger so he could relinquish care of it to his fiancée. He found her in the chicken coop, loving on her spunky chicks that were happily exploring their swanky digs.

"Look at my babies!" Aspen was sitting cross-legged on the ground, petting one of them. "Aren't they wonderful?"

Wyatt knelt down, scooped up a chick and held it in his hand. The chick took a liking to him, and it curled up in his hand, preened its feathers, then tucked its beak into the crevice between his thumb and pointer finger.

"Let me get a picture of that," Aspen said, pulling out her phone and snapping a picture. Before she stood up, she had already posted the picture to all of her social-media accounts.

"I'd like to spend some alone time with you," he said, helping her up and then kissing her hello.

"You're about to get so much more alone time with me than you bargained for."

Holding hands, Wyatt led them to the path that led into the nearby woods. They walked along the path until they encountered the boulder marking the spot where he'd first proposed.

Wyatt stopped, knelt down, already having pulled out the ring box and hidden it in his hand.

"What are you doing?" Aspen asked him.

"This is the very spot I first proposed to you. I meant it then, I mean it now and I will mean it forever. I am fascinated by you, intrigued by you, and I love that we can be together and not feel the need to fill in the empty space. I love how you love animals and your family. I have more fun with you than anyone I've ever known, and the days that I have spent with you have been the best of my life." Wyatt opened the box he had been concealing in his hand, showing the ring he had chosen for her. "So, Aspen Hernandez, will you please marry me and be my wife for every single day for the rest of my life?"

Aspen was crying happy tears; she nodded her head and held out her finger and he slid the ring onto it. "It's beautiful, Wyatt."

"You're beautiful," he said, admiring the ring on her hand before he pulled her into his embrace and kissed her.

"I can't wait for the honeymoon." Wyatt had to make a slight pant adjustment.

"You?" Aspen put her hand in his as they walked back to the central area of the ranch. "What about me? I've had a thirty-year dry spell—I am *super* thirsty."

"Are you ready for Hitch?" Charlotte opened the recently installed screen door to their porch.

"Yep," Wayne said, securing the last landing pad on a handmade cat tower for Hitch.

Hitch was wailing loudly and persistently. Charlotte opened the carrier door and let Hitch out to explore his new home. Hitch saw Wayne, and with his tail straight up in the air he sauntered over to him and rubbed up against him. Wayne reached down to pet the cat; then, Hitch went straight to work breaking in a sisal-rope scratching post and jumping onto the platform and then onto the next and the next until he had reached the very top of the cat tree.

Hitch meowed loudly and then flopped over, his hind legs hanging off the side, and he turned over to his side happily.

"I think he's good." Charlotte laughed.

"He'll be fine here."

Although the cabin was ready with all of the appliances delivered and even the back-ordered claw-foot tub installed, Charlotte and Wayne wanted to sleep in the cabin for the first time on a meaningful day. The soft opening was looming, and they both agreed that the night of the event, they would sleep in the cabin, all four, as a family.

Together, they moved to their living room and sat down on the love seat, taking in the view. From this vantage point, they could see the horses grazing in the pasture, and Charlotte felt that she would live in this cabin for the rest of her life. It was cozy with low ceilings, but it fit her, and she had been elated to discover that Wayne felt the exact same way. At last, she felt secure in her relationship with the cowboy. She didn't have to hide her true feelings or worry that he was going to pull up stakes and head on down the road to the next town.

"I saw Aspen's wedding dress yesterday," Charlotte said. "She is going to make a stunning bride."

"A lot of things coming to a head," he said. "The wedding, the soft opening—"

"Us moving into this cabin."

After a lengthy but comfortable silence, Wayne asked her, "Does all of this wedding talk make you feel a certain way about us?"

She shifted her body position, draped her legs over his lap and smiled at him. "Mr. Westbrook, are *you* starting to feel a certain way about marriage?"

"I don't know. Maybe."

Charlotte sat upright. "Are you serious?"

"Would it be the worst thing if we *did* get married?"

She mulled it over, her brow crinkled, her lips turned down. "I guess not?"

"You know, I actually thought I was too old to get my ego bruised."

Charlotte laughed and leaned forward to kiss him on the cheek. "Look, I was never *that* girl. While my sisters were playing Barbie dolls, I was learning how to drive an excavator. When Danny and Ray were planning out their weddings and mooning over some boy in school, I was herding cattle. I've never been married, so I guess I figured my time had passed."

When he didn't respond and was still looking a bit hurt, Charlotte said, "Let's give this topic some room to breathe. It's not off the table—of course it's not. I just didn't know that you were even in the market for a bride."

"Well, I'm not in the market for just *any* bride, but I am in the market to marry you."

Two days before Charlotte's sisters were scheduled to arrive in Montana, Aspen and Wyatt's wedding was held. Charlotte was seated on the family side next to Wayne's stepmother, Beverly. Mrs. Beverly Hunt Westbrook was a slender woman with white-blond hair pulled back with a clip covered in crystals. Her makeup was flawless but applied with a heavy hand, and she was draped in diamonds; eight fingers were adorned with two- and three-carat diamonds, and she wore a choker encrusted with diamonds and large wrist cuffs inlaid with emeralds and diamonds.

"Charlotte!" Beverly moved from her seat to the empty one next to her. "I recognized you from the pictures Wayne sent me."

"Nice to meet you, Mrs. Westbrook—"

"Beverly or Bev."

"Wayne has sent pictures of me to you?"

Beverly touched her hair lightly to make sure it had stayed in place. "Oodles."

"Oodles?"

"Honey, do you always answer a question with a question? I do believe that would get on my nerves."

"I don't usually, no."

Beverly patted her on the arm. "Well, don't you worry about that for one tiny little second, you hear me?

"Now, have you seen my soon-to-be daughter-in-law?"

"We're friends."

"Oh, that is so wonderful to hear," Beverly said with her heavy Texas drawl. Everything Beverly said just sounded *better* because of that accent.

"She is the most gorgeous creature. From my lips to God's ears, if Aspen had a Texas drawl, she would be such an angel she'd have to go straight to heaven."

The organist began to play the wedding march, and Beverly spun her head around, craned her neck and said, "That's my handsome boy."

Wyatt, dressed in a Texas tuxedo, walked ramrod straight with an air of confidence that made Charlotte feel proud of him.

Beverly slapped at Charlotte's hand. "Isn't he the most handsome boy you've ever seen in your whole entire life?"

People around them were shushing Beverly, but she was blissfully unaware as she continued to critique the small wedding party in her unrestrained volume.

Wayne, also dressed in a Texas tuxedo, with his hair trimmed neatly and his goatee shaved close to the skin, walked down the aisle to stand next to his brother. It didn't matter how many times she saw Wayne, every time she thought he was the most handsome man she had ever seen. He was a perfect match for her.

Beverly grabbed her arm, shaking it. "Look at my Wayne! You look like a million bucks, Wayne!"

The bride's side of the aisle was definitely staring disapprovingly at the groom's side. But she was not Beverly's keeper; she had no intention of getting on Wayne's stepmother's bad side. She was important to Wayne, and Wayne was important to Charlotte; therefore, Beverly was important to her as well.

"Oh my, oh my," Beverly said when Aspen appeared at the back of the church on the arm of her father. "She's too pretty. Just look at her. She's shining like a disco ball."

Beverly started to cry, and it just so happened that Charlotte had tucked some tissues in her pocket because her allergies had been acting up. She retrieved them and handed them to Beverly.

"Oh bless you, you sweet, darling thing." Beverly blew her nose loudly a couple of times just as another hush fell across the congregation. The minister looked directly over at them, and as they all sat down, Charlotte said a prayer for Beverly to make it through the ceremony without causing any more unwanted attention from the officiant or the bride's family.

"Who gives this bride to this man?"

Santiago said in his booming voice that echoed in the nearby empty vestibule, "Her mother and I do."

From her pew, she heard Santiago say, "*Te amo mucho, mija.*"

"*Te amo*, Father."

Wyatt held out his hand to Santiago, and Aspen's father shook his hand before heading back to the pew to sit by his wife.

The minister then began the ceremony, saying, "Dearly beloved, we are gathered here today to witness this man and this woman joined together in holy matrimony…"

Charlotte couldn't explain it, but the moment Wyatt and Aspen took each other's hands, standing before their friends and family so sure of their path together, she began to cry. Beverly saw her tears, gave her an elbow in the ribs and handed her one of the unused tissues in her hands.

"It gets me every single time," Beverly told her. "Every single darn tootin' time."

At the reception, Charlotte made the rounds on Wayne's arm.

"You look very handsome tonight, Mr. Westbrook," she said. She had been staring at him all night because she had never seen him this dressed up. It was like seeing him again for the first time, and she *loved* what she saw: he was a good, hardworking man who also happened to look sexy in a tuxedo.

Wayne led her to the dance floor and swung her into his arms. "Hang on, darlin'. We're about to show these Montanan folks how the Texas two-step is done."

They danced off and on all night, filling the rest of their time eating good food and mingling with the other attendees. For Charlotte the best part of the evening was getting to know Beverly. Yes, she was loud, boisterous and flamboyant. She was also incredibly accepting, complimentary and full of positive energy. And she had always been kind to Wayne, taking him under her wing and teaching him a trade that he was deeply committed to, to this day.

Before they left the reception hall, Wayne and Charlotte made their way over to the bride and groom's table.

"Congratulations, Wyatt." Wayne hugged his brother and then hugged his new sister. "Welcome to the family, Aspen."

Charlotte took her turn hugging Wyatt, and then she had a quick moment with Aspen. "I'm so happy for you, Aspen. You make such a beautiful bride."

"Thank you." Aspen hugged her again. "It wouldn't be my special day without you."

Charlotte was about to leave the table area when Aspen asked, "How are my babies?"

She was talking about the chickens, of course. "They're good. Healthy, growing, social."

"That's good," Aspen said with the tiniest of frowns and genuine worry in her eyes. "I was watching the video feed of the coop this morning, and I was concerned that Bashful wasn't getting enough grain."

"She's fine."

"Are you sure?"

"I am beyond sure." Charlotte gave her friend one last

hug. "You enjoy your much-deserved honeymoon with your husband, and I will send you frequent updates of your babies."

"Thank you," Aspen said. "I just worry about them."

"I know you do," she said. "That's what makes you you."

Wayne offered her his arm. On the way out they said a final goodbye to Beverly, confirming that she would be coming out to Hideaway Ranch to see the place she had heard about from all of her sons.

"That was a beautiful wedding." Charlotte climbed into the passenger seat and kicked off her pumps.

"Yes, it was."

"And you know what happened to me? It was the strangest thing… I actually started to imagine myself in a wedding dress."

"Is that so?"

"But I guess I would need a proposal first. Maybe even a ring."

On that dark night with only a sliver of moon in the sky, Wayne said in that gravelly, deep voice that always sent a chill right up her spine in the best of ways, "I'm just the man who can help you with that."

Chapter Eighteen

Charlotte felt completely overwhelmed with the soft opening of the new and improved Hideaway Ranch. Yes, she had been able to split up the workload with her sisters, the Westbrook brothers and the Hernandez twins, but that didn't change the ongoing and ever-growing list of must-dos prior to the tour and the part that was slated for tomorrow. Fall was in the air, but they hadn't had their first snow yet; they were lucky in that the forecast tomorrow was for cloudless blue skies, sunny and seventy degrees. She had been hiding out with the horses as she always felt relaxed when she was with them. She had wished that she could have tagged along with Wyatt and Waylon, who had taken two of the geldings to do a final test run of the new trails for the rides the following day.

"Charlotte!" Rayna called out to her from the front porch of the main house. "Are you ready?"

The three of them had decided to take a picture at the bluff; they had all changed out of their work clothes and got themselves dolled-up for the occasion.

Charlotte signaled to her sister that she was coming and then gave all of the horses in the paddock hugs and love. Danny and Ray had arrived a week ago to help her prepare for the festivities, and they had promised to make time to visit the bluff to have a quiet moment together to honor their parents as well as the generations of Brands before them who had first settled this land.

She met her sisters at the bottom of the porch steps, and they all piled in to Danica's four-wheel drive rental. Danica was driving while Charlotte sat shotgun and Ray was in the back with the tripod. They had decided against a selfie stick because they wanted an image that was straight-on and framed to capture the scenery around them.

"Danny, I do believe this ranch is wearing off on you," Charlotte teased her. Danica had arrived with a suitcase full of designer jeans, Ralph Lauren button-ups and blinged-out cowgirl boots.

"Bite your tongue, Charlie," Danica said, her straight blond hair grown long enough to pull back into a bouncy ponytail.

"Where's Wayne? Didn't he want to come with?" Ray asked, looking thinner and gaunter than the last time she had visited the ranch after their mother had just died. The divorce had been particularly tough on Rayna, and Charlotte hoped that Hideaway Ranch would be a place of rebirth for her youngest sister.

Charlotte turned around so she could look at Ray. "He did, but he had to take some equipment back to Sugar Creek. They've been real nice to us, and we don't want to burn that bridge by hanging on to their equipment and holding them up."

"He had no choice," Danica said. "He had to go."

Wayne had cleared the road that led to the bluff, and they were all grateful for his hard work on their behalf. The bluff had become a special, reverent place for Wayne ever since they had sprinkled Mick's ashes there.

"This is a whole lot different than the first time we came here." Danica shut off the engine.

"It really is," Ray agreed, opening the door and stepping outside.

As Charlotte got out, her phone dinged with a text message from Wayne. "He's just delivered the equipment, and he's about to start back home."

"Thank you, Wayne. I can cross that off the list." Danica took her place in between her sisters. Ever since they were kids, they had lined up in birth order. It was a habit that seemed to persist without much thought.

Charlotte texted Wayne back, letting him know that they were heading up to the bluff before the three of them began the slow, steady climb up to the spot where their father had proposed to their mother. After they spread Mick's ashes at the bluff, Wayne had personally returned to the overgrown path and beat back the saplings, weeds and foliage. Charlotte believed that he had been powered by his grief for the loss of Mick when he had cleared the path, but she was grateful for his effort.

"This looks so different to me now," Ray said from the rear.

"Different time of year," Charlotte said, "and the path was cleared by Wayne. And he comes here periodically to keep it at bay."

"I have a lot of respect for Wayne," Danica said, her

breathing beginning to be labored. "He works harder than anyone I've ever known, other than Dad."

The rest of the way, they climbed the winding, rocky path in silence; as Charlotte came closer to the top of the hill, her mind was occupied with thoughts of Rose and Butch. She missed them every single day, but when she was at the bluff, she actually felt their presence very clearly. In this place, Charlotte felt a greater connection to her parents—and to Mick.

At the top of the hill, Charlotte paused and waited for her sisters to catch up. Even though both of her sisters worked out and were fit, they weren't accustomed to the altitude.

Danica joined her at the crest, her face red from the excursion, her breathing deep. Hands on her hips, she coughed a couple of times and looked down at the ground while she shook her head.

"You'd think I never worked out," she said, standing more upright.

Charlotte handed her the bottle of water she had been carrying.

"Thank you." Danica took a swig.

Rayna arrived—she had been taking the hill much more slowly, but her breathing was less labored. Danica handed Rayna the water.

Once her sisters caught their breath, Charlotte continued on the path through the dense forest and around the corner that would take them directly to the rocky outcrop that created the bluff.

Charlotte turned the corner and then stopped in her tracks. Wayne was standing on the large granite shelf that was the bluff; his facial hair was trimmed close to his face, and he was wearing his best cowboy hat, the one he used only for special occasions.

Wayne smiled at her: he had wanted to surprise her and he had succeeded. Danica and Rayna joined her; when she looked at both of them, she could tell by their expressions that they were not the least bit surprised that Wayne was at the bluff.

"Hello, darlin'." Wayne held out his hand and beckoned her.

Charlotte looked over at her sisters, and they were giddy with excitement, hugging each other tightly and doing their best to keep quiet. Ray had quickly set up the tripod and was capturing the event on video.

"This is why you wanted us to get dressed up?" she asked them.

"We didn't know how else to get you up here in clean clothes," Danica said.

"Wayne wanted it to be a total surprise," Rayna added.

"Mission accomplished," Charlotte said to her sisters before she walked over to Wayne, her eyes locked with his. Her heart was beating so quickly and forcefully that she could feel the pounding in her ears. Her legs suddenly felt like wet noodles, and her hands were shaking.

"What are you doing here?" she asked him. "I thought you were in Bozeman."

"I decided to be here instead." He lowered his head, his eyes full of love for her. "I'd like to hold your hands."

The calmness in his voice, the certainty in his eyes, did little to settle her nerves. Now her stomach was acting up. She put her shaking hands in his; his were rough, strong and warm. The steadiness of them did lessen her shaking, but not so much her stomach or mind.

"Charlotte." Wayne said her name with so much affection that it, as it always did, made her smile.

"I've been on the road for half of my life. I thought I was running from something, but now I know I was running *to* someone…"

"What are you doing, Wayne?" she asked in a whisper.

He continued without answering her question. "The minute I drove onto this ranch, I felt at home. I didn't know why. But now I do. It was because of you. I felt at home with *you*."

"You will always have a home here," she interjected.

"You are my home, Charlotte," Wayne said. "I love you…"

Charlotte's eyes welled up with joyful tears. "I love you."

"So." Wayne let go of one of her hands to fish a ring box out of the front pocket of his jeans and then knelt before her. "Charlotte Brand…it would be my great honor to call you my wife. Will you marry me?"

Wayne opened the box and revealed a ring in the shape of a horseshoe with bright white bezel-set round diamonds; in the center of the horseshoe was a deep purple amethyst.

"My mother's birthstone," she said, touched by Wayne's thoughtfulness. He was not a naturally romantic man, and she had accepted that about him because she wasn't a very romantic woman. But he always caught her off guard with sentimental touches that made her realize the true depth of his love for her.

"Say *yes*!" Danica and Ray called out to her.

Charlotte smiled through her tears. "Yes, Wayne. I *will* marry you."

Wayne slipped the ring onto her left hand before he stood up, pulled her into his loving embrace and kissed her.

"Thank you," Wayne said after the kiss.

She put her hands on either side of his face, looked into his eyes and said, "It will be my honor to call you my husband, Wayne Westbrook. I will love you for the rest of my days."

Wayne kissed her again, and then her sisters yelled "Congratulations!" and ran over to engulf them in a multiples hug, Danica hugging from one side and Rayna hugging from the other.

There was laughter and tears, and her sisters admired her ring, and Wayne thanked them for helping him carry out his plot. Then, after the initial excitement ebbed, Wayne whistled his signature call.

"Who are you whistling for?" she asked, looking around for another surprise.

"Patience, darlin'," Wayne said.

A few minutes later, from the other side of the hill, on a path that led to a valley on the other side, Wyatt and Waylon walked Cash and Atlas into the small clearing.

"And you were in on it too," Charlotte said, knowing that her face was flushed and her eyes were shining from sheer delight.

Wayne walked over to his brothers, shook their hands, and then gave them a quick hug and pat on their backs. Then, Waylon and Wyatt gave her a hug and welcomed her into their family.

"Thank you," Charlotte said. She had always felt a unique connection with Wayne's brothers; it was, in its own way, the same instant, innate comfort she had felt with Wayne in the very beginning of their friendship.

Wyatt took a quick couple of pictures of her with her sisters: they were all dressed up, so they might as well get that picture. After they were happy with one of the shots, Charlotte hugged her sisters again.

"You will be seeing them again," Wayne reminded her. "I'm not kidnapping you."

Charlotte laughed; Wayne could always make her laugh. She walked over to her fiancé and took Cash's reins from him.

"You're full of surprises today, aren't you?" she said.

He kissed her before he gave her a boost into the saddle. "I suppose I am."

Wayne swung into his saddle, and then they both waved to their four siblings before they turned their horses and headed along a path that would take them through scenic woods and down the other side of the hill to a valley.

Wayne and Atlas led the way; at times, it was nice to let Wayne lead. And he was a perfect fit for her because he was man enough to follow her as well. For an old-fashioned cowboy, he had many modern ways of thinking.

Charlotte was mesmerized by the sounds in the woods: the wind rustling through the leaves of the trees, the call of birds flying overhead and chirping to each other high up in the canopy created by the glorious oak trees. She felt relaxed and totally happy, and she hoped that this feeling of deep satisfaction was setting the tone for her married life. Of course there would be bumps along the road, but if they faced them with respect, love and honesty as they did now, she was certain that they would make each other happy, as they grew old together.

"Look at that." Charlotte rode up next to where Wayne had halted Atlas in a clearing that gave them an unfettered view of the valley below.

The valley was bursting with color from the blooming

of wildflowers; the bright blues, oranges, purples, reds and yellows of the flowers made it seem as if a colorful blanket had covered the valley floor. And this eruption of wildflowers was a perfect contrast to the sharp edges of the mountains off in the distance.

On the way down, Charlotte took the lead, having ridden this trail a hundred times. She knew where the footing was best for the horses, as well as any boulders or holes that needed to be avoided. Cash slipped several times on smaller bundles of rocks that rolled beneath his hooves, but she kept her body leaned back to counterbalance.

At the bottom of the trail, at the head of the valley, Charlotte stopped, gave Cash a well-deserved pat on the neck and verbal praise while waiting for Wayne to join her. When he brought Atlas up beside her, she reached out her hand for Wayne to hold. Together, they sat quietly, taking in the majesty of the scene that was unfolding before them.

"Now, that is damn near as pretty as you are." Wayne tipped the brim of his hat up.

"I love you," she said.

"I love you."

She smiled a flirty smile at him. "Are you up for a race?"

"You bet I am!" Wayne said. "And this time, I'm gonna win!"

"Not a chance, cowboy!" Charlotte held on to her hat, gave Cash his head and asked the muscular quarter horse to move off at a gallop.

She heard Wayne curse when she got the head start. She slowed down to let him catch up, and then right when he thought he could pull ahead, she asked Cash to gallop again, laughing happily as she left Wayne behind.

At the other side of the valley, Wayne caught up with

her. They were both laughing, winded and flushed from the exhilaration of the run.

"Would it hurt you to let me win once in a while?" he asked, pretending to be sore about losing.

"Now, Wayne." She laughed, feeling happier in that moment than she ever had in her life. "What would be the fun in that?"

Wayne had managed to pull off a great surprise proposal, and with Charlotte willing to be his bride, he didn't feel that dark cloud on the horizon anymore. His future was full of blue skies, and this was the first time that he didn't consider himself a rambling cowboy. From now on, he was a big sky cowboy, setting down roots in the Montana soil.

"Not bad for an old dog." He examined his reflection in the mirror. He didn't look half-bad with a clean-shaven face and a goatee that had been tamed.

He finished drying off his face, ran a comb through his hair and then walked out of the small trailer bathroom.

Bowie was waiting for him, wagging his tail; he had been Wayne's ride or die from the get-go. Hitch was the first to move into the Moonshine Cabin. Wayne felt relieved because Hitch never felt comfortable leaving the camper and now he had a bigger territory to enjoy.

"We're getting married." Wayne bent down, ruffled Bowie's ears and gave him a kiss on the head. "What do you make of that?"

The dog barked loudly while Wayne put his hat on and made sure it was square.

"Come on, Bowie," Wayne said. "Let's go find our girl."

At the door, Wayne paused. He had slept his last night in this trailer. It had served him well, but now it was time for him to make a life with his pride and joy: Charlotte. She was a gift from heaven above, and whatever he had done to deserve her, he had made a promise to his God to keep on earning her love every day until he took his last breath.

Wayne opened the door and stepped out into a bustling scene. Charlotte hadn't known that she was planning her own engagement party when she was planning the event to introduce the new-and-improved Hideaway Ranch to family, friends, neighbors and potential clients. Wayne felt his posture straighten as he walked across the ranch yard already filled with people. He had helped transform this ranch with his beloved. And he was proud of the role he'd played and to call Hideaway Ranch his home.

"Wayne!" a man called out to him in the crowd.

Wayne stopped, looked around to locate the person who went with the familiar voice and then spotted Jock Brand.

He made his way over to the elder man and stuck out his hand. "Jock! So glad you could make it!"

"Glad for the invite," Jock said. "This is my wife, Lilly. Lilly, this is the cowboy who got away."

Lilly Brand was a lovely woman, reserved, with wise brown-black eyes and long, thick raven hair laced with silver threads. She held out her finely boned hand to him, her handshake firm.

"It's a pleasure to meet you, Wayne." Lilly smiled at him kindly. "My husband has been complaining for months about losing you."

Wayne smiled back at her. "Well, I have to tell you, ma'am, this is the first time in my life that I'm in high demand."

"We took a look at that cabin you restored. That's mighty fine work, son," Jock said.

"I appreciate that," Wayne said, "I really do. We wanted to finish it before this soft opening but there were plenty of times that I thought we were going to fall short."

Jock looked over to his wife and asked, "Now do you see why I didn't want this one to get away? Wayne understands the value of hard work."

Wayne chatted with the elder Brands for a few more minutes before he shook Jock's hand again, tipped his hat politely to Lilly and then set out to find his fiancée. Bowie stuck by his side.

He stopped by the chow tent and found the newlyweds working together to keep the plates filled and the food line moving along.

"Have you seen Charlotte?" he asked Wyatt and Aspen.

"No." Wyatt shook his head.

"I saw her in the main house," one of the people in the line told him.

He thanked the stranger and then headed over to the house, up the porch steps with Bowie bounding up ahead of him. He opened the door and found his bride-to-be getting her pictures taken for the website.

"Wayne!" Charlotte broke away from her sisters and headed over to greet him.

"Charlie!" Danica and Rayna complained. "We almost had the shot!"

"Sorry," she apologized but then turned to him, an appreciative look in her eye for his attire and his neatly trimmed goatee. "Hello, handsome. Going my way?"

"Always." He kissed her quickly so her sisters would stop giving him the stink eye.

Charlie returned to her spot in the renovated kitchen and linked arms with Danica. Then she said to him over the photographer's head, "We decided to dress alike. Don't get used to it."

"Charlie!" her sisters moaned again.

He blew her a kiss and then went back outside so he wouldn't distract her. They had a plan for a ribbon cutting for the main house, then they would have dancing with music provided by a local bluegrass band. Charlotte had told them about his harmonica playing, and he got roped into playing with them for a least one song. They had a game of Pin the Hoofprint on the Cowboy's Backside. Waylon had been volunteered for a Win a Date with a Cowboy auction, with the proceeds going to the Montana historical society. They had a supervised petting zoo with the chickens, goats and miniature donkeys, and there was face-painting and hayrides for everyone. After satisfying food, good music and fun dancing, a giant Hideaway cake made into the shape of three massive fillies, each horse containing the favorite cake flavor of each Brand triplet, was presented. The hayrides all looped around in front of the renovated Moonshine Cabin that was now their home. After the renovation of the main house, Charlotte never moved back in. It didn't feel like home anymore, but what they were building together at the old cabin did. And tonight would be the first time they slept in their new home together.

Wayne made the rounds awaiting the appearance of Charlotte, Danica and Rayna to cut the massive red ribbon that Aurora had wrapped around the two porch posts at the top of the stairs. Aurora blew a horn and then laughed about how loud it was in her own ear. She waved to everyone, asking them to gather around the house.

"Ladies and gentlemen! Thank you so much for coming to celebrate with us. Please put your hands together for the three women who had a new vision of what this five-generation ranch could be!"

The crowd cheered and Wayne whistled, clapping his hands in between whistles. His mind flashed back to the first day he had laid eyes on Charlotte and Bowie. She was strong and fearless, and yet so incredibly beautiful and feminine. He knew, without a doubt, that it was love at first sight for him. She pulled a gun and threatened to shoot him, and he fell in love.

His fiancée came out onto the porch with her sisters; they each wore a black cowgirl hat, a blue button-up shirt with a Hideaway Ranch logo designed by Danica's PR firm, black jeans and studded black boots. They were all attractive women, but his eyes always found their way back to Charlotte.

Aurora handed the triplets a giant pair of scissors. The crowd counted down, and when they hit zero, the sisters, now business partners, cut the ribbon. Wayne moved through the crowd and lifted his arms to Charlotte, and she jumped down into them.

"I'm proud of you, darlin'," he said, slowly lowering her until her feet touched the ground.

"Thank you, handsome. I'm proud of us both." Bowie appeared at their feet, and they both leaned down to give the dog some love. "He's always loved you. Way before I had decided to keep you."

Wayne rested his arm over her shoulders. "I've said it before, but it does bear repeating. That is one smart dog."

Charlotte felt like she was floating for most of the day. The opening of the ranch had been a bigger success than she had ever imagined. Danica was a pro at design, branding and all of the mind-numbingly boring financial stuff that made her want to bang her head against a wall. And Rayna had worked with Aspen to pull together an incredible menu that both honored the history of the ranch while still elevating the food choices to be mindful of modern dietary needs. The menu was, in Charlotte's opinion, a masterpiece that included plants on the ranch that could be picked on a nature walk and put into a salad served that night.

"I like to see you happy," Wayne said as he took her for a spin around the dance floor.

"Get used to it," Charlotte said easily.

Charlotte couldn't imagine how her life would have been without Wayne. He was her best friend, her lover, her partner and her sounding board. She loved him when he was sweaty, dirty, frustrated or sad. She loved him when he was on the stage making bluegrass music or making her feel like a desirable woman when he danced with her, keeping his eyes—always—on her.

"You looked mighty sexy up on that stage, Mr. Westbrook."

"Is that right?"

"Yes, it is."

"Well, maybe I should give you your own private show."

"If you're ready, we can catch the last hayride home."

Wayne whistled, and through the crowd, Bowie found them.

Wayne put his arm around her and she put hers around him. "Let's go home, darlin'."

"Music to my ears."

They climbed onto the back of the trailer filled with sweet-smelling hay and called for Bowie to jump up with them.

"Are you folks ready?" Waylon asked the small group on the trailer.

Everyone indicated they were, and Waylon turned on the tractor and slowly took them home. At the designated stopping place for the tour, Wayne, Charlotte and Bowie jumped out of the tractor.

"Thank you, Waylon," Charlotte said.

"Not a problem, Charlie."

Wayne shook his brother's hand, and the family of three approached their new home. Charlotte could hear everyone praising the work they had done on the cabin; it was gratifying, but what meant more was that they had built their forever home together.

On the porch, they waved to the final tour group. Then, Wayne opened the door and unexpectedly swung her into his arms.

"Thank you kindly for coming. We surely do appreciate it. But now it's time for you folks to move along."

His last words drew a lot of laughter, and the crowd waved as Wayne carried Charlotte across the threshold of their home and then kicked the door shut with his foot.

"Welcome home, darlin'." Wayne kissed her sweetly.

"Welcome home, handsome," she said. "For now and forever."

Epilogue

"Honey?" Bowie barking awakened Charlotte from a sound sleep: there was urgency, a warning, in his bark as he stood at the large picture window they had installed in the loft bedroom. Hitch, who had been asleep on her pillow, growled and jumped off the bed.

"Wayne?" She shook Wayne's arm before she sat up, her eyes working to focus in the sparsely lit room.

When Wayne didn't awaken, she threw off the covers, still groggy, and went over to the window to stand next to Bowie. Through the branches of the trees, Charlotte could see the flickering of headlights appearing and disappearing from view as they traveled on the winding gravel drive that led to the main hub of the ranch. It was the middle of the night; this car had no business being on their property, and the ranch wasn't booked for the current week.

"Good boy," Charlotte praised the dog.

She took her handgun out of her nightstand drawer, went down the stairs and quickly unlocked the gun safe housed in the back corner of the living room to get her pump-action shotgun. She grabbed her father's coat off a hook by the door and put it on over her flannel night-gown, slid on her snow boots and a wooly hat to keep her head warm. Bowie tried to push his way through the front door, but she pushed him back with her leg, stepping out onto the snowy front porch. Her feet made a crunching sound as she walked quickly toward the main house with the gun in her jacket pocket and the shotgun slung over her shoulder. She kept her head down, trying to stop the large flakes of snow from landing on her face.

"Charlotte!" She heard Wayne call her name, and she stopped to wait for him to catch up. "What are you doing out here?"

"Trespassers," she said.

Her cowboy had rushed out of the house without a jacket or shoes.

"Damn it!" Wayne said. "Let me get some clothes on, and I'll be right back."

"Okay," she said, turning back to the slowly approaching headlights.

"Don't go anywhere!" he called out to her before he went back inside the cabin.

"I won't!" she responded in a loud whisper, the skin on her face beginning to turn cold and her nose running. The fallen snow was lofting frigid air up her nightgown, and she was starting to shiver.

She started to walk around in a small circle to generate some body heat. "Come on, come on, come on!"

A minute later, Wayne was dressed and by her side.

Together, both armed, they walked to the entrance of the inner sanctum of the ranch.

"Can you make out the model?" she asked him.

"No," he said. "I don't recognize it."

They had positioned themselves in a spot that was obstructed from the driver's perspective: they definitely had the advantage.

No matter how she tried, she just couldn't make out the intruder. All she could ascertain was that the driver was alone and appeared more feminine than masculine. The driver parked the car and shut off the engine, which turned out the headlights. The uninvited guest got out of the vehicle and shut the door.

"Let's go find out who this is," Wayne said, keeping his handgun concealed in one of his jacket pockets.

Not caring if she was overreacting, she swung the shotgun off her shoulder, pumped it once and approached the vehicle with her shotgun pointing at the person, in lockstep with Wayne.

"This is private property!" Wayne said in a menacing tone.

"Charlie? Wayne?"

Charlotte lowered her shotgun when she immediately recognized the voice. "Ray? Is that you?"

"Yes!" Her youngest sister walked toward them.

"What are you doing here? After midnight, in a snow-storm, with no winter clothes?"

Rayna wrapped her arms around Charlotte and hung on for a couple of long moments; she felt frail in her arms.

"She's cold," Charlotte told Wayne. "Let's get her into the warmth."

"I'm so sorry I woke you," Rayna said as they walked the short distance to the main house. "I thought about texting so many times but just *didn't.*"

"Let go of that. You're here, safe. That's what matters." Wayne unlocked the door and turned on the light to the kitchen, and Charlotte and Rayna entered.

"Put on a pot?" she requested of Wayne.

"Sit down," Charlotte said to her sister. She took the seat next to Rayna and held on to her hand. Her sister looked so fragile and detached it scared her. She went to the hall closet to retrieve one of her mother's handmade quilts and covered Rayna's shoulders with it.

"This will help you get warm." Charlotte sat back down at the table.

"Thank you." Rayna slid her stiff fingers along the finished edge of the quilt.

"What happened, Ray?"

"I was visiting the boys in Oregon," Rayna said, shivering beneath the quilt. "I had flown in, but for some reason I thought it would be fun to drive back to Connecticut." Her expression indicated regret and dejection. "When I was younger, I used to love road trips. Do you remember that about me?"

Charlotte held on tight to her sister, feeling like if she didn't, Rayna might just float away. "Yes, Ray. I do remember."

"So I rented a car and ended up at a crossroad in Idaho," Rayna said before thanking Wayne for the warm cup of coffee. "And for some reason, I just…went left instead of right and—" she shrugged her shoulders "—I wound up here."

Rayna took a sip of her coffee then held the cup to

warm her hands before she continued. "I guess… I just wanted to come home."

Charlotte stood up and put her arms around Rayna's shoulders. "I'm so glad you did. Welcome home, Ray. Welcome home."

* * * * *

#3035 THE COWBOY'S ROAD TRIP
Men of the West • by Stella Bagwell

When introverted rancher Kipp Starr agrees to join Beatrice Hollister on a road trip, he doesn't plan on being snowbound and stranded with his sister's outgoing sister-in-law. Or falling in love with her.

#3036 THE PILOT'S SECRET
Cape Cardinale • by Allison Leigh

Former aviator Meyer Cartell just inherited a decrepit beach house—and his nearest neighbor is thorny nurse Sophie Lane. Everywhere he turns, the young—and impossibly attractive—Sophie is there...holding firm to her old grudge against him. Until his passionate kisses convince her otherwise.

#3037 FLIRTING WITH DISASTER
Hatchet Lake • by Elizabeth Hrib

When Sarah Schaffer packs up her life and her two-year-old son following the completion of her travel-nursing contract, she's not prepared for former army medic turned contractor Desmond Torres to catch her eye. Or for their partnership in rebuilding a storm-damaged town to heal her guarded heart.

#3038 TWENTY-EIGHT DATES
Seven Brides for Seven Brothers • by Michelle Lindo-Rice

Courtney Meadows needs a hero—and Officer Brigg Harrington is happy to oblige. He gives the very pregnant widow a safe haven during a hurricane. But between Brigg's protective demeanor and heated glances, Courtney's whirlwind emotions are her biggest challenge yet.